KIDNAPPED BY THE MAFIA KING

MAFIA KINGS
BOOK 6

BELLA MOONDRAGON

For Belvin

CONTENTS

ONE
COLD BLOOD

Angelo

SWEAT DRIPS *from my forehead into my eyes as I run through the streets, in too much of a hurry to even consider finding a car or waiting for someone to come and pick me up. Traffic would only slow me down, and I can't afford to lose a single second.*

My heart beats so fast that my chest hurts. My legs grow weak as I try to push forward, shoving away the worst-case scenarios in my head. I force my lungs to take in as much air as possible because I certainly need it.

More than that, I need to be able to focus. I can't risk making a single mistake.

The streets are empty, proving everyone who says New York City never sleeps wrong.

I round a corner and see my final destination—but I'm too late.

The air is thick with the smell of gunpowder and blood. Several bodies litter the ground. I step over them, afraid to look down in case I recognize some of them.

I can guarantee the person I'm looking for doesn't lie among them.

Some of the Saints men arrive right after me. I was nearby, so I got here first. But instead of waiting for orders, or for my boss to arrive and tell me what the plan is, I followed my instincts.

They should have predicted this would happen.

They should have seen this ambush coming.

They should have guarded this safe house better.

I should have seen it coming, for that matter. I should have protected my brother. The time for planning has slipped through our fingers, and now, all we can do is react.

I need to find Luca before it's too late.

"I'll take a look inside," someone whispers behind me, but I'm already moving forward.

However, as soon as I turn into the alley, hoping to get inside through the back door, I stop dead in my tracks, too horrified by the sight I encounter.

My baby brother's eyes meet mine, filled with unshed tears, so terrified that my blood instantly turns to ice.

Oleg Romina, the motherfucker who runs the Romina Empire, the Russian mob, grips Luca's hair, forcing his head backward. When Oleg spots me, he forces my brother down to his knees, causing a whimper to escape his mouth.

I clench my jaw so hard that I hear a cracking sound. "Let him fucking go," I snarl through gritted teeth, hoping my voice doesn't reveal how on edge I am right now.

But Oleg only smirks at me, clearly enjoying the leverage he has over the situation. I have no idea why he thinks my brother is worth anything to him, but he is an asshole, a cold-blooded monster, so I doubt he even cares who he has under his control now. He just wants the Saints to be over with and done. The bastard gets off on seeing other people suffer.

"No can do, muy drug," Oleg retorts, his raspy voice and thick accent making me feel sick to my stomach. How dare he call me his friend? "The boy has seen too much. Can't risk it. You know how it works in our line of business."

"Let him go, or I'll rip your fucking head off," I threaten, striding in their direction.

Luca looks at me with pleading eyes, but even in this situation, he's so brave. He doesn't utter a single word. He doesn't try to do anything that could cause the situation to worsen. This is exactly what I taught him to do should he ever got caught.

Oleg smirks at me again, but when I try to lunge at him, something holds me back. Strong hands wrap around my arms, forcing me to stay put.

"We have to get out of here, Angelo," someone informs me, but they must be out of their fucking minds if they think I'll simply run away and leave my brother here to die.

"Let me fucking go!" I roar. I clench my jaw harder, struggling against their grip, not even bothering to look over my shoulder and see who the bastard is holding me back. My eyes are glued to my brother and Oleg. I study every single movement of theirs, racking my brain to come up with a strategy to take Luca out of his control and away from him.

"They will blow this place up," someone else warns me on my other side.

"Shut the fuck up," I growl back. "I'm not leaving him behind."

As if I should have to tell them that. Luca is my only family. He shouldn't be here. He shouldn't be in this situation. The only reason he is here is because of me. This is my fault. All of this is my fault. I should have protected him, and yet, the enemy managed to get to him before I could. I know my fellow capos have lost loved ones, and we probably have had casualties from today's fight judging by the amount of bodies I walked over a moment ago, but my only family is still alive and right in front of me. There's no way I'm turning my back on him.

I'd rather die.

I have to get Luca out of here. Even if it costs me my life.

"You Saints boys have always been so stubborn, never knowing *when to take a step back," Oleg snarls, a cold and calculating gaze emanating from him as he watches me and my men arguing. Then, as if tired of the little show, he takes a gun from the holster and points it at Luca's head, his eyes still on me.*

Bile threatens to climb up my throat, but I force it down. I need to stay strong. "Let him go," I try again, this time forcing my voice to sound less threatening and more... pleading. "He has nothing to do with this. He's just a kid."

Reasoning with a monster is useless. I know that much, but I can't do anything from here. If I take a step forward, Oleg could pull the trigger before I have the chance to even take a breath.

A chuckle escapes the monster's throat, and I can sense what's to come. But I have no chance to say anything else before he cocks the gun.

"Consider this a lesson, Messina," Oleg replies, his eyes hungry for more blood. "Maybe next time your boss will teach you not to fight those you can't beat."

The gunshot sound rips through the night, and my entire world shatters as I watch my baby brother's body fall to the ground, lifeless.

My knees buckle beneath me, and I let out the most raw and desperate scream.

THE SAME SCREAM jerks me awake.

It takes me a second to realize I'm staring at my bedroom ceiling instead of the dark sky of that fateful night. Cold sweat pours through my every pore, and I shiver, my hands trembling uncontrollably. My heart pounds against my ribcage, and the walls of the room press in around me, stealing my air and making my vision darken.

"Fuck," I hiss, forcing myself not to vomit. The smell of blood is so strong in my nostrils that it's like I'm still in that alley.

I grip the soaked sheets, forcing myself to inhale and exhale slowly. My throat is dry, my chest hurts, and my head is pounding as if someone is bringing down a hammer on my fucking skull.

It was just a nightmare, I tell myself.

But that's the stupidest thing I could say to calm myself down.

Because it *wasn't* just a nightmare.

It was reality–coming back to bite me in the ass. Again.

I've lost count of how many times I had to relive this scene over and over. Most nights, I'm too terrified to even attempt to fall asleep. I lay awake until I can't stop myself from falling into a fitful slumber, knowing the dreams will come.

I probably need professional help to deal with this–as has been suggested to me several times before–but I've always been too proud to admit I have a problem. Maybe I need to admit I'm not always the hard ass I pretend to be.

But I don't want to see a shrink because, the truth is, they will try to make me believe I'm not to blame, that what happened was a tragedy, that only Oleg is to blame. After all, he's the bastard who killed an innocent kid because of his greed and god complex. They'll try to tell me that I couldn't have done anything differently.

But that's not the truth.

The truth is that Luca died because of me. Because I joined the mafia. Because my gang faced an enemy that we couldn't beat.

Because *I* was too late.

And no one will ever be able to convince me otherwise.

I'll have to live with it for the rest of my life.

But maybe that's the punishment I deserve.

Maybe I should simply accept that this is what I get for not finding a way to save my baby brother's life.

TWO
WELCOME TO NEW YORK

Tatiana

AS SOON AS the plane touches down at JFK airport, a wave of anxiety washes over me. This is my first time leaving my home country of Russia. I've spent my entire life looking over my shoulder, waiting for my asshole uncle, Oleg Romina, to show up and finish the job he started twenty years ago when he murdered my parents in cold blood. Now, he's summoned the only parents I've ever known, Lev and Ilya Ivanov, to return to America. I insisted they bring me along, but as we deboard the plane, a sense of unease settles into my chest.

My biological father, Petr Romina, used to be the boss of the Romina Empire, a smaller Russian mob that has territory in several countries, including New York where Oleg resides. When I was old enough to understand the kind of life our family used to have, Lev and Illya told me the truth about my parents' deaths. My mother was my dad's mistress, and when Oleg learned that they were planning on getting married, his greed made him murder both of them, preventing them from building a family and carrying on with the legacy.

Instead, Oleg took over, becoming the boss of the Romina Empire for over two decades now.

He never knew of my existence, though, because my parents made sure I would be safe with Lev and Ilya before they died so that I could have a normal life.

Lev is still one of Oleg's capos, working in Russia, but he's always been loyal to my father, and he promised him he'd take care of me, even if he had to risk his life for it to happen.

That's something I will not allow.

So, when Oleg summoned them to come to America, I threw a tantrum and said I was coming with them. It took me a long time to convince them this was the right thing to do, and they only agreed because I promised I'd be hidden and would make sure I wasn't seen with them.

But I could never live in peace back home, knowing they'd be here, so close to my uncle and at risk of being tortured or killed.

Probably both.

I have to be close to them. To keep an eye on them and take care of them. It's the least I can do after everything they've done for me.

As I walk through the airport and head to the luggage claim, my stomach twists into a tight knot. I have both my parents in my peripheral vision, making sure they don't leave my sight for a second.

We're walking separately from each other in case someone is watching us, but we have a plan to meet at our new building. We've rented apartments in the same complex so we don't draw too much attention to the fact we're always coming and going into the same space.

It upsets me to have to live away from them, but I guess it's better than staying back in Russia and not knowing what's going on here.

I already hated Oleg with every fiber of my being, but now that he's ordered my parents to come here, fury threatens to consume me, and it's all I can do to keep it tamped down. Why did he have to summon them here after so long? What does he want them for? What is he planning?

Unease coils in my gut like a snake about to strike.

Someone asks a worker how to get to baggage claim, despite all the signs. The older gentleman who has probably worked here longer than I've been alive says, "Right this way. Follow the signs." He's not as abrasive as I've heard most New Yorker's can be, but he's not exactly the picture of hospitality either. I follow the crowd toward the baggage claim, keeping a steady pace.

It's my first time in an airport as large as this one, so it's a bit disorienting. I don't know exactly where to go, but the signs are clear enough. I glance to my side every once in a while to make sure Lev and Ilya are still close to me.

Lev taught me how to be on high alert all the time, looking for anything that could be considered out of place, anyone who looks suspicious. He also taught me skills to defend myself. So far, I've never had to use them, but the closer we get to Oleg, the more likely it is I'll need them.

We grab our bags and head out separate doors, still within each other's eyesight. I'm only a few steps out the door when two black vans come screeching to a halt in front of me, their tires so loud that it attracts the attention of everyone around me. Shock and fear overcome me, and I don't have time to scream for help or check on my parents before a large man jumps from the vehicle and shoves a black sack over my head, forcing me inside the van.

So much for knowing how to defend myself.

As soon as my brain catches up with the situation, I begin to kick and punch blindly at whoever is holding me, but it's all in vain. Soon, they have my wrists restrained behind my back and my legs wrapped together with some kind of a cord. "Let me go!" I growl, trying to be as loud as possible so maybe someone will hear me.

But the van is already moving, and I doubt anyone will be bothered to call the police. Even then, the police likely won't come to my rescue. If I'm being kidnapped by the bastard I think I am, no one would dare try to stop him.

"This one is feisty." The deep voice next to me has a Russian accent, which is no surprise. I shove him hard with my shoulder since I can't crack his jaw with my fist. It seems to do nothing. I hear two other men next to me, a trio of devils that makes my skin crawl with disgust tinged with a hint of fear I refuse to acknowledge.

"Pity she already has an owner," someone else muses. "I'd love to take her for a ride, if you know what I mean."

My heart drops to my stomach, and I fear I might throw up the terrible vegetable lasagna I had on the plane.

One doesn't grow up exposed to this life the way I have without ever hearing about the horrendous acts the mafia commits against their enemies, but I wasn't expecting to be a victim. Not today. Not ever. Lev and Ilya have always made sure to take good care of me. To keep their promises to my parents. To keep me safe. All of this is happening because I was stubborn, insisting on coming here with them.

"Where are my parents?" I grunt, starting to feel suffocated. Struggling has my lungs burning. I'm unable to draw a deep breath.

"You'll see soon, pretty little bitch. Just make sure you behave because I don't want to hurt you. The boss gave us specific directions not to–but if you get out of line, well, I guess I'll just have to take a scolding," the deep voice to my left informs me.

I swallow a curse, deciding to play nice for now since I need to be awake when we get wherever it is they are taking me. Also, I'm scared to death of what they might do to me if I black out. They might be following orders, but I doubt they have the ethics and decency to keep their hands to themselves if I make their job too easy.

We drive for what seems like about fifteen minutes before I lose track of all the turns we've taken. I don't have a clue of where we are since I've never been to New York City before, but it's worth a try.

My hands and legs are numb by the time the van comes to a stop.

Rough hands tug me from the van. I prepare to put up a fight until a familiar voice has my blood freezing in my veins, all the fight gone out of me.

Dad.

"Let her fucking go! It's me that he wants! She has nothing to do with anything!" he shouts.

I want to tell him to shut up. Oleg won't take it easy on him if he keeps arguing.

Fucking narcissistic prick.

"Please, just let her go." Mom's voice is weak, raspy, and I can hear the tremble in every word as they leave her mouth. She's terrified. Not for herself–but for me.

I swallow the lump in my throat, pushing aside the voices in my head saying that we should have escaped when we had the chance.

What were we thinking? Of course, Oleg didn't invite my parents here for a fucking spot of tea.

But how did he find out about me? As far as I know, he's had no idea that I even exist. Even in Russia, we were always extra careful to avoid detection.

My thoughts are interrupted as I'm guided across a patch of concrete, another of grass, and up some steps. When they finally remove the bag from my head, it takes a while for my eyes to adjust to the brightness of the room.

But when I do, I wish I couldn't see anything. The man staring back at me looks so much like my birth father–which I only know because of the pictures I've seen of him. One feature is decidedly different, though. His eyes are two blue ice spheres piercing through my soul.

The callus smirk on his lips causes my legs to falter under me, but his men still have a tight grip on both my arms, so I try to pretend like I'm just struggling again. I can't afford to show him any sign of weakness.

White marble floors grace the living area, with two enormous leather couches, a massive grand piano, and a bar in the corner.

White curtains clue me into a potential way out–until I see the bars. I won't be getting out that way, and the door behind me is blocked by two enormous men.

More of Oleg's henchmen manhandle my parents into two folding chairs, jarringly out of place in this room. They're pushed down and tied so tightly, my mother begins to whimper as the assholes pull the ropes much harder than necessary.

Tears form in my eyes, forcing my weakness to show. "Stop!" I shout. "Please–stop!"

"Tatiana Ivanov." Oleg rolls my name on his tongue as if he's tasting me. His Russian accent is heavy, even though he's lived here for over two decades. "My beautiful niece. What a pleasure it is to finally meet you."

I bite the inside of my cheek, forcing myself to stay quiet. I don't want to give him the satisfaction of hearing me beg anymore. Not yet anyway.

"It's a pity that we have to meet under such dismal circumstances, but in my defense, I didn't know about you until... well, only a few weeks ago."

Oleg paces back and forth, a pistol in his hand, but he is so nonchalant, holding the weapon flippantly, one can tell it's become an extension of his body.

"My brother was always the smartest of the two of us. Even dead, he managed to keep me in the dark. But he's been taken care of. And since you came all the way here and made my job so much easier, I have chosen a path for you that is much better than what I originally had in mind." He turns and looks at me with those icy eyes, letting me know he'd planned to kill me originally. Somehow I doubt what he's up to now is any better.

My jaw cracks, I'm gritting my teeth so tightly. But I don't bulge. I lift my chin, glaring at him, daring him to continue.

"But first things first. I don't hold grudges, but I also have to show you I'm not someone to be trifled with," he continues, turning his back to me and heading toward my parents.

I sense what's about to happen before he lifts his hand, and a scream escapes my lips. "No!"

One gunshot followed by another echoes through the room. The sound is deafening, but I hardly notice the ringing in my ears. My mind falters, trying to comprehend what I'm seeing. Two crimson pools stain the white marble beneath the misplaced folding chairs, both of their heads hang limp, but my mother's eyes are wide open—frozen. Staring at me.

Raw desperation pours out of me, a guttural scream followed by sobs I cannot control. With every fiber of my being, I will time to reverse, to rewind a few moments, an hour or two, to put me back on that plane, making different choices. Better choices.

But that can't happen, so here I stand, staring at another set of dead parents and the fucking bastard who has now taken everything away from me.

The sickening sound of his low cackle has my stomach churning, and when I return my gaze to his callous face, I feel like I might vomit all over his fucking marble floor.

"Asshole!" I manage to bite out. "You fucking bastard!"

"Now, now," he says, stepping toward me. "Watch yourself, or my plans for you might change again. You wouldn't want to follow them, would you?"

I would like to, actually. I wish he would raise that gun and put a bullet through my forehead. That's my initial thought, anyway. But then... I wouldn't have the chance to watch him cringe in pain as I rip him limb from limb.

I bite my tongue, tears still stinging my eyes.

"As I was saying, I have other plans for you." He continues to talk, but I can't rip my eyes away from the limp bodies of my parents. "You see, traditions mean a lot to me. Eventually, I will have to retire, and the Romina Empire should be kept within the family. I can't be the last of my family line to rule this syndicate with an iron fist."

He realizes I'm not listening and moves so that he's situated between myself and my parents' bodies. I blink a few times and focus on his icy stare. He chuckles another low rumble, and the temptation to spit directly in his smug face is almost unbearable.

My parents died to protect me. They gave everything in a failed attempt to keep me safe. I cannot let this bastard win.

One callused finger slips beneath my chin, yanking my face up to look at him. I grit my teeth, staring back at him in defiance. Nothing he can say or do can possibly cause me more harm than what he's ever done.

With a wide smile, Oleg declares, "You will marry my son, Yakov."

Without another thought, I hock back and let fly a wad of phlegm that hits him directly in the center of his left eye.

The slap across my face sends me reeling, but it doesn't hurt.

I'm beyond pain now.

THREE
PRISONER

Tatiana

I SPEND most of my time in "my" room. Images of my parents bleeding out fill my mind, whether I'm awake or asleep. Even sitting by the window, staring out at the serene garden behind the mansion, I can't shake the overwhelming sadness and revulsion that fills my body with every shuddering breath I inhale.

No one comes into my room except for the maids–and that's a good thing. When I have to see Oleg again, it will be all I can do to keep from lunging at him and trying to take him out right now. I will kill him–but I can't be impulsive, or I'll spoil my chance. Something tells me he won't hesitate to kill me if he feels it's necessary, regardless of all of his plans for me.

No, I need to bide my time. Lie in wait. Strike when the timing is right.

When I'm not picturing my parents' pale bodies sitting in those chairs, I imagine what it will be like to kill him. That's the only time I allow myself a bit of happiness, a small smile, when I think about what it will be like to have his blood coating my hands.

A few days after my parents were murdered, there's a knock on my door. I'm summoned to come downstairs. I hesitate. I don't want to see Oleg or anyone–but I know I don't have a choice. Taking deep breaths, I make my way downstairs to the parlor. This is a different room than the one where my parents' were slaughtered. Still, I know that room is right down the hallway, which makes me uneasy.

I walk into the elaborately decorated room, shades of burgundy and forest green blending with dark woods and heavy furniture, to see a man a bit older than me standing next to Oleg. I know immediately who he is. He looks like a slightly younger version of his father. Yakov. The man I'm going to marry.

He's smiling at me in a way that makes me think he'd devour me if he could. His nose is too big. His hair, while styled, is coarse and already beginning to thin on top. What's most unsettling of all are his eyes.

They're the same icy orbs his father stares me down with.

I swallow hard and stop a few steps away from him. I don't want to touch him.

His eyes roam over my body, taking their time, lingering on all of the places I'd never want him to touch me. When he finally reaches my face, a ghastly smile crinkles his already-wrinkling face at the corners. "You've chosen well, Father," he murmurs.

I narrow my eyes into slits and keep my distance. I refuse to entertain the thought that this man will someday be my husband.

He takes a step toward me. I don't retreat, though it's all I can do to keep myself from doing so. "We will marry soon," he says, his Russian accent not nearly as thick as his father's but still there. "I'm looking forward to it, Tatiana."

Rather than responding to him, I turn to Oleg. "May I go back to my room, please?" It's difficult to get that last word out, but I have to behave myself, or else my parents–all four of them–will have died for nothing.

"What's the matter, *milaya*? Don't you want to spend some time getting to know your husband?" Oleg cackles, rocking back and forth from heel to toe.

Swallowing down bile, I say, "No, I think we will have time for that later." I return my gaze to Yakov and realize I've been able to surmise everything I could ever need to know in this one meeting.

He's repulsive–possessive and cruel.

He's also unintelligent. I can tell by the foolish smirk on his face. That's not something I want in a husband, but in this situation, it will work in my favor.

"Go," Oleg says, still chuckling under his breath.

I don't hesitate to turn and march out of the room, but I haven't even reached the hallway when I hear Yakov say, "That's a fine piece of ass, Father. Thank you for acquiring her for me."

Oleg says, "You should have the best son. Just don't fuck it up."

Back in my room, I sink down into a chair and rack my brain for ways to escape. This place is heavily guarded. I have nothing–no money, no phone, not even a change of clothing that belongs to me. If I managed to get out the window from the second story and past the guards, then what? There's a fence around the property, and from what I can see out the window, we seem to be far from the city. Where would I go? What would I do? No, I have to bide my time. Even if I went to the Russian embassy, there's no guarantee I wouldn't run into one of Oleg's friends and end up right back here– or dead. If I am patient, the opportunity will present itself. One way or another.

DAYS TURN INTO WEEKS, and now I've been here for nearly a month. Every day, I sit by the window, staring outside, watching the world go by, wondering when I will be faced with marrying Yakov. It's coming. I know it is. Oleg won't put this off for long. He's likely gathering all of his minions and the other syndicate leaders, trying to make this seem like some sort of royal affair instead of the shot-gun wedding it really is.

The longer I'm held captive, the more desperate I become. I need to find a way to get out of here. In order to do that, I need to know the mansion better. Where are the exits? I'm not locked in my room, so one day after lunch, I decide to explore the estate. No one is paying any attention to me anyway. They seem to think I've given up on any hope of getting out of here.

As I make my way down endless hallways, no one asks me what I'm doing. I keep an explanation at the tip of my tongue just in case someone questions me. I bump into a few guards when I get to the second floor. It's no surprise he has his men patrolling all over the place–inside and outside. Every step I take, eyes follow me.

How the hell am I supposed to get out of this place?

Inhaling slowly, I remind myself of my purpose. Firstly, I must stay alive. I can't vindicate my parents if I'm dead. Secondly, I need to escape. I'll have to get away and then figure out the best way to take Oleg out for good.

I take a detour and head toward the kitchen. Lunch churns in my stomach, threatening to come back up. I need a glass of water to keep it down.

Once I reach the kitchen, I hesitate before pushing through the door. I've never been here before. The maids said I should ask them if I need anything. I haven't made a single quest, but I know it's a means of making sure they know where I am at all times.

The room is empty except for one maid. I think her name is Lily. Lila? I haven't been in much of a mood for socializing, so I'm really not sure what any of their names are. They are nice enough, but I'm not here to fucking make friends.

"Oh, uh... hi," I say awkwardly, fidgeting with the hem of my shirt. "I just, uh, wanted a glass of water."

Flashing me a smile so large it seems out of place, she moves to the fridge and pours me a glass of ice water from a pitcher. She hands it to me, and I regret not being polite to her before. She seems... nice.

"Thank you," I say, clearing my throat. "I... don't remember your name," I confess, embarrassed.

She chuckles, shrugging. "It's okay. I doubt Mr. Romana knows it either. We're supposed to be invisible." She rolls her eyes. "I'm Laura."

Ah... I was close.

"It's nice to meet you, Laura," I reply. "Despite the circumstances." I'm not in a situation to trust anyone, but so far, Laura seems kind. I may as well be polite to her. I take a sip of the water and feel marginally better.

She stares at me and sighs, her eyes darting to the door for a second as if to make sure no one is coming. "Listen...." She leans forward, her mouth so close to my ear, I can feel the warmth of her breath. "I don't know you, but I think I know what I'd do if I were in your situation." I raise an eyebrow, and she continues. "Don't do it. It won't work."

I frown, narrowing my eyes at her. "What are you talking about?" I try to keep my voice nonchalant, but I hear the quiver in it.

"No one escapes Mr. Romana. Believe me, I've seen so many die because they dared to try."

My heart skips a beat as I realize what she is saying. I swallow the lump in my throat and nod. "I'll keep that in mind." It's all I can say. I have no doubt my uncle is used to keeping dangerous people prisoners here, people he's at war with. If they can't get away from his clutches, what are my chances?

Not good.

Laura offers me a small, sympathetic smile before heading back to the stove. I'm about to leave the room when a glint of silver catches my eye.

A wooden block full of knives sits on the counter. Blades of various shapes and sizes stick out of the slots, everything from a paring knife to a meat cleaver. Without hesitation, I reach over and grab one of the larger steak knives and slide it under my shirt, into the waistband of my pants. I have no plans to use it at this point, but it won't hurt to have it with me–just in case.

I fucking know how to use it, after all.

"Thank you, Laura," I say before rushing out the door.

I'm halfway down the hallway when an unpleasant odor hits my nose. Yakov appears in front of me about the same time I place that sweaty, spicy scent. My stomach turns over, and I wish I'd stayed in the kitchen with Laura.

When he sees me, a crooked smile tugs up one side of his face. He approaches, flanked by bodyguards. "Ah, Tatiana." His eyes meet mine, and I look away as my skin begins to crawl. Even his voice disgusts me. "What a surprise to see you walking around the house. I hope you're not getting too attached to it, though. I plan on moving to a different estate after the wedding." He chuckles, and his body-guards mimic him.

I don't give him the satisfaction of answering. In fact, I hope he finds me dull and unintelligent enough that he decides not to marry me. Unfortunately, my plan doesn't seem to be working. Even with me standing here staring blankly at him, his smile widens, and a glint in his icy eyes tells me he's thinking repulsive thoughts. Once again, bile rises in the back of my throat, but I choke it down.

Disgusting.

"What's the matter, *kukolka?* Cat got your tongue?" I drop my eyes to the floor, praying he'll leave me the hell alone. He takes a step toward me. I brace myself as his stubby fingers lift my chin. It's all I can do to keep from pulling away. Seeing my reaction, he tightens his grip, forcing me to look up at him. "That's another thing I'll have to fix once we're married," he continues through gritted teeth. His anger radiates from every pore, but I don't budge. "Look at me when I'm talking to you."

I want to tell him to fuck off because I couldn't care less, but he shoves me backward, his nails scratching my face as he does so.

I bite down the rage boiling inside me. One swift move from me, and the knife hidden in my waistband would be sticking out of his chest. But that would leave me dead before I have a chance to kill my true target–his bastard father.

I need to wait for the right moment, for the right chance, to get my revenge.

In the meantime, I glare back at his icy eyes, imagining all the ways I'd like to rip this asshole apart.

Soon.

FOUR
GROOMZILLA

Tatiana

A TACKY, overly poofy white gown hangs on the back of the bathroom door next to the full-length mirror. I take a deep breath and drag a hand down my face. How the fuck am I getting out of this?

I hoped I'd have more time to escape, but this day has come more quickly than anticipated, and now, here I am. The fuckers got me to the church on time.

"What do you think?" one of the maids who will be helping me get dressed asks, a timid smile on her face.

Arching an eyebrow, I say, "I think I'd be better suited to black."

She laughs nervously and pulls the fancy frock down off the hanger. I have to assume this contraption cost thousands of dollars and was designed by one of New York's biggest names in fashion.

It's a death trap to me.

It would look so much better with a spray of vomit across the front.

Telling myself I need to focus, I listen to the maids prattle on about how they're going to do my hair and makeup and other such bullshit I couldn't care less about.

"This dress is magnificent," one of the maids whispers to the other. The other woman agrees, and I resist the urge to roll my eyes.

Unfortunately, Laura is not here. Just another tally against this morbid day. She's the only one in the house I like—or trust. These two keep making eyes over the top of my head like I can't see them in the mirror.

The maids begin to style my long, wavy brown hair, pulling it from side to side, deciding what to do with it. I ignore them, tugging at one of the straps of this vicious gown. It's so fucking tight, my lungs are burning.

Another woman I don't recognize comes in and starts laying out makeup brushes on the vanity in front of me. She's older, with a stern face. Not exactly the kind of person one dreams about getting them ready for their wedding.

Fuck... I miss my mom....

"I'd have to live a thousand lives to be able to afford something like this," the maid to my left notes, fingering the strap of my gown. "Are these... diamonds?"

Her eyes nearly pop out of their sockets as she reaches down to finger the shining jewelry embroidered on my corset. They look like diamonds for sure, but I've never been into fancy shit like that, so I'm really not sure if they're real or fake. Too bad I can't rip them off the gown and tell these ladies to make a break for it. Maybe I'd go with them.

They continue to chat amongst each other as the stern woman with the bird nose begins to apply makeup in garish colors to my face, making me look like a clown—or a bride from the 1980s, more like it. I don't give two fucks. Maybe Yakov will think I'm hideous and call the wedding off.

I have to stifle a yawn as she begins to apply lipstick in a hot pink hue. I was up most of the night, trying to figure out a way to escape, but I was being kept in a fortress with dozens of brutish guards around every corner.

The whole way to the church, I bided my time, praying I'd have the opportunity to jump out of the vehicle, but I had a guard on either side of me. So, I've been trying to come up with a plan for the wedding reception. With my luck, there will be just as many armed men there to ensure I can't even pee without being watched.

I watch the hands on the clock on the wall behind me. Two hours? Fuck. Why is this taking so damn long? But then... I'm not in a huge hurry to marry my cousin. That's so fucked up.

"You look so lovely," the maid who wanted the diamonds off my dress says, giving my hair a final poof.

"Thanks." That's all I can say. What else could I tell them? That they are dolling me up for a man who will probably beat me and threaten me every day of our lives? That I'm on my way from one prison to another? They work for Oleg and the Romina family. They already know what those bastards are like. I don't need to remind them.

"You look like a princess," the other one muses beside me.

"She really does," the first one agrees.

I offer them a small smile. My vision blurs as tears threaten to spill down my cheeks, ruining Beak-face's hard work. I can't let them see me cry. Besides, I'm sure Oleg would punish them if I got to the wedding looking anything less than how he's envisioned.

"Are you sure you don't want to eat anything before you go, Miss Ivanov?" one of the women who did my hair asks. "You haven't eaten anything at all, and I'm sure the ceremony will be long. You need to be able to stand up there without passing out."

She is right about that. Although, I wouldn't mind ruining the wedding because I fainted.

"I'm okay, thanks," I reply. Besides, I couldn't put anything in my stomach right now. Bile rises in the back of my throat again.

They all excuse themselves, leaving me alone in the room.

Someone is supposed to come pick me up and take me to the chapel, so I wait seated in front of the mirror, staring back at my reflection.

I don't even look like myself. Maybe that will make it easier to pretend this isn't me—that I'm not the one marrying Yakov. I'm just temporarily caught in someone else's nightmare.

Back in Russia, I used to imagine who I'd marry, a handsome man who loved me. I'd wear a beautiful gown I picked out with my mother—my mother standing behind me, smiling proudly as we gazed into the mirror, both of us beautiful and blushing.

I'd rather go back to constantly looking over my shoulder in Russia than be here now—with my parents dead. I never really expected Oleg to find out about me, and I still don't know how he did. None of that matters now.

A knock on the door pulls me out of my reverie, and I get to my feet, not even bothering to tell whoever it is to come inside. I know they came for me.

One of Oleg's capos is outside, his eyes narrowed in annoyance that he has to be the one to escort me. Maybe he thinks I'm beneath him. Maybe he'd rather be out killing innocent people rather than shadowing me down the hallway. I don't wait for him to order me to march. Instead, I brush past him into the hallway, silently hoping he steps on the ridiculously long train of this dress and tears it so the wedding will be off.

Tears announce their presence with a sharp sting, but I will them back, pushing away the intrusive thoughts and walking alongside this brute, the maids rushing behind me to help adjust the dress's train.

The hallway stretches on forever; though it's as short as the plank on a pirate ship. I watch the blurred faces gathered on either side, staring at me, and try to remember this isn't over yet. If I keep my wits, maybe I can find a way to get out of here.

One thing is for damn sure. I can't cry in front of these bastards. Weakness has a scent, and they'd eat me alive.

When we arrive in front of the chapel, the doors are open. Unlike my dress and makeup, the decorations here are glamorous.

Beautiful flowers in crisp white and scarlet red bloom from large vases near the dais. Smaller ones are attached to the end of every pew. A large archway decorated in flowers and ivy stands behind the priest.

The priest... too damn bad he's not here for my fucking funeral.

With just one glance, I can tell there are more than three hundred guests packed inside the chapel, not to mention the bastards lining the hallway and stationed outside to keep me from running. I'm sure the most elite mobsters of New York and the surrounding area are all congregated here to see Yakov anoint me as his queen.

The music shifts, and all eyes turn to me. People whisper to each other behind their hands as I make my way to the entryway.

"Miss Ivanov, come right here, dear." A middle-aged woman with way too much jewelry gestures for me to take my place. I'm assuming she's the wedding planner. I wonder if she chose this dress. If so, I may just have to spit in her eyes. She hands me a bouquet, and I begrudgingly snatch it out of her hands.

I maintain my composure and stop where she's pointed. Taking a deep breath, I finally allow myself to look at the other figure standing at the far end of the aisle, near the priest.

Fucking Yakov. He looks like the smarmy bastard he is, standing up there, rocking back and forth from heel to toe, his hands folded in front of him. He reminds me of a cobra, ready to strike.

God, the thought of a large snake makes my mind jump elsewhere. That asshole better not think I'm sleeping with him. I'd rather die first. Of course, Oleg has already explained that he must have an heir to his legacy. The mere thought of having to give Yakov a child, to watch my flesh and blood be raised under the influence of those two bastards, makes me double down on my threat—kill me now.

"You can go," the woman whispers, and I realize the wedding march is already playing and everyone is staring at me in anticipation.

I take a deep breath and force my legs to move forward. My hands tighten around the bouquet, and my gaze finds a spot behind the altar. I can't look at Yakov again or that puke I threatened to splatter all over my dress will end up on him, too.

God, how I want to turn and run. I'd be caught before I could blink though, and it'd only worsen my situation.

As soon as I reach the end of the aisle, Yakov yanks my arm with his, forcing me to stand next to him. The overwhelming stench of his spicy cologne burns my nostrils. I grit my teeth, trying not to grimace. I can feel Oleg behind me, and I know he has his eyes on me. He's fully prepared to deal with anything I might try to pull off.

"No one will save you, darling," Yakov murmurs into my ear, and my stomach twists with his foreboding threat. "You're stuck with me, so you better stop fighting it. Otherwise, what I have planned for us tonight will be a lot less pleasure, and a lot more pain."

The priest clears his throat in front of us and opens his mouth, but not a single syllable comes out before the ground beneath my feet trembles and a large boom has me dropping my flowers to cover my ears. Panic bubbles up in my throat as I quickly turn to see what's going on. Gunfire rings out from the back of the church, followed by screams, shouts, and the sound of hundreds of people scrambling to escape.

Chaos erupts all around me.

Smoke burns my eyes, momentarily disorienting me. I crouch down the best I can in this fucking dress, trying to ascertain what the hell is going on. Everywhere I look, I see people trying to find the closest exit. In the back of the church, bodies slump over the pews.

I need to do... something....

Spinning around, I realize Yakov is no longer beside me. I hear his voice somewhere across the chapel as he yells orders to his men. The smoke clears for a moment, and I see my betrothed cowering behind a pew while he waves at the guards to run into the gunfire.

I look back at the pew where Oleg was seated, and he's gone, too. Knowing him, he's in the thick of things. Unlike his son, he's not a coward.

And then... everything becomes crystal clear. I have to do what these other motherfuckers are doing. It's my one chance.

Gathering up my garish gown, I do exactly what I've wanted to do since the day Oleg killed my parents.

I run.

FIVE

BLOODY BRIDE

Tatiana

HOW THE HELL am I supposed to escape this place when I have no fucking idea where I am? Running toward the back of the chapel seemed to make the most sense to me since the fighting is all happening at the front—at least for now—so I sprint toward the door the priest likely used and pray it's unlocked.

Thankfully, it is. I slam through it, looking around to ascertain if there's any danger here. I see the priest huddled in the corner and almost roll my eyes. Hiking my skirt up, I take off toward a door I believe has to be an exit.

"You shouldn't go that way!" he shouts. "They're out there, too!"

But my momentum carries me through the door before I can think, and I nearly run into a couple of Oleg's men who are defending the back entryway against what appears to be another syndicate—one of the many groups of enemies Oleg has accumulated over the years, no doubt.

"How the fuck did they find us?" one of the men in front of me shouts to the other in a thick Russian accent. I just have time to hide behind a marble column before they see me.

"This is the Saints we're talking about, man," the other one replies, his breathing erratic. "They were probably waiting to attack as soon as they thought we were distracted."

Another barrage of gunfire has them occupied enough that I decide it's time to make a break for it. I have no idea where I am or where I'm even going, but at this point, I have no choice but to run. I pull my dress up so it doesn't trip me as I run in the only direction that seems to lead away from the onslaught. There might be a route to a different part of the garden—somewhere I can disappear from view until I can get my bearings.

Oleg will realize I'm gone soon, and he'll have his capos after me in the blink of an eye. I don't stand a chance against them, especially unarmed and unfamiliar with my surroundings, so I'm at a complete disadvantage here. If I'm going to take advantage of this situation, I have to get as far away from here as possible while his attention is on the Saints.

I have no fucking idea who the Saints are, but at the moment, they're my new best friends.

If Oleg survives this—and I hope he doesn't, but I'm certain he will—I have to keep running. Hiding under his nose might sound like a good idea, but he'll have the entire chapel turned upside down to find me.

As I sprint across the open ground, I'm constantly looking over my shoulder, hoping no one is after me. So far, I don't see anybody. It's so fucking hard to run in these shoes, but at this point, my feet are numb, so at least I don't feel them biting into my heels. My heart is in my throat, beating so hard it's about to break free. And this goddamn dress has to weigh at least three hundred pounds.

In front of me, I see what looks like a small wooded area. I have no idea how many of these places are left this close to the city, but I can't imagine there are many. Maybe I'll get lucky and this will lead to a park or some other place where I might be able to get help.

As I take off for the trees, I ponder kicking my heels off, but running barefoot in the forest might not be a good idea either. The last thing I need is to step on something sharp that will leave me a sitting duck.

I rush between trees, dodging what look like thorny bushes, and cut through a pile of leaves, nearly tripping over an exposed root. I gather my dress again and move toward a grove of cedars. My foot catches on something buried in fallen pine needles, and down I go.

"Fuck!" I catch myself with my hands, but a pain in my calf reminds me that I'm not completely unarmed. Ever since the day I stole that knife from Oleg's kitchen, I've been carrying it around with me, just in case I have an opportunity to use it. Now, despite the fact that I wrapped it carefully before securing it to my leg, it seems to have scraped me. I can't think about it now. I pull myself up from the ground and start running again.

The screams and gunshots behind me get quieter as I distance myself from the chapel. However, I hear a few muffled noises in front of me that sound like panicked people doing the same thing I am—trying to get away. I'll have to steer clear of them, just in case they decide to sell me out, but it's hard to be quiet in this fucking getup as I traipse through the forest, running for my life.

I see sunlight up ahead and realize I'm almost through the woods. Without looking too closely where I'm going, I rush forward. A snapping sound and another rough fall later, I realize I've broken the heel off one of the designer torture devices on my feet.

"Fucking A!" I shout, pawing at my gown to pull it out of the way so I can see. I take the shoes off as quickly as I can and toss them into the bushes, hoping they won't be easily spotted when Oleg comes looking for me.

On my feet again, I take off running, only to see another obstacle in my way.

I step out of the woods and am met with an iron fence that apparently runs around the entire forest—maybe the whole property.

"Are you shitting me?"

"The gate's over here!" someone shouts from my left. I know he's not talking to me, but that's good to know. Quickly, I dash back into the trees, trying to use the larger trunks as shelter so that whoever else is in the woods doesn't see me. In the distance, I see a couple of men dressed as waiters and a maid scrambling through an unlocked gate.

"Thank God," I mutter. As soon as they are out of sight and I don't hear anyone else nearby, I'll take my shot.

One by one, they squat down and crawl out from under the fence, and when the last one passes, I count a minute in my head before I follow them.

Now that I have an opportunity to break free, I'm in such a rush I'm not being as careful as I should be. My dress is so wide, I have trouble clearing the opening, and the back of my dress snags on what appears to be a rusty shard of fence that's let go from the main column. I tug at it, using all my strength to detach myself, but these layers refuse to rip.

I'm fucking stuck!

I look around, assessing any threats and considering what to do.

Standing still, I feel more of my injuries than I did while running, and my calf begins to throb. Oh, yes! The knife! With a wicked laugh, I reach down and grab it from its hiding spot and use it to hack through the stuck material. Once I'm free, I attempt to tug the telltale fabric off the fence, but it won't budge—and I can't stand here all fucking day.

Deciding it's not worth it to continue to struggle, I lift up what's left of my skirt with one hand and keep the knife at the ready in the other, just in case.

In front of me, I see a narrow path and decide to take it. I still have no idea where I am, but any place is better than that chapel or Oleg's prison.

The path leads through another wooded area, and I realize the chapel must've been on another one of Oleg's various estates. We have to be close to the city because we didn't drive far to get here, but we are far enough away that I can't hear the sounds of congestion or smell the smog.

Trees line the side of the path. I rush down it, hoping it takes me to someplace public. Rounding a corner, I think I see another open area in the distance.

And that's when I'm knocked to the ground.

"Fuck!" I fall hard, rolling a few times but managing to keep my grip on my knife. The sound of laughter to my left has me scrambling to my feet.

A man in a suit grins at me, the pistol in his hand pointed right at my chest.

Where the fuck did he come from?

"Well, well, well. Look what the cat dragged in," he says in an American accent. I know he's not one of Oleg's men because I don't recognize him, and most of them are Russian, but the fact that he's pointing a gun at me tells me he must work for one of Oleg's allies.

"Let me go," I say in as calm a tone as I can muster. I hope he doesn't notice the hand I'm holding the knife in is trembling just a bit.

"I don't think so, sweetheart," he says. "You think I don't know who the fuck you are?"

"I'm not a part of this," I tell him. "I'm not part of the Romina Empire."

"I don't give a fuck. You're the bride. You gotta be worth something." He takes a step toward me. "Now, be a nice little princess and drop the knife."

Instead of tossing it aside, I raise it higher, pointing it at him. It seems I have, indeed, brought a knife to a gunfight, but Lev taught me what to do in this situation. Granted, that was years ago, and I've never once had to use any of the combat skills he taught me in real life, but the muscle memory should still be there—I hope.

If not, well, I'm fucking screwed.

"Fuck off," I tell him.

His eyes widen slightly in shock, but then he laughs again and takes a few steps toward me. I anticipate his move as he goes to grab me, knowing he won't shoot me outright because my uncle would kill him. I dodge to the left, twisting around to grab the arm that holds the gun. I completely take him by surprise and manage to wrench the gun from his hand. He raises his other fist to hit me, but I'm still holding the knife. With a quick slice, he's pulling back, screaming. Blood squirts everywhere—covering his suit, spraying me in the face and all over the front of my hideous gown.

Well, it's not puke, but it might still be an upgrade.

"You fucking bitch!" he shouts, holding his arm. I must've hit a pretty good artery because that's a hell of a lot of blood.

With him distracted and bleeding, I grab the gun off the ground and point it at him. "You were saying?"

Clearly, he's not the tough guy he's been pretending to be. With his arm bleeding profusely and his own weapon pointed at him, he takes a few steps back toward the tree he was hiding behind. I guess he was put here to secure the perimeter during the wedding. He's done a miserable job.

Still keeping my eye on him, I take a few steps backward, debating whether or not it would be a good idea to shoot him in the leg so he can't follow me. But the gun doesn't have a silencer, and I don't need to announce to my uncle that something's happening in the woods right now. When I'm satisfied he's not going to chase me, I turn around and run as fast as I can toward the path, my knife in one hand, his gun in the other.

Above me, the sun beats down, causing beads of perspiration to sting my eyes. I can't pause to wipe them away, though. At least the wedding wasn't a nighttime event. While it would have made it easier to hide, I wouldn't have been able to see a fucking thing out here. I probably would've broken an ankle—or worse, my neck.

Eventually, the path ends in an enormous green space dotted with a few trees, some flowers, and what appears to be a little pond off in the distance.

"Holy fuck," I mutter. "This is a park."

Glancing around, I see a few people here and there, but no one near me. On the other side of the park I see a parking lot and what appears to be some baseball diamonds. I don't see any buildings right away, but they have to be close by. Maybe there's a neighborhood. But then... where the fuck do I think I'm going? Am I just going to waltz into the police station and tell them I've been kidnapped by the Russian mob?

No, that's not a good idea.

Fuck. I'm still screwed.

I start walking down a trail that seems to lead to the parking lot, though it's a winding path that goes out of my way before it returns to a straight shot to where a few cars are parked. I round a corner and come eye-to-eye with a woman about my age dressed in athletic clothes with her earbuds in.

Her eyes widen in horror as she takes me in.

"Shit," I mumble. I can't blame her for looking at me. I must look worse than the Bride of Frankenstein wearing this dirty, torn gown with a huge blood smear across the front.

Not to mention I'm barefoot and have twigs in my hair.

She says nothing and takes off running again. I'm thankful she didn't scream, honestly. With nothing else to do, I continue to walk, praying that my uncle isn't already coming after me.

Even if he's not yet, he will be soon.

Another jogger sees me, turns around, and sprints the other direction.

Glancing down, I realize there's a whole lotta blood on this fucking dress.

I have to get rid of it. Now.

SIX

BLENDING IN

Tatiana

GETTING someone to help me proves to be an almost impossible task, even once I wander into a populated area of New York City.

I know literally no one in this city, and it's not like I can trust anyone. While I'm fairly certain my adoptive parents had allies here, I have no fucking idea who they are or how to find them. Oleg must have eyes and ears everywhere, so it makes me hesitant to approach anyone.

But in this dress, I'm an easy target for anyone who might be helping him. New York is a crazy place, but I'm probably the only woman in a bloody, ripped-up wedding gown on the streets today. If the mob doesn't get to me, the police certainly will.

My stomach is beginning to ache from the knot that formed in there weeks ago, but I force myself to take deep breaths. At least I'm able to hold back my tears—for now. My whole life turned upside down in a blink of an eye, and having to suppress my feelings so I don't show my weakness to Oleg and Yakov has taken its toll on me.

Picking up my bare feet is becoming more and more trying. I'm hungry, tired, and just want this nightmare to be over. My hurried pace is fueled by adrenaline and the awareness that if I don't get away now, I never will.

"Are you all right, sweetheart?"

I blink, staring at the kind face of an old lady, concern furrowing her brows as she stands a good five feet from me on the sidewalk.

"Do you need any help?" Her eyes roam past my wide eyes to my shaking hands. It was probably a wise decision to drop the gun in a dumpster a few blocks back. At least, she won't think I'm going to murder her–probably.

My mouth opens and closes a few times before I answer. What if the Rominas sent an innocent looking elderly woman to lure me in and then trap me so they can dive in and take me back to the mansion? It seems a bit far-fetched, but I wouldn't put it past Oleg.

Would it be a mistake on my end to trust her?

Timidly, she moves closer, grabbing my hand and squeezing it. "Did someone hurt you?" she asks, lowering her voice.

"Yes. I mean, no, I-I..." I look around, considering what to tell her. I don't want to incriminate her by telling her more than she needs to know. If she really is just an angel who was sent to aid me, Oleg could get to her and find out she helped me, and I can't even begin to imagine the things he might do to her. "Could you just get me some clothes?" I ask instead.

The corners of her mouth turn down as she studies me. I glance down at my ruined gown, and her eyes follow mine. Maybe she expected me to ask for money, but I couldn't bother her with such a request. Not when I know she might be killed for even speaking to me.

"Are you sure? Do you need me to call the police or something? You look like you were... attacked," she whispers the last word, cautiously watching my reaction.

I shake my head. "I'm all right," I tell her, looking over my shoulder. The sooner I get new clothes, the better my chances of escaping will be. "I just need to get changed. Please. I need people to stop staring at me."

She studies me for a couple of seconds before she finally nods. "Okay, I can help you with that. I live in a condo a block from here. You can come with me if you want," she offers kindly.

It astonishes me that she would trust someone as suspicious as I am enough to show me where she lives, but I guess there are still good people in this world.

Or maybe she's leading me straight into an ambush.

Nodding, I follow her down the sidewalk. I *need* to trust her. She's the only one who can offer me a chance of escaping Oleg for good right now. I ignore the glances I get from people on the street. The old lady doesn't say anything else to me, which I'm thankful for. She looks like someone I could get attached to, and right now, that's the last thing I need to do.

Anyone who gets close to me automatically has a target on their back.

Soon enough, we reach a brick building on a surprisingly empty street, and I tell her I'll wait outside while she grabs something for me to wear.

Five minutes later, she comes back with a plain black T-shirt and a pair of jeans in one hand and some flip-flops in the other.

"These are my daughter's," she explains, handing them to me. "She's about your size. They should fit."

I smile in thanks, taking them and moving to the small alley beside the building. She turns her back to me, watching the street in silence, glancing from side to side to make sure no one is approaching while I change. I slip the jeans on under the dress so I'm not completely naked, and then tug the dress off over my head, thankful to be wearing a bra that leaves much to the imagination.

Once I'm dressed, I bury the dress in a dumpster, hoping no one digs through and finds it and then return to her side. "Thank you so much," I say. She turns to face me again. Her eyebrows are still furrowed, and her mouth is drawn into a tight line.

"Are you sure you don't need any more help?" she offers again.

I shake my head, giving her a small smile. "You've done more than enough already. I can't thank you enough."

She takes a step forward, shoving something in my hand. I look down, spotting a fifty dollar bill now in my palm.

"You really sho—" I begin.

She waves a hand at me dismissively. "I want to. There's a small deli a few blocks from here. You could hide in there for a while until you figure out what to do. They have delicious croissants there, and you look like you need to eat something. You don't want to pass out in the middle of the street."

She's not wrong. I'm lightheaded and clammy, and my pulse is racing. However, food is the last thing on my mind right now. I do need to think about where to go or what to do though, and I can't do that out in the open like this. Maybe her suggestion will come in handy. "Thank you," I say again, tears dampening my eyelashes as I take her hand and hold it for a moment.

She nods at me before urging me to go on. She turns her head to watch down the street in the direction we came, just in case I'm followed.

I don't look back.

I already feel my heart tightening with pain as I turn my back on the first person who's been kind to me after so long. Laura was somewhat nice to me, too, but she would never be someone I could blindly trust since she works for Oleg.

I miss my parents.

I miss my home.

I miss my freedom.

God, why does everything have to be so hard?

It takes me about ten minutes to get to the deli she told me about. Spinning around, I make sure no one has followed me and let out a small sigh of relief before I approach the door.

It was premature.

Before I have the chance to enter the establishment, I spot a black SUV pulling up in front of the door. Several men get out and look around, searching for something... for *someone*.

"Fuck," I hiss, running to hide behind some trash cans in a nearby alley. Turning around, I see a brick wall behind me.

Good God, of all the fucking alleys in New York City, I had to pick one that's a dead end.

I hear footsteps in the distance and lean around the corner to peek at the deli. Several men walk inside, others going around the back. Another group splits up to go into nearby establishments.

Exhaling sharply, I close my eyes for a brief second to calm my racing heart. Is the mafia everywhere in this fucking city? I don't think I recognize any of the men I just saw, but they could be more of Oleg's allies.

I open my eyes again, take a deep breath, and dart my head around the corner for another check.

I'm staring at a broad chest covered in a black button-down.

I blink twice, trying to make sense of what I'm seeing.

"Fuck," I mutter, lifting my eyes.

His rugged jawline tenses, the muscle in his cheek protruding slightly as he stares down at me, his eyes hard and cold. My first instinct is to turn and run, but he's muscular and probably much faster than I am. His curly hair is styled and professional. The guy looks like a fucking gangster for sure.

"I don't know who you're looking for bu–" Before I can finish my sentence, he grabs me, pushing me up against the wall, holding both of my wrists with one of his enormous hands. My arms are pinned above my head, useless. He leans in so that his nose is only a fraction from mine. Brown eyes pierce right through me as a grin spreads across his lips.

"For someone who was just getting married a few minutes ago, you're pretty good at blending in," he murmurs, the smell of mint and a hint of whiskey brushing my face. "I have some questions for you. I hope you like Upstate New York," he adds before lifting his other hand and covering my nose with a cloth, knocking me unconscious.

SEVEN
KIDNAPPING THE RUNAWAY BRIDE

Angelo

"I'VE GOT HER," I inform the rest of my men, who are all wearing earpieces. "I'm taking her to the car."

"Roger that," Dice replies right away. "We'll meet you there."

I toss the woman's limp body over my shoulder and step out of the alley, ignoring the curious and frightened stares I receive from pedestrians bustling by on the street.

The SUV is parked in front of the deli, and when Sal spots me, he climbs from behind the wheel and rushes to open the back door for me. I place the woman into the back seat—carefully, even though I don't need to be—and go around to the other side so I can sit beside her. I buckle us both in and wait for the others to load up.

Even though I knocked her out, and she probably won't wake up in the next few hours, I still need to keep a close eye on her, just in case she wakes up and tries some funny business. I'll watch her the entire way until we're out of this part of the city and safe in our territory where we're less likely to be attacked.

"That was easier than I expected," Kian murmurs as he sits in the passenger's seat in front of me. He glances over his shoulder, scrutinizing her where she lays limp, almost lifeless, on the seat next to me, and then his eyes dart to mine. "Are you sure that's her?"

I nod sharply, glancing at her sideways. This is her all right. I've seen her picture before, and that's not a face anyone would easily forget. In a word, she's beautiful. Her long, wavy brown hair is somewhat disheveled, which isn't a surprise after everything she's been through. Her makeup is a bit over the top, but she was supposed to get married today, and a lot of it has come off–from sweating as she made her escape, no doubt. Her eyes, even though I can't see them now because they are closed, are still imprinted in my mind like a permanent stamp, as is the way she looked at me before I knocked her out, her sapphire blues shining up at me with the sparkle of tears as she silently pleaded for me to let her go.

"Wasn't she wearing a wedding dress?" he continues, returning his attention to the road ahead now that are back on the move. "A bloody one even. Sal said she managed to cut his arm, and the blood splattered on the dress."

"She must have found a way to change clothes before we got to her." I'm stating the obvious. No longer wanting to talk about the sleeping beauty, I abruptly ask, "Did we have any casualties?"

I had to leave from the chapel where the ceremony was being held before the mission was completed since we were informed that the bride managed to escape. The boss ordered me to go after her, so I have no idea how it all ended, although I heard that Oleg and Yakov also ran away.

"Thankfully, no." Dice turns onto a street that has the red lights on. "Just Sal's bloody arm. That's what he gets for being so fucking aggressive." Dice chuckles, but I don't think it's funny.

God, how I hate the traffic in New York.

"Some of the other guys got minor injuries, but nothing too serious," he continues, checking his watch out of habit.

"What about the Rominas?" I press through clenched teeth. I still can't believe they escaped.

"The motherfuckers were fast. We got two of their men down, but I don't think they were that important, to be honest," Dice explains, equally annoyed at the outcome.

"We did catch them off guard, though," Kian muses proudly. "I doubt they saw it coming. They are just... fast and skilled. Just like cockroaches when you flip on a light switch in a shitty hotel."

I nod slightly, even though they are not looking at me. That's exactly what I think of them. Although, not even cockroaches are as vile and repulsive as the Rominas. Oleg has got to be the most cruel and vicious person I've ever had the misfortune of meeting. His son isn't far behind, though he's too dumb and cowardly to do as much damage.

"We need to fucking end them, once and for all," I grumble. Just thinking about them is giving me a headache. I squeeze my forehead, knowing that won't do any good.

"We will, man," Kian encourages me. "We'll avenge your brother and everyone that we lost because of that motherfucker. You can mark my words."

His voice carries as much anger and hatred as I feel inside. All of us have enough reasons to hate those motherfuckers, and we're all in this together. We will end Oleg and his legacy once and for all. None of us will rest until they're all dead. I look at the girl next to me. She's also part of the Romina syndicate, after all....

I'm glad I still have the Saints to keep me grounded. After losing my brother, they were the ones who helped me move forward. Now, they're the only people I can call family. I'm truly grateful to have them by my side.

"Where is the boss anyway?" I ask, clearing my throat and changing the subject again. I'm not good with emotional talk, and I'm definitely not prepared to discuss my brother right now. Even after so many years, I still find it hard to talk about *that* night.

"Franco is driving him to the safe house," Dice answers, his eyes focused on the road as he drives us out of town.

We're supposed to take the girl to one of our safe houses in Staten Island, and until we get there, we can't lose focus. As far as we're concerned, the mission only ends once we're safe inside our own territory.

Today's operation was risky, and even though we didn't get to take down Oleg or his son, we managed to get *her*, which could lead to the outcome we all want. Since she was going to marry Oleg's son, she might be able to give us the information we need to finally get our revenge. It leaves a bitter taste in my mouth to imagine myself having to torture her, though.

I glance at her once more and watch as her chest rises and falls slowly, a few stains of dry blood smudged on her neck and chin. I can't imagine having to use my most forceful means of extracting information while those wide blue eyes stare into my soul. I've never struggled to force people to spill what I need from them, but her... I shake my head, my eyes darting to the window. She is the fucking enemy and was going to marry into the family that murdered my brother. I should be thrilled to finally have a chance to start my revenge after so long. Instead, dread coils in my stomach like a snake, waiting to strike me down.

"Is the boss going to interrogate her himself?" I force myself to sound casual.

Tony is definitely the best man for the job. He might not want me to be the one to do it. After all, he hates the Rominas as much as I do, and I wouldn't mind if he were the one to break her instead. It would mean *I* wouldn't have to do it, and we'd most likely be successful because his skills are also... effective.

"Uh, not really. He's taking the couple of men we got our hands on to a *different* safe house." Kian glances at me over his shoulder once more as if to see my reaction. "He said it's best to keep them apart in case Oleg comes for them. He'd have to split his men, which might give us an advantage, though we are also split at the moment. Although–" He hesitates, moving in his seat uncomfortably. "The bride is probably who they'd come after first. But that's just a guess." He shrugs.

I consider his words, my brows creasing. "All right. So, what are his actual orders?" Tony didn't get to pass them to me directly since I was involved in putting together a task force to go after the runaway bride.

Dice clears his throat, his jaw clenched. "You're supposed to take care of her until she spills something," he relays, his voice firm and professional.

"When we finally have something on the Rominas, we can take Oleg down and his empire with him." Kian flashes me a toothy grin.

I roll my eyes, sensing where this is going. I know why Tony wanted me to be the one to squeeze information out of her. Out of all his men, I'm the one who is most eager to kill Oleg after what he did to my brother. Sure, a few other members of our syndicate also had their loved ones murdered by him and his gang, but none of them have been consumed with vengeance the way that I have been. Tony knows I can do it. However, I'm afraid it won't be that easy.

This girl seems fragile, so delicate, but since we have no information on her whatsoever, she could also prove herself to be a tough one to break. She did manage to run away from us, after all. We have no idea who she is or why she was going to marry into the Romina family, but I plan on finding out as soon as she wakes up.

"So, in other words, you're babysitting the pretty girl here until we get something useful," Kian adds in a teasing tone.

"And you're staying to help, I assume." I narrow my eyes at them. Dice and Kian share a glance, and I clench my jaw.

"Sure, man," Kian finally says. "Just don't make me torture a pretty girl. You know I can't stand seeing a woman cry."

I grunt, leaning my head backward against the seat, feeling the exhaustion finally take over my body.

My brother's face emerges in my mind's eye, and I tighten my fists, determination coursing through me.

If this is what it takes to get closer to finally putting Oleg in the grave, so be it.

EIGHT
I WILL BREAK YOU

Tatiana

I FEEL like I must've gotten run over by a truck. My head is pounding so hard, I feel like vomiting, but even so, I force my eyes to open. There's no light here except for a dim stream coming through a tiny window near the top of the wall in front of me, so it's difficult for my eyes to adapt.

There are strands of hair in front of my eyes and face, and when I lift my hand to push them aside, I realize my wrists are tied behind my back in what feels like a very thick, tight rope. My legs are also strapped to the chair, both my ankles tied. I can barely move.

Panic starts creeping through me as I realize what's going on. Images of the recent events flash through my mind, making me remember how I ended up here, wherever I am.

I look from one side to the other, taking in my surroundings. Even though it's dark and humid here, I spot some tools and boxes that make me think this has to be a basement. The place is quiet, and there seems to be no one around, although I doubt they'd leave me here alone, unwatched and unguarded. I can't get out of here, after all. Not even the lessons I learned from Lev can help me get free of these fucking knots around my wrists. They're so tight that struggling against them cuts off the circulation to my hands.

"Shit," I hiss to myself, uncomfortably moving in my seat.

My head is pounding, and my stomach twists, reminding me I haven't had much to eat today. With all the wedding preparations, I didn't eat much before the ceremony. And then everything else happened. Whatever that guy used to knock me out has left me nauseated.

I rack my brain to remember what he said to me. He mentioned something before he knocked me unconscious.

"I have some questions for you. I hope you like Upstate New York."

Well, if he had asked me politely, I'd tell him that I have nothing to tell him. Whatever it is he thinks I might be able to help him with, he's wrong because I know nothing.

Does he even know who I am? What could they possibly want from me?

All of a sudden, my life's turned into a cat-and-mouse chase that I can't seem to break free of. Why has everyone decided I'm the best person in the universe to fucking kidnap? First Oleg, now this guy... whoever the fuck he is.

Bastard! My mind returns to those twinkling eyes, that bright smile, that strong jawline, as he cruelly knocked me out. Why is it that the hottest man I've ever laid eyes on is also the one to take me hostage? I shake my head, shoving those thoughts aside. *What is this... fucking Stockholm syndrome?*

As if someone's heard my thoughts, a creaking metal sound to my right makes me turn just in time to see the door opening and a shadow coming through. I recognize the form immediately.

"Ah, you're finally awake." That low, raspy voice reaches my ears, and I instantly tense up. Fear mingles with curiosity, coiling in my stomach and trying to slip lower, but I won't let it. I'm not one of those fucking idiots who falls in love with their kidnapper.

His firm footsteps echo through the room as he approaches me, and when he crosses the stream of light coming through the window, I'm able to see his face. Just as I suspected, it's the same guy who knocked me out.

And he is just as hot as I remembered.

His cold aura compels me to keep staring at him, forcing me to study his every movement. He's wearing the same black outfit, only now he's taken off the jacket, his short-sleeved shirt revealing his sculpted biceps and an anchor tattooed to his forearm.

His jaw is clenched, and judging by his countenance, I'd say this man has probably never smiled in his entire life. His brown eyes roam my face, and now that he's close enough, I can see his hair is no longer perfectly styled back. Whatever styling product he used earlier has failed him, allowing the curls to fall softly over his eyebrows, giving him an even sexier, mysterious aura. *Fucker.*

He clears his throat, bending forward so his gaze is level with mine, his eyes narrowed into slits. "Now, I can finally get some information from her," he says, a grin forming on his lips. His soft, warm, inviting lips....

Shut the fuck up, Tatiana!

"Are you going to tell me your name, or will I have to extract it from you?" he adds, standing up again and crossing his arms over his muscled chest.

I fight the urge to frown. So, he doesn't know who I am. Or maybe he has an idea of who I am, since he must have seen me at the wedding, but he doesn't know my name. Which makes me assume he isn't sure I'm the person he needs.

I press my lips together, forcing them to remain shut, remembering everything Lev taught me about self-defense and how to behave if I ever got caught and taken for interrogation.

I won't give in. I won't tell him a thing. He'll have to fucking drag it from my dying lips.

I have no idea who he is or why he thought he needed to kidnap me, but I can't trust him.

I can't trust anyone.

I should be thankful he managed to get me out of Oleg's clutches, but I can't be grateful if I don't know what his plans are for me. And judging by the way I'm tied to this chair, I don't think he has good intentions at all.

"Okay, your name is not the most important piece of information right now." He shrugs, starting to pace in front of me so calmly that frustration begins to gather in my gut. He doesn't seem to be in a rush, so I can assume this will take a long time. I need to come up with a plan, and fast.

I don't think my body can handle much torture. I feel weak, exhausted, drained. I might be able to fight just him, no matter how tall and well-built he is, but I doubt I'd be able to handle more if he calls for backup. But first things first, I need to get out of these ropes. They are killing me.

My skin is burning from the friction, and I'm sure my left wrist is bleeding from my struggle to release the knot, but the adrenaline pumping in my veins is doing its work and preventing me from feeling too much pain—so far.

"I know *who* you are, and most importantly, I know what you represent for the Rominas, so your name should be the least of your concerns right now," he explains, not stopping to look at me. It's like he's reading me a story, his tone bored and contained.

Fucking cowardly asshole.

"Being the bride to the heir of the Romina Empire, I must assume you were taught a thing or two about interrogations." He comes to a halt in front of me, his massive body turning toward me once more.

I don't know why I'm surprised, since he obviously saw me at the wedding, but I wonder what else he knows about me. Is he aware I was forced into this marriage? Or that Oleg killed my parents?

Would it be too much to assume he took me to use me as a bargain against Oleg?

If that's the case, I have some bad news for him—Oleg couldn't care less about my death.

Sure, it would ruin his plan of keeping the legacy of "his" empire within the family, but his son still has Romina blood. He could take any other woman to marry Yakov and keep running his businesses.

I clench my jaw even harder, gritting my teeth with such pressure that I hear my bones crack. When he lowers to my level again, his face so close to mine that I have to hold my breath, I accidentally breathe him in. His cologne is intoxicating, but the last thing I need right now is my judgment to be clouded. His dark eyes study every inch of my face so carefully that I wonder what he is thinking.

"You know, I respect—even admire–a woman with resilience," he continues, his minty breath fanning against my lips.

Can't he keep his distance while he speaks to me? It'd be easier to take his threats seriously instead of wondering what he can possibly do to me if I keep refusing to answer his questions. He seems to be the type of guy who'd know what to *do* with someone like me. In every sense of the word...

What the fuck are you talking about, Tatiana? The guy would probably cut you into pieces and offer your body to the dogs if you push him too much. This is not a steamy romance, you fucking idiot!

Scolding myself doesn't help when a smirk appears on his lips, causing shivers to run down my spine, only serving as fuel to my delusional thoughts.

"Fine, suit yourself," he concedes, unbothered. "But let me warn you, just in case you're thinking you can wear me out, it might take me longer than usual, but I can and *will* break you."

NINE
INTERNAL BATTLE

Tatiana

OKAY, *fuck*, that does sound like a genuine threat.

He's definitely not new to any of this, and he's used to stubborn people like me. He's probably faced worse in his years in the mafia, assuming he's from another syndicate. Judging by the way his eyes are hungry for information, I doubt he's just a normal person Oleg owes money to or had a bad business deal with.

Lev taught me how to hold on during an interrogation as long as I could in several of our lessons in the past, but he never really *tortured* me while doing so. How am I supposed to act when the real deal is actually happening? I thought I was prepared for this, but maybe I'm not?

Am I ready for this man to cut my skin, hold my head under water, pull my nails out of my fingers, and all the dreadful things these people are known for doing? How long until I break?

Panic creeps through me again, and I realize I need a plan B before I lose the grip on my self-control and have to start pleading for my life. I don't wanna beg, but who knows how I'll react once he actually starts forcing the words out of my mouth?

"I don't know what you think you can get from me, but you took the wrong person," I finally say, watching his brows shoot up with curiosity.

"Ah, so you do speak," he muses, the grin on his face widening as he returns to his standing position. "Well, I hate to break it to you, but you might want to try a different approach because everyone says the same thing once they're tied to that chair," he explains, gesturing with his head to where I'm seated.

"You should have done your research better," I retort, doing my best to keep my voice calm and steady. But the way he looks at me makes it hard for me to focus. How is it fair that an evil man is so fucking handsome, even in the shadows? "If you had done that, you'd know I'm telling the truth."

He narrows his stunning eyes at me, considering my words. "Right. You want me to believe that you were running around in a wedding dress, escaping *from* a mafia wedding ceremony, because you, what... ended up there by accident?"

I sneer, fighting the urge to roll my eyes at him. "Who said I was in a wedding dress? You took me out of an alley in the middle of New York City wearing jeans and a T-shirt. Does this outfit look like something a mafia bride would wear?" I ask, knowing he won't buy my bluffing, but just spitting out whatever I can think of to buy my brain some time to come up with another way out of here. This whole place is a fucking prison cell. How am I supposed to run from here without being caught by possibly hundreds of men waiting outside? Not to mention getting past this guy....

Besides, I'd have to get him to untie me first. At least that way, I'd be able to try and fight instead of just sitting here, waiting for death to come and claim me.

Because that's what will happen to me once he realizes I'm of no use to him.

"Very funny," he murmurs, huffing and cracking his knuckles in annoyance.

An idea comes to mind, and even though it makes me feel ashamed to have only thought of something as lame as this, I'm not in a situation to be picky. It's not like I have any options either. I need to fight with what I have, and right now, it's the only thing my mind can come up with in a moment of desperation.

"Listen, I know there's no way for me to get out of here, not alive and not before telling you what you want to know, but I really need to pee," I tell him, trying to press my legs together, pretending I'm desperate. Which I am, but for different reasons. It doesn't help to be under his intense gaze like this. Now's not the time for that, though.

I need to survive, not surrender to my hormones and dirty thoughts, especially not with someone who will kill me in the blink of an eye. Someone who kidnapped me and knocked me unconscious.

He snorts, smirking at me. "Couldn't you have thought of something better than that?" he asks, not buying my bluff as predicted.

"I'm serious," I argue, contorting in my seat. "Unless you want me to pee in my pants while you interrogate me, could you please let me use the bathroom? It's not like I can escape from there either," I lie, hoping he buys it this time. I do my best to use the female charm I like to think I have, but his face doesn't crack, not even for a second. "Please," I plead. "I will tell you what you want to know when I'm done. I promise."

He tilts his head up to the ceiling, tapping a finger against his jaw, debating whether my word means anything in this screwed up world he lives in.

I'm about to accept that my plan B sucks as much as plan A did, but eventually, he sighs and takes a step toward me, squatting down in front of me, his hands reaching for my ankles.

I swallow hard at his proximity and how my intrusive thoughts imagine him kneeling in front of me for completely different reasons.

"Let me just warn you. If you try anything, *anything* at all once I release you, I won't hold back, hear me? There are more men outside of that door than you could possibly count, so I'd think very carefully if I were you before doing something stupid. I'm being generous. I don't give a fuck if you piss yourself. Got it?"

My left leg is released, and I feel the blood returning to my foot, slowly reanimating it. I nod sharply at him, pretending I take his threat seriously.

I don't know if it's the submission I show—the way I bow my head and lower my gaze in surrender—or maybe he just really thinks I won't be so stupid as to try and escape him, fully confident of his capacity to put me down if I do something–but he unties me almost as if I am a nuisance to him.

Once my hands are free, I take a deep breath, licking my lips before standing, being careful so as not to make any sharp movements that will cause him to contain me again before I have the chance to get away.

I feel his eyes on my back, and when he moves to stand beside me, I launch a punch straight to his face.

I'm fast, but he dodges the attack, gripping my fist with only one hand. He does it so effortlessly that I have no time to even react before that fucking smirk appears on his face once again, and he's manhandling me, but his creased brows show me how pissed off he is by my attempt.

"Bad move," he murmurs in a deadly rumble.

I can't back down now, though. I've come too far.

With that thought in mind, I use my other hand to punch him in the ribs, which he doesn't see coming since his eyes are on my face.

Only a grunt escapes his throat as he tightens his grip on my hand.

I use my last resource, raising my knee to his groin, this time managing to have him bend over, groaning in pain.

"Bitch..." I hear him murmur behind me, but I'm already at the door, so I don't dare to look back and see if he's going to be able to catch up to me.

When my fingers wrap around the doorknob, I'm swept off my feet and fall to the ground, my back slamming into the cold, concrete floor, causing my lungs to give out for a second, stars filling my field of vision.

I try to inhale and fail, wishing I could catch my breath. His body pins me down to the floor, his weight forcing me to remain still. Not that I'd dare do anything else now because I can barely think with him on top of me—and it has nothing to do with the lack of air in my lungs or the darkness clouding the edges of my vision.

An intense heat gathers deep inside of me, and a groan escapes my lips that is only partially due to the pain in my head and back.

His eyes roam my face with a mix of hatred and something else, something deeper that I can't put my finger on.

I'm sure my face must be reflecting something perplexing because he narrows his gaze and frowns as if he is just as confused as I am about how our bodies are reacting to one another.

What the fuck is going on here?

TEN

FRIEND OR FOE?

Angelo

THIS GODDAMN WOMAN is not only beautiful but also clever as fuck. She definitely knows how to use her appearance and charm to her advantage, blinking those beautiful eyes at me. Even in a T-shirt and jeans, she looks sexy as hell. She doesn't need to wear anything seductive or whisper dirty words in my ear. Just being under her gaze is enough for my dick to start twitching inside my pants. *Fuck!*

I don't know why the hell I fell for that, believing she actually needed to go to the bathroom. Maybe, deep down, there's still some good left in my corroded heart. Or maybe I just didn't want to believe that she'd be able to trick me.

But she almost broke free from me, which would've been fucking embarrassing when the guys outside had to bring her back to me, seeing me rolling around on the floor with my smashed up cock in one hand. Needless to say, the pain she caused me made my blood boil. But even so, I couldn't force myself to strike her. Not yet. Instead, I'd pinned her to the floor.

And that was the biggest mistake I could have made.

I'm surprised, confused, and fucking annoyed at how my body reacts to having her beneath me. The way her blue eyes roam my face, the way her long hair spreads around her head like a halo, the way she feels so tiny and perfectly molded to me...

Fuck, fuck, fuck...

It's not the first time a woman who is supposed to be the enemy has caught my attention, and I'd always explained it by saying I'm just attracted to strong women who can hold their own, who are smart and confident, who know what they want and are willing to do whatever is needed to get it. But this is... *different.*

She challenges me with just one look, and the way my body screams at me to undress her right here and now and claim her, on this dirty tile floor, it's almost overwhelming.

She squirms under me when I tighten my grip on her wrists, holding them above her head, preventing her from punching me again. My legs hold hers together, forcing them to remain still so she's unable to kick me anymore.

My cock still aches, although I'm lying to myself when I say it's only because she racked me. The tension between us right now is mind-blowing, and her struggling under me is not helping with the need growing deep within me.

"I told you not to try anything stupid," I snarl, our noses practically touching.

Her breathing is quicker now, her chest rising and falling with a disconcerting speed. I swallow hard, forcing my eyes to remain on her face, which doesn't help much either, since her eyes hold invisible reins threatening to put me under submission.

"Get away from me," she hisses under her breath.

"You might think I'm an idiot, but I'm not," I continue, not daring to move away. I know she'll try something else as soon as I release her wrists, and honestly, I'm too tired and pissed off to chase her right now.

Tony assigned me this mission, and even though I'd rather be chasing Oleg and cutting him into pieces, limb for limb, I'm not going to be ungrateful. I need to trust the process... and Tony. He knows what he's doing. I'm sure of it.

I can't deny that I'm frustrated to have to deal with this insufferable woman, though. Or maybe I'm just fucking angry at myself for being so weak when I'm this close to her.

"Who the fuck are you?" I try again, my voice low and firm.

"Why the fuck would you kidnapped me if you don't even know who I am? I'm not going to tell you jack shit," she retorts angrily, her Russian accent thick. "You're clearly shit at your job." She grins at me, defiant, as if she is not clearly at a disadvantage here.

"I know enough to understand that you're useful to me, so you might want to cooperate, or this situation is going to get really ugly for you," I inform her, thankful that my brain is starting to ignore the reactions she causes in me and focus on the exchange of information instead. If I force my mind to pay attention to her words, I might be able to get something useful out of that beautiful, tempting mouth of hers.

"I don't know what you think you can get from me, but I'm not useful to you," she insists, as if she wasn't supposed to be marrying that son of a bitch, Yakov, earlier today. I hate that fucker almost as much as I hate his father. And it pisses me off that he almost had this beauty as his bride.

"Someone who was marrying into the Romina family should be aware of some of their weaknesses, if not all of them, so... I'd start spitting out whatever the fuck you know, if I were you. Unless you want the blood to stop circulating to your wrists. It'd be a pity to have those delicate hands stop functioning properly," I threaten, glaring down at her.

She sighs heavily, causing her breasts to brush against my chest, and I can immediately tell she's wearing nothing beneath that thin T-shirt. Glancing down, I see taut nipples hardening and have to look away.

Fuck...

"Fine, what is it that you want me to tell you? Is it Oleg you're after?" she asks, narrowing her eyes at me.

I raise my brows at her, curious. "See? You do know what I want."

"I will help you destroy him," she offers, and this time, when my eyebrows arch in surprise, I can't hide it from her. She might be bluffing, but the spark of hatred I see in her eyes can't be a figment of my imagination. "If you let me go, that is," she concludes, lifting her chin in defiance.

I sneer, shaking my head slightly. "Do you really think I'll buy that again? Please, try a better line of bullshit." I smirk, keeping my eyes locked on her face—and nowhere else.

"It won't help me to tell you I want him to rot in hell as much as you do because you clearly won't believe me," she continues in a steady voice, attempting to shrug the best she can beneath me as her eyes hold my gaze.

She stops struggling under me, which I appreciate. It's hard to think about anything else when she keeps squirming under me with that tiny body rubbing against me in all the right—or wrong—places....

"But I can help you," she adds.

I study her face, looking for any sign that she's lying. She seems genuine though, her jaw clenching and her nostrils flaring as she stares at me, waiting for my response. Does she really hate him as much as I do? Why was she marrying his son then? Was she forced to do it?

I shake my head. Oleg wouldn't be stupid enough to force someone to marry his son. That would mean he'd have to be looking over his shoulders all the time inside his own house. How could he risk his empire by forcing an intruder into his own home, into his family? There's no way he'd make such a horrendous mistake.

But one of the cardinal rules of this life is to keep one's enemies closer. Maybe that's what he was doing? Did he want to have her near him so he could control her?

If that's the case, why? Why would he want *her*? What could she possibly have to offer him?

"If you really want me to believe you, you'll have to give me more than that." I keep my face stoic as I watch her. "Something that will buy your way out. I can't just trust you. I'm sure you know how this works."

She nods. "I do. I'll help you, and you'll help me," she agrees.

I stare at her, wondering if I should give her the benefit of the doubt. If I fail, if she ends up betraying my trust, I'll have caused the whole mission to fail because of my bad judgment. If I fail, Tony will be disappointed in me since this is the first time we've gotten close to the Rominas in years. I'd be putting everything at risk if I decide to believe this woman whose name I don't even know.

However, my instincts tell me I should do it. I should take that leap of faith and see what she can offer me. If she can give me anything useful, anything at all, that will help us get to Oleg and his son, that'll already be a win. I have to trust my instincts because they are the only thing I have right now.

And I refuse to accept that she's gotten to me so deeply I can no longer trust myself.

I can see the same hatred for the Rominas in her eyes, that same spark of disdain I'm so familiar with from seeing it staring back at me in the mirror every morning. There's no way she can fake such rage. If I'm right, I'd bet she hates Oleg as much as I do.

And that leaves me fucking curious to find out why.

ELEVEN
TRUCE

Tatiana

MY EYES DON'T MOVE as I watch my kidnapper's face contort in confusion at what I just said. It was a gamble, but it was my last shot since I came to terms with not being able to escape from this place unharmed–if not fucking dead as a doornail.

I doubted it would work at first, but I seem to have hit a sensitive topic when I offered to help him with information about Oleg. It's not like I have much on him anyway, since I was barely ever in the same room as him while I was his prisoner, but if it's Oleg that he's after, I'm more than happy to help him with his vendetta.

My determination seems to do its job because my kidnapper climbs off me and extends his hand to me. I hesitate, staring at his large hand while wondering what the hell might have made him change his mind.

Maybe he's playing games with me, pretending to believe me so he can tie me to that chair again.

"Come on. I won't tie you up again." Is he a fucking mind reader?

His brows shoot up as he waits for me to grab his hand or do anything other than just stare at him, dumbfounded.

In reality, other than just being suspicious of his true motives, I'm more concerned about how disappointed I felt when he got off me and I could no longer feel the weight of his body on mine.

What the fuck is the matter with me? He kidnapped me! He's a dangerous man.

I should be feeling relieved instead of wishing he'd kept me trapped between the floor and his rigid body.

Great. I'm a psychopath.

With one last hesitant look at his hand, I accept his offer and take it. He yanks me to my feet so that I'm standing in front of him. He takes a step back, putting a little distance between us, but the tension surrounding us is palpitating. It's like an electric current that will ignite if either of us moves a muscle.

He seems somewhat uncomfortable with the situation as well, but it might just be my delusional brain playing tricks on me.

I pull my hand back from his, taking one step backward. We're an arm's length away from each other, so I could try to run again now that he has given me some space.

But for the first time since I got to New York, I don't feel like running or trying to escape. For the first time, I feel... *safe.*

That's fucking insane. I'm a prisoner in a basement with an unknown man. Nevertheless, the way his eyes have softened and his frightening posture has relaxed now makes me feel like I can trust him.

If we have the same goal—to end Oleg—maybe we *can* become allies. It wouldn't be completely delusional.

"Am I wrong to assume you're offering to throw Oleg under the bus because you hate his guts too?" he asks me, his eyes narrowing into slits as he studies my reaction.

I take a deep breath, deciding that I need to be truthful with him if I want to survive. I don't doubt for a second that he'll kill me if I try to fool him again. Mafia members are not known for being merciful.

I've heard a lot of stories through the years to know that's the case. And even though his very presence is confusing to me, I have to find a way to trust him.

"I fucking hate him." I have no trouble admitting that, clenching my teeth. As much as I try to push away all the bad memories I have of Oleg, and all the suffering he's caused me, so my emotions don't get the better of me, that's nearly impossible. That bastard took everything from me.

My parents, my adoptive family, the life I had back in Russia, and the life I could've had someday....

He left me with nothing, not even my dignity. I was given to his son like a dog who would become his breeder just because Oleg has this sickening obsession with creating a legacy. As if he's done anything to earn the empire he now claims.

I was too young to remember it, but Lev told me the whole story of what happened to my parents when I was old enough to understand. Oleg stole everything from my father. Otherwise, he'd have nothing other than his ambitions. He'd just be another capo, answering to my father's orders.

"Care if I ask you why?"

His deep voice brings me back to reality. I blink a few times, formulating a response. "I don't think I can trust you enough to tell you why yet. Let's just say I want him dead and buried so I don't have to look into the bastard's fucking eyes ever again for the rest of my life." My voice drips with ice.

His eyes widen almost imperceptibly at my words, but as usual, he's skilled at hiding his true emotions. I wonder what he's had to face in his life to become this cold and detached. "Fair enough. Well, if we're going to be partners, I think it's only fair that we at least know each other's names." The corner of his mouth turns up slightly into what I could almost describe as a smile.

God, he's insanely handsome.

He offers me his hand once more. "Angelo Messina." His raspy voice sends an electric bolt down my spine.

Fuck, woman! Get yourself together!

I nod sharply and grip his hand, ignoring the tingling sensation that shoots up my arm. "Tatiana Ivanov." It didn't even occur to me to lie to him. He could find out easily who Yakov was supposed to marry. Lev did a great job keeping me off the radar, but who knows what these guys can discover with their network?

His calloused hand contrasts deeply with my soft and smooth skin, and somehow I feel like a fraud. This is what the hand of a true fighter should feel like. The things he must have seen, faced, and done... I can't even begin to imagine. Despite Lev's best attempts to prepare me, practice is never the same as real life.

When our eyes meet, it's like everything I'm debating within myself vanishes from my brain, and I can only focus on the way I feel under his gaze. Not only does my body feel bare beneath his heavy gaze, but so does my soul.

Get your shit together, woman!

I've never felt like this before. Not that I've had a lot of chances to meet guys back in Russia under Lev's watchful eye, but I've... been around. I went to college. I've had a couple of boyfriends. I'm no fucking virgin.

But no one has ever made me feel like this.

Angelo clears his throat, probably thinking there's something wrong with me, the way I'm staring at him. I yank my hand out of his grip. "Well, I... I bet you must be hungry and thirsty." He shoves his hands into his pockets.

I nod at him, feeling an enormous void where my stomach should be and realizing I'm actually starving.

"Okay, so let's go get you something to eat. Then, we can talk."

He walks toward the door, and I rush after him to keep up with his long strides. Angelo knocks on the door twice, and another man opens it. I ignore this new guy and follow Angelo closely, observing my surroundings as we climb a set of stairs and step into the bright hallway of what appears to be a mansion. Several men stand guard, all of them wearing suits similar to Angelo's, their expressions serious, but also confused, as they watch me walk freely with my hands untied.

Angelo doesn't bother explaining the situation to any of them, though. He heads toward the end of the hallway where I hope we'll find the kitchen. Now that he's mentioned it, I can't stop thinking about how hungry I am.

I'm momentarily lost in my surroundings as I observe the luxurious, spacious house. It's not as extravagant as Oleg's—even though I hate to admit he has good taste, with his modern art pieces and paintings all over the place—but this mansion, in a way, is cozier and looks more like a home instead of a prison. Weirdly, I feel like I could get used to living in a place like this.

Soon enough, we get to the kitchen, which is empty except for the two of us. Angelo gestures at the stool by the counter, and I take a seat, watching as he opens the fridge and grabs a jug of orange juice. He pours me a glass, then proceeds to prepare a sandwich. I remain silent the entire time, watching the way his muscles strain against the fabric of his shirt as he moves. His brows are creased as he focuses on his task, but even something as simple as preparing a sandwich makes him look hotter and sexier than he should be allowed.

A couple of minutes later, he places the plate and juice glass in front of me, and it doesn't even cross my mind that he may have secretly poisoned my food. I'm so hungry right now that if I die eating a turkey and cheese sandwich, I'll die with a smile on my face.

He sits on a stool on the other side of the counter, watching my every move, not saying a word until I finish. I'm far from being satisfied, but this will do for now, I guess. I don't want to push his kindness too far.

"Do you think you're ready to tell me about Oleg now?" He crosses his arms, his eyes narrowed as he observes me from the other side of the counter.

I consider what to tell him. Of course, I can't give him all the information I have at once because this may be the only thing keeping me alive right now. Also, I'm not exactly sure what he wants me to tell him. It's not like I know Oleg's secret plans and schemes.

"I lost everything because of Oleg," I rush out. "Because of his fucking greed. I never wanted to be involved in any of this. I hate the type of life he is so fond of."

Angelo nods silently, taking in my every word. "I can relate to that, in a way," he confesses, standing. "Listen, you must be exhausted. And I'm sure you're dying for a shower. You still have dry blood on your neck. Why don't you take a hot shower and get some rest? We can talk tomorrow. If you're going to cooperate with us, you have to be all in. I can't go back to my boss with empty promises. Being vague isn't going to help you. Just because we have a truce right now doesn't mean that things can't change in a heartbeat. *Ponyatno?*"

Yes, I understand what he's saying. I've already racked him and tried to run away–I could've been slaughtered for much less. He's been merciful to me, nice even. He must have a good heart, deep down, because any other mobster would've put a bullet in my head after all the trouble I've caused him.

"Okay, thank you," I murmur, genuinely grateful. I feel awful. Dirty. Stained. Luckily, I can't see the blood, but I can still smell it and feel it on my skin.

I follow Angelo to the second floor where he leads me into a big bedroom with a ginormous king-size bed and a large wardrobe in the corner. There's also a small table by the window and an armchair to enjoy the view, but it's the bathroom that takes my breath away. The floor and every surface is covered in white marble tiles. Everything is opulent–especially the huge jetted bathtub.

"We keep clothes in a variety of sizes in the closet over there. I'm sure you can find something that fits," he offers, gesturing to a door on the far side of the bathroom. "I'll be back when you're done."

That should sound like a warning; instead, my filthy mind goes crazy with images of what he might do to me when I'm done.

I shake my head and watch him leave before walking to the

closet. I find a T-shirt and sweatpants in women's sizes, although they are a bit large for me. Thankfully, I find a pair of new panties with the tags still on that will work. Looking around, I take a deep breath, realizing this is the first time I've been alone in ages.

Turning on the shower to heat up, I strip off the clothes that kind woman gave me and then step beneath the stream. The hot water against my skin is invigorating. I wash away all the dirt, blood, and sweat from my skin and hair, watching the water run pink then clear, but even so, I'm unable to completely relax.

How can I, when I'm still a fucking prisoner?

Granted, Angelo is already treating me better than Oleg did, but that doesn't change the fact that I don't have my freedom.

I finish my shower, dry off, and get dressed. When I return to the bedroom, Angelo is there, comfortably seated in the armchair.

"You can take the bed," he tells me, that cocky smirk on his face.

"Are you going to stay there?" I ask, trying hard to hide my surprise.

He snickers like I've just asked him the stupidest question imaginable. "I'm not supposed to let you out of my sight. And until I have something useful for my boss, I don't think I can leave you alone, especially in a bedroom with windows."

I roll my eyes at him, pulling the blankets back and lying on the bed, too exhausted to argue with him. If he wants to kill me in my sleep, so be it. If he wants to watch me while I sleep–possibly dreaming of him–that's his prerogative. I don't have the strength in me to be on alert right now. I just need to sleep.

And for some crazy, unexplainable reason, I know he won't do anything to harm me.

That thought alone is enough to help me fall asleep as soon as my head hits the pillow.

TWELVE
GUARD DOG

Angelo

TATIANA FALLS ASLEEP AS SOON as she gets into bed, despite being suspicious of me watching her. I didn't really think she'd try to escape through the window, not only because it'd be a hell of a fall if she tried, but also because I have men outside, guarding every inch of the safe house.

But for some reason, I don't want to leave her alone. Despite her tough exterior, there is a sadness in her eyes that just makes me want to be here for her, in case she needs something.

She probably doesn't trust me yet. I'm not entirely convinced I can trust her either, but still... it's nice to think we might be able to get along and help one another out. Her hatred for Oleg seems genuine. I can see the same pain I feel reflected in her eyes whenever she mentions him. What are the chances she's just an extremely good actress? Not likely.

I watch the blankets move up and down slightly, her breathing even. I answer some texts and emails, trying to keep myself busy and kill two birds with one stone. She's been asleep for an hour or so when she groans quietly. Leaning forward, I see her brows are creased as if she's having some sort of nightmare. My hands itch to touch that soft spot in her forehead, wanting to somehow ease her mind and clear away the bad dream she might be having, but that's not my place

I can't lose focus. No matter how fucking hard it is.

As if on cue, my phone buzzes. I take one last look at her and then check the screen. Tony's name flashes across it. I walk to the door and out into the hallway. Closing my eyes, I take a deep breath before answering the call, bracing myself. I'm sure one of the guys told him about Tatiana walking freely out of the basement earlier, so I'll need to explain my thinking.

"Yes, Boss," I say, pressing the phone to my ear and leaning against the wall.

"I thought you'd have the decency to call me and explain yourself instead of letting me be the one to come after you," Tony grumbles. He sounds irritated, although I note the tiredness hidden in it. He likely went through a lot today as well.

"Sorry, man. I was waiting for her to fall asleep before I called you," I explain. It's not a lie. I just didn't feel like asking for his permission before I made my decision since he gave me full authority to get information out of her by whatever means necessary.

"Care to explain what the fuck is going on?" he asks bitterly.

So much has happened today that I need a second to put all of the events together in my head before I can narrate them to Tony.

"The bride cut the shit out of Sal's arm and slipped him, but we managed to trail her. We caught up to her in a neighborhood near the park. I cornered her, knocked her ass out, and brought her here. When she came to, I started to interrogate her, as ordered, but she decided pretty quickly to cooperate. I think we need to take a different approach with this one, Boss. Give me some time."

Tony remains quiet the entire time I'm telling him the story, but once he speaks again, he still doesn't sound convinced. "We need information on Oleg and his businesses. You let her out of the basement?" he scolds me. "What the hell do you think you're doing? If it's 'cause she's attractive, Angelo, I can find you another woman. You don't need to fuck our witness." He spews one accusation after another in an angry tone, not even giving me the time to respond to any of them.

I should be offended at what he's implying, but I'm not because I know Tony, and this is his way of taking out his frustration. I've been on this side of the conversation enough times by now to know that.

My attraction to Tatiana has nothing to do with needing to get laid. I can't put my finger on why I feel so out of control when I'm near her, but so far, I'm handling it, and I have no time to dwell on it right now. "Boss, come on, now. You know me better than that. I'm a professional, after all. She seems willing to help. Apparently, she hates Oleg as much as we do."

I hear a sharp inhale of breath before Tony continues, this time a bit calmer. "You need to be careful," he warns me. "We don't have a lot of background on who she is. For all we know, she could be lying straight to your face. Until we know for certain, you can't lower your guard. I'm sure I don't need to tell you that, but we both know very well how a woman can blind us."

"Trust me, Boss. She's not a threat. I can feel it." I'm sticking my neck out based on a brief conversation with the woman, but I need to trust my instincts. That's all I have. "I'll get something useful soon. I promise you. You know I'm just as desperate to get my hands on Oleg as you are. I just need you to trust me this time."

"I do," Tony says firmly, and I believe him. It's one of the many reasons I trust him with my life as well. "That's why I need you to be careful. One wrong move, and we're back to square one. Or worse, dead."

I swallow the bitterness in my mouth, gripping the phone harder. "That won't happen," I insist through gritted teeth.

"Fine. Okay. Call me as soon as you get something. And have the guys back you up if you need them." Tony hangs up before I have the chance to say anything else. I close my eyes again, leaning my head against the wall and allowing myself a moment to breathe. I should get some sleep, but how can I do that when I need to keep an eye on Tatiana?

I'm putting everything at risk here, and as Tony mentioned, I can't make a single wrong move, or this whole mission is over.

"Fuck," I breathe, running my fingers through my hair. "Sal?" I call, heading toward the stairs.

I find him on the bottom floor, looking up at me with curiosity in his eyes.

"Can you watch her room while I take a shower and grab something to eat?" I ask. "I'll take the night shift. I just need a few minutes."

He looks a little leery, and I see the bandage peeking out underneath his sleeve, but he knows his place. "Sure thing. Take all the time you need."

"Thanks, man." I pat him on the shoulder as he passes by and heads toward Tatiana's door, positioning himself against the wall just like I had been a minute ago.

Less than an hour later, I'm clean, fed, and back at my station.

"I'll sleep on the couch. Call me if you need my help," Sal offers.

"What? Do you think I can't handle her on my own?" I tease, a smirk forming on my lips.

Sal grins back at me and shrugs. "Not if she pulls a fucking knife on you." He chuckles and walks away, disappearing around the corner.

I step into the bedroom again and return to the armchair. Tatiana is still in the same position as before, so I take that as a sign that she's deeply asleep. She might not wake up any time soon, so I allow my eyes to close for a few minutes, trying to rest my mind.

What seems like only seconds later, a scream pierces the darkness, and I'm suddenly wide awake, my eyes searching the room for a threat.

I'm used to waking up to screams—but before, they've always been mine.

My eyes adjust to the darkness, and I can now see Tatiana sitting up on the bed, breathing heavily, her hand on her chest as she forces air into her lungs. Her hair is wet from sweat, plastered to her forehead and cheeks.

"Hey, hey, hey." I approach her cautiously, not sure if she's fully awake. Her wide eyes find my face. I sit beside her on the mattress, trying to be as cautious as possible so as not to freak her out even more, but she barely moves when I touch her shoulder. Heat radiates up my hand, so I slowly pull it away.

"Everything is fine. It was just a nightmare," I reassure her softly.

It takes her a couple of seconds to meet my gaze, her eyes out of focus as she stares at me.

"You're safe," I tell her firmly. "I'll get you some water."

I stand and head to the mini-fridge across the room, grabbing a bottle and bringing it to her.

I watch as Tatiana slowly lifts the bottle to her mouth, lavishing the water as if she's been in the desert for days. Some of it drips from her mouth down her neck, and I look away, scolding myself for letting my perverted thoughts get the better of me.

I could lick that water right off her jaw.

She gives me back the bottle, now empty, and her eyes soften a little. "I-I'm really sorry about that," she says, her voice raspy from sleep, and perhaps from screaming. "I don't normally have nightmares."

I dismiss her with a shake of my head. "It's only natural after everything you've experienced," I reassure her, guessing that must be true.

She nods slightly, but says nothing.

"Listen, I know this situation isn't ideal, and you probably don't feel safe here, but as long as you're with me, and we can help each other out, you don't have to worry. You also don't have to trust me completely. Just trust that I hate Oleg more than anyone, and I'll do everything in my power to stop him—once and for all. So, you can hold on to that."

She holds my gaze like a tether that reaches deep down inside of me and anchors somewhere behind her eyes I may never see. Her tongue darts out to lick her dry lips, and I swallow hard, trying to focus on her eyes, but whenever I look into those blue pools, I'm sucked into oblivion, so lost and numb that I don't even know where I am.

Tatiana lifts her hips slightly, settling on the bed, and the madness that has plagued me since I first saw her trembling in the alleyway has my cock twitching and my mind racing.

Pulling myself away, I head toward the window and open it a crack, letting the cold breeze call me as best it can.

"You should go back to sleep," I suggest, not daring to look back at her. "I'll be here, so don't worry. Nothing will happen to you. We can talk tomorrow." I end the conversation before she can even think of extending it.

I can't do this tonight, not when my entire body is screaming at me to climb into that bed with her and pull her against me, making her forget about all the shit she went through today.

I'm beyond fucking screwed.

THIRTEEN
COMBAT TRAINING

Tatiana

I WAKE up in a strange room, my entire body sore, my head pounding, my leg muscles weak from all the running yesterday, and to make it all worse, nightmares kept me up all night, so I'm also groggy–and irritable.

Visions of my parents being murdered flashed before my eyes all night long–the blood dripping down their faces, Oleg's vicious grin, a silent scream stuck on my lips. I'd wake up in a cold sweat, only to fall back asleep and start the cycle all over again.

Each time I screamed, I woke up my babysitter. It wasn't fair to him, and at one point, I considered staying awake. But I couldn't do that. I was too exhausted to keep my eyes open.

Still in bed, I look over to find that the armchair Angelo stayed in all night is empty with no sign of him ever being there, other than the fact that it is closer to the bed than it originally was. My screaming must've alarmed him enough so that he moved it closer.

Was he concerned about my well-being or annoyed that he had to keep crossing the room to get me to stop screaming?

I shake my head and run a hand through my hair. Thoughts of Angelo have me more confused than ever before. We have a common goal, but I'm still being kept here against my will. Not that I have anywhere else to go, and I doubt I'd be able to return to Russia without Oleg finding out. I'd either be kidnapped or killed before I reached the airport.

In any case, I doubt Angelo will let me go before I give him the information he needs. He clearly answers to someone—probably the Boss of whatever mafia gang he belongs to, if that's even what they are—and since I have given them no reason to believe me so far, I'm stuck here.

I rack my brain for anything I can use to sell out Oleg and his empire. Anything at all—businesses, names of establishments he owes, future plans... but nothing comes to mind.

The few days I stayed in his house, I wasn't near them enough to have overheard what he was planning or anything related to any of his businesses. All he included me in was the wedding planning, and even then, I wasn't allowed to give my opinion.

Still sitting on the bed, I go over everything I know about Oleg again—and something pops into my head. Lev and Ilya used to tell me stories of how Oleg got to where he is today—stories about what he did in the past, and business deals he had made with people all over the United States.

Why the hell can't I remember any names now that I so desperately need them?

A knock on the door has my hand darting to my chest, clutching my heart. With everything that's happened, I need to cut myself some fucking slack, but I'm still embarrassed at my startle reflex.

"Yes?" I answer, my voice hesitant and low.

"Can I come in?" Angelo asks from behind the door.

"Sure."

I look down to make sure I am presentable, even though he saw me quite a mess yesterday, and throughout the entire night really. The T-shirt I picked out from the closet is a bit large for me, so I don't have to worry about showing any skin. My intrusive thoughts whisper that I don't mind having Angelo's eyes on me, but I force them away, focusing on the way he looks this morning instead.

Holy fuck! He looks even better in the sunlight. His dark curls are damp and falling over his eyes. He's dressed in black joggers and a form-fitting, long-sleeve shirt that clings to his frame, revealing how well defined his arms and abs are.

"Good morning," he murmurs, closing the door behind him and shoving his hands into his pockets. "I'd ask if you rested well, but we both know the answer to that question."

I nod, my cheeks burning with embarrassment. My gaze travels back down his body. He clears his throat, and I look back at his face, scolding myself.

Get a fucking grip, Tatiana. His eyes are up there!

Clearing my throat, I say, "Thank you for taking care of me, though." My voice cracking doesn't make me sound any more confident.

He smirks and dismisses me with a shake of his head, heading for the window and pulling the blinds open. He lifts the glass, letting the cool breeze invade the room, and I shiver, pulling the blankets up to my neck.

He doesn't seem to notice. "Listen, I know we have a lot to talk about, and that none of this is ideal for either of us," he begins, turning to look at me again. He leans against the wall and crosses his arms. "But, unfortunately, there's nothing we can do about it. Let's just say you're collateral damage."

I nod, following his train of thought. I've come to terms with my current situation. Right now, I'm better here as a prisoner than I'd ever be as Yakov's wife—or Oleg's victim.

"I understand," I tell him.

He changes the subject, catching me off-guard. "Feel free to wear whatever you want out of the closet and use whatever products are available here. If you need anything specific, let me know, and we might be able to get it for you." He sounds slightly more chipper than before–maybe because we aren't strictly talking business.

"I appreciate that." I manage a small smile, meaning it.

He shrugs, and that glum disposition slips back into place, the corners of his mouth turning down a bit. "Honestly, I'm doing the best I can with what I have. It's not as if it's ideal to keep you here for any of us, but I've got to believe I can trust you to help us out."

I feel guilty when he puts it that way. I can't even imagine what he had to say to convince his colleagues and boss that I'm worth their time. "I can't think of anything I need at the moment, thank you," I reply genuinely. It's much more than I got at Oleg's. Sure, he lavished me with couture clothing but kept me under suffocating and overwhelming surveillance. The fear I felt when I was in that house, terrified that he'd suddenly get tired of me and put a bullet to my head, was sickening.

At least here, I feel like Angelo is really trying to see me as someone who can help him instead of an enemy. And I truly appreciate him for it.

He nods and kicks off the wall. "You can get changed and head downstairs. Breakfast is ready. Just... ignore the ugly stares you might get. They'll eventually come to terms with the situation," he informs me. I watch him intently, noticing the way his jaw clenches and he shifts his weight from one foot to the other. I wish I knew what's going on inside that head of his–that sexy, handsome, attractive head.

"You okay, Tatiana?"

Maybe it's because I haven't gotten laid in far too long, but my body has fucking betrayed me again. I nod. "Are you, uh, going somewhere?" I gesture at his outfit. "To work out?" Judging by his damp hair, I thought he had just taken a shower, but maybe it's sweat?

He shakes his head. "That's the plan. I'll just wait until you get breakfast, and then I'll ask Dice to stay with you."

I ignore the way my insides churn at the idea of having another man watch me, but it's not like I can do anything about it. And I can't expect Angelo to be my guard dog twenty-four/seven either.

"Can't I go with you? I'd like to vent my pent-up energy, too." The words come out of my mouth before I have the chance to think them through.

He tilts his head to the side, his eyes slightly wider than normal. "As long as you're not planning to throw a gym weight at my head and knock me unconscious, I don't see why not," he replies, his brows lifting slightly at me.

Why does he looks so fucking sexy when he does that?

"I'm not that stupid." I can't lie—the idea did cross my mind, but then, other ideas crossed my mind that I wouldn't ever follow through with either. Thoughts of his body on top of mine yesterday flash before my eyes. I have to look away from him.

"Okay, then. You can get dressed, and I'll be waiting in the kitchen."

Angelo leaves the room, and I get up from bed, glad to have something to do with my time other than rot in this room the entire day.

Finding something to wear that won't be a nuisance at the gym is harder than I expected. I end up choosing black leggings that more-or-less fit me, although they are slightly baggy, and a woman's tank top that is a bit tight on my boobs, but it does fit. Whoever the woman is that these clothes belong to, she's a bit taller and possibly a bit heavier than me, but at least I can get into her clothing.

I walk out of the room, glad not to be followed by any thugs, and head toward the scene of food, which I hope brings me to the kitchen. I find Angelo sitting at the table by himself, drinking a protein shake.

"You said I'd get ugly stares, but I didn't bump into anyone on my way here," I note, watching as he turns to look at me.

His eyes scan me from head to toe, darkening instantly as he takes me in. He swallows what's in his mouth and clears his throat, putting down his glass.

"Everyone else had to leave for a meeting with the boss," he tells me. "But don't get any funny ideas. I can handle you all by myself." The way he grins at me and that cocky confidence causes shivers to run down my spine to my core, leaving me astounded for a second.

Why does everything he says sound... so sexual? Or is it just me? God, I'm like a desperate, horny teenager.

"I'll just grab a cup of coffee and a banana, and then we can go," I tell him, walking toward the counter. "I don't like to work out on a full stomach."

Angelo patiently waits for me to finish, and ten minutes later, we're in a training room. I'm astonished at how large and equipped it is—free weights, kettlebells, barbells, and a large mat that covers half of the room for combat training, with punching bags hanging from the ceiling.

"Wanna start warming up with one-on-one combat?" Angelo suggests, turning to face me.

The idea of having physical contact with him sounds risky for several reasons, the worst of them being the fact that I don't trust myself near him. But maybe Angelo can teach me a thing or two since I'm rusty and don't have my dad to train me anymore. Memories of the countless lessons I had with him cross my mind, and I have to push the tears that form in my eyes away.

"Sure, okay."

If he notices my change in emotion, he says nothing. Angelo and I cross over to the large mat, but instead of stopping in front of me, he walks to my left side.

"I thought I could teach you some tricks first. You seemed able to hold your own when you attacked me last night, but I noticed some flaws in your technique." He starts showing me some moves, asking me to mimic him, and then he comes close to me, eventually adjusting my stance or how I position my hands for defense.

For thirty minutes, I barely have the chance to pay attention to our proximity because whenever I lose focus, even if just for a second, he tosses me on my back to the mat, breathless.

"You need to keep both feet rooted to the floor. Otherwise, your attacker will knock you down in the blink of an eye every time," he explains, walking behind me.

He grabs me by the waist, and I fight the need to gasp in surprise. My skin burns with the touch of his fingers.

"Now, raise your hands in front of your face, protecting your head," he instructs me, his voice hoarse, his body rigid behind me. I peek over my shoulder and see his eyes slightly dilated. When his hands settle on my hips, the electricity between us is so palpable, I can't possibly be making it up–can I? Maybe it's just that this room is so warm, and there's not much ventilation, rather than that we're both attracted to one another. Sweat from all the effort we're putting into combat ripples down both our bodies, making my skin slick– making him glisten.

His breath fans against my bare skin, and I regret having pulled my hair up into a ponytail. I can feel his mouth so close to my neck and ear that I need to close my eyes to steady myself.

"What do I do now?" I ask in a whisper.

He stiffens even more behind me, but his hands don't move away from my hips. Instead, his grip tightens on my skin.

"Oh, fuck it," he hisses, and with a swift movement, he spins me around to face him, and the next thing I know, his mouth is on mine.

FOURTEEN
THAT'S NOT TRAINING

Tatiana

AT FIRST, I'm shocked by what's going on, barely reacting to Angelo's lips on mine. But it lasts less than a couple of seconds before I groan against him and grant his tongue the access he so desperately wants.

Angelo pulls my body against his, his hands wrapped around my waist, keeping me trapped against him. His kiss is so delicious, so enticing, so... sexy. He knows exactly what he's doing, his tongue dancing inside my mouth as if it wants to commit this moment to memory.

When he sucks my bottom lip, I forget all the reasons why this is completely wrong. I shouldn't let this happen, but right now, I can't find any answer within me as to why not.

A moan escapes my throat when I feel his hands moving from my hip, down to my ass. He grabs and squeezes before pulling me tightly against him.

He's already hard for me, and that's the only sign I need to know he wants the same thing I do. I wrap my arms around his neck, pulling him down and deepening the kiss even more. Angelo doesn't let go of me while his hands start roaming my entire body, from my ass to my ribs, and up to my chest.

The thin fabric of my tank top makes it easier for me to feel his touch, and when his palms brush over my nipples, my eyes roll to the back of my head, and I melt in his arms.

I moan again, feeling no shame. I'm only enticing him more, considering the way his dick is hardening against my stomach.

He pulls away from my lips, lowering his mouth to my jaw and neck then up to my earlobe, where he sucks it, leaving me momentarily numb with pleasure.

My core is already throbbing with need. Only one thing will satiate the burning inside of me.

I'm not beyond begging at this point. I don't think I can hold on much longer. It's been so long since I've been touched like this, desired this way, been so fucking horny....

My face is on fire, not from embarrassment but from need.

He starts walking backward toward the weight bench. He knows exactly what he's doing, and the next thing I know, he's sitting down and pulling me onto his lap.

Fuck, the pressure this applies to my already sensitive area is almost too much to bear.

He kisses me again, his hands darting to my ass and yanking me forward. My leggings and his joggers are still in the way, but the friction is enough for me to release some of my need.

My panties are soaked, and I wish I could get rid of them immediately, but since I can't, I slowly start to rock my hips back and forth against his hardness.

He hisses my mouth again, tightening his grip on my hips and assisting me by guiding me on top of him.

"Fuck, you're so hot," he whispers, and I smirk to myself, kissing him again.

If I'm about to die in the next few hours, at least I get to experience this first. Not that I want to die, but I'd rather go out in a blaze of glory.

I don't know if this will end with full satisfaction, but I'm willing to take it as far as he'll let me.

My head falls backward, and I close my eyes. He reaches down between my legs, his fingers dancing over the fabric of the leggings. His thumb caresses my clit, and I have to bite my bottom lip so as not to moan loudly.

"Oh, God. That feels so good," I groan, speeding up on top of him.

My thoughts are cloudy as my orgasm approaches. I barely remember what it feels like–it's been so long since I've been with a man—but when that electric current creeps up on me, from my toes to my stomach, I dig my nails into his shoulders, holding on for dear life as I release myself.

When the wave of pleasure dissipates, I lean my forehead against his shoulder, trying to compose myself and steading my breathing.

"That was..." I trail off, unable to speak or even think of something coherent to say.

"Great?" he offers, and I can hear the note of amusement in his tone.

"I was going to say amazing, but that works, too." I laugh, pulling back to look at him.

I should say that was a huge mistake, but I can't force the words out of my mouth. Because no matter how wrong this was, I don't regret it. I do wish I could've returned the favor for him, though.

At this point, my life is hanging by a thread. If I can't get out of here alive, start anew somewhere, I'll at least enjoy the few things that still make my heart race.

A voice from outside the door has me jerking off his lap, and I take several steps backward to get some distance from him in case someone enters.

"Angelo, are you in there?" a man calls.

"I'm here. I'll be out in a second," Angelo answers, adjusting himself through his pants and standing.

"Okay, we'll wait in the living room to brief you on the details from our meeting with the boss," he says. "Don't take too long, though, because we need to leave in an hour."

"Got it," he calls, sounding a bit annoyed. "We should... go." He clears his throat. He scans me, running a hand through his hair, just as out of sorts as I am.

"I'm sorry about that," I say, although I'm not being completely honest. I don't regret it, but I feel like I put him in a bad spot somehow. "I got carried away. I-it won't happen again," I add, starting to stammer.

Angelo's eyes darken. "You have nothing to apologize for. And we'll talk about that later," he replies in a raspy voice, gesturing for the door with his head.

I take the hint and follow him out of the gym, trying as hard as I can to ignore the way my body seems to gravitate toward him.

"Stay in your room until I come to get you," he orders, not turning to look at me. I watch as he heads to the living room, and with a deep breath, I take the stairs to my room.

It's frustrating to feel this way after I've had the best orgasm of my life. And I didn't even have to be undressed for it.

Why do I feel guilty? Why do I feel bad for Angelo? He was the one who kissed me first. If he didn't want things to go so far, he shouldn't have done that in the first place.

He also kidnapped you and is keeping you here against your will, that stupid voice inside my head reminds me.

Why do things have to be so complicated?

Shaking my head, I decide to take a shower and get rid of all the sweat on my skin, not to mention Angelo's scent. I can't think clearly while I can still smell his cologne all over me.

The cold water helps me focus. I wanted to take a hot bath instead, but I don't need to relax right now. I need to keep myself on alert as much as possible.

The water runs over my head, and I close my eyes, thinking about how drastically my life has turned upside down in such a short amount of time. I'm so frustrated. I'm anxious all the time, unsure of what the future holds. How am I supposed to live like this?

You need to find something useful to tell them.

Of course. That's what I should be focusing on. I need to remember something important about OIeg. Otherwise, I could be dead in the blink of an eye if they decide to believe I'm just stalling and wasting their time.

Why can't I remember a single thing Lev told me about Oleg, though?

The fact the Rominas are involved in shitty illegal businesses everywhere is not a secret, but I can't remember a single name that will buy me a ticket out of here.

I try to go back to the last conversation I had with Lev and Ilya before we left Russia. They told me to keep my eyes open all the time and not to trust anyone. They said they had some allies here, but they never gave me any names.

They also told me to stay away from Chinatown.

I frown, opening my eyes and staring at the wet tiles in front of me.

Chinatown.

That could be a hint.

A very vague one, but I could start from there. Maybe Angelo and his guys have a way to investigate further and see if there's something suspicious there.

I rush to finish my shower, suddenly excited to talk to Angelo. I wrap myself in a towel and run to the bedroom, grabbing clean underclothes, some shorts, and another T-shirt from the closet and get dressed. I'm brushing my hair when Angelo knocks on my door.

"Just a sec!" I yell, tossing the brush aside and pulling the door open.

I'm ready to step outside when I notice he has a tray of food in his hands.

"I thought you'd be hungry after the... workout," he says, a grin spreading on his lips as I move aside for him to enter the room.

He's also showered and changed into jeans and a plain white shirt.

God, have I mentioned how I love when his hair is wet, the curls falling over his eyes? It's mesmerizing.

"Tatiana?" he says, setting the tray on the desk, and I realize I've been staring.

"I'm back to being a prisoner in my room?" I ask, closing the door and walking toward him.

He shakes his head, gesturing at the food. "No, but I didn't think you'd like to eat with a bunch of men staring at you, so..."

I nod, appreciating the gesture, even though I feel there's something off. I sit down to eat while Angelo remains on his feet, his arms crossed as he stares out the window.

"Are you not eating?" I glance at him, taking the first bite of a delicious steak. I'm actually surprised I'm allowed to have such a nice meal while being a prisoner–especially for lunch. But again, he also gave me an orgasm an hour ago, and I doubt that's how he normally treats his prisoners.

"I've already eaten," he replies coldly, not looking at me.

Frustration boils within me, and I drop the fork on my plate. The clatter echoes through the room.

He looks at the plate and then at me, his brows creasing.

"Did I do something?" I blurt out before he has the chance to say anything. "Why are you treating me like this all of a sudden? I know I'm your prisoner and all that, but—"

"It's not your fault, I'm sorry." He cuts me off, his eyes softening as he reaches to brush a strand of hair from my face. "I just have a lot going on right now. And I'm—"

"You regret what happened," I finish for him, bitterly.

"No, I don't," he replies right away, his gaze never wavering from mine. The intensity in his eyes is almost too much for me to bear. "I'm not apologizing for kissing you–or anything else."

FIFTEEN
MAKE ME FORGET

Tatiana

"THEN WHAT IS THE PROBLEM?" I stare into Angelo's eyes, waiting for him to explain why he's suddenly being so cold to me.

His body language is fucking confusing as hell. I see desire in his eyes, but he's keeping his distance from me. I wish he would stop playing games and just be upfront with me. I don't have time for bullshit right now.

"Listen, you already know the situation we're in. I don't want to lie to you or pretend everything is okay because it is not," he begins. The weight of this presses down on him enough that his shoulders slump a little.

"I know," I state firmly. "I'm not a child. I understand the situation we're in right now. Trust me, you don't have to worry about that." If he only knew the things I've seen.... I take another bite of my steak, but I'm no longer hungry. I force myself to eat anyway since I don't know when I'll have another chance to. If this conversation goes south, this might be my last meal of the day, so I'd better force it down.

Angelo sighs, running his fingers through his hair and leaning against the wall, facing me. "I need to give my boss something so he gets off my back," he explains. "I need to prove I'm not making the wrong decision by trusting you."

His words hit me hard. Not because I'm offended. I know better than that. I just hate that I've put him in this position because I can't come up with any information.

"I'm trying the best I can to remember something useful," I tell him, equally frustrated. "I just haven't had that much contact with Oleg. I only met him a few weeks ago."

Angelo narrows his eyes at me, and I can't blame him for it. I'm sure he thought I have been part of the Rominas' circle for longer than that.

"I remembered something while I was in the shower, though," I continue. I can't take another bite, regardless of how desperately I want the protein for later. Angelo arches an eyebrow at me as I push the plate away and stand.

He perks up, crossing his arms. "What did you remember?"

I take a deep breath. "My parents told me to stay away from Chinatown when we came here. They never said why, but I assume our enemies were there."

"Chinatown?" Angelo tips his head to the side, stroking his chin in thought.

"Yes, but they never said anything else. I know my parents had allies here, but I don't know who they are or *where* they are. I don't think everyone who works for Oleg is loyal to him, but I can't tell you who might turn on him because I honestly have no idea." I hope this is enough of a start for him to believe I wasn't bluffing when I said I wanted to help.

He seems to consider my words. After a minute in silence, he says, "I'll be right back."

He takes off, the door slamming behind him. I inhale deeply, sitting on the bed, wondering what he plans on doing with that information.

It takes him half an hour to return, and by that time, I'm lying on the bed, staring at the ceiling and racking my brain once more for information.

"I asked the guys to do some digging," he tells me as he closes the door behind him. "If we can discover who is willing to turn their backs on Oleg, we will have a chance to end him."

I nod slowly, following his train of thought. "I'm trying to remember more. I promise you I'm doing my best."

"I know," he replies, his voice soft. He sits beside me and places a hand on my leg. My entire body heats with his touch, but I don't make a single move, afraid to misread his intentions.

But there's no way he isn't aware of this suffocating tension between us. He has to be feeling this need and desperation that's coursing through me. My stomach clenches with want as I yearn to finish what we started this morning.

God, he's fucking driving me crazy...

His eyes roam over my face as if he is searching for an answer to an unspoken question. Why is he so hard to read? What is it that he wants from me?

"What?" I ask, too anxious to remain quiet. My body is so tense and my heart is beating so quickly that I fear Angelo can hear it from where he's seated.

"I don't want you to think I'm taking advantage of you." I can hear the guilt in his low voice, an indicator that he means every word.

I believe him. The situation isn't ideal, but we're attracted to each other. Sometimes the body wants what it wants.

I can't blame him. I'm not fighting it either, so if anyone is to blame for this, it should be both of us. He shouldn't be feeling guilty.

"That thought never crossed my mind. Not even once," I tell him, my eyes focused on his. "You don't have to worry about that. I know none of this is ideal, but you didn't force me to do anything.

You might kill me after all of this, but right now, after everything I went through, I honestly don't seem to give a fuck."

And that's the truth.

I meant it when I said I'd be happy to die like this. At least it's not with Oleg or Yakov. The idea of giving them the pleasure of killing me makes my blood boil with rage.

Angelo seems surprised by my confession, his eyes widening slightly as he takes in my words.

"I'm not going to kill you," he whispers, scooting closer to me.

I push myself up on the bed, our faces so close now I can see flecks of gold in his irises. "You can't promise that yet." I smile softly, brushing our noses together in a gentle touch.

He closes his eyes, taking a deep breath, cupping my cheek, caressing my skin so gently with his thumb that I lose myself in him. "What have you done to me?" he asks, his voice barely audible.

I open my mouth to answer, though I don't know what to say, but his lips are on mine before I have the chance to respond anyway.

What starts with a gentle kiss turns into a desperate, rushed attempt to get rid of our clothes and pick up where we left off in the training room earlier.

Angelo's mouth trails down my neck as he kisses and nibbles at my skin, and I swallow a moan. I find the hem of his shirt and tug at it, forcing him to break away from me so I can pull it over his head. He helps by throwing his arms up, and the shirt is on the bedroom floor before we know it.

He removes my shorts next, tossing me on my back on the mattress. I raise my hips to help him, and when I'm about to tell him to get rid of his pants, too, he grabs the back of my thighs and pulls me toward him.

His eyes never leave my face as he slowly hooks his fingers through my panties and pulls them off.

I can't tear my eyes away from his face. The way his eyes darken while he undresses me is intoxicating. Every inch of my body is in flames, and we've barely even started.

A gasp escapes me when, in a swift movement, he spreads my legs apart and places his face between them. The sensation of his hot tongue against my already burning folds is too much for me. He laps at me with such hunger that I'm speechless, only able to take in all the pleasure he's providing me.

"Shit, that feels so good," I murmur, my eyes rolling back.

He chuckles against me, the hot burst of air causing me to shiver. "You taste pretty good, too,'" he teases before his tongue lashes out again. He speeds up, and I arch my back from the bed, granting him more access to me. I swear this is a thousand times better than what I experienced this morning, and that had been my best orgasm so far.

I can't even imagine how he'll make me feel when he is inside of me.

As if hearing my thoughts, Angelo pulls away from me, his eyes studying my reaction. I follow his every movement, captivated, as he takes off his belt and unbuttons his pants. I can't look away, watching as he strips completely naked in front of me.

"Are you sure about this?" he asks in a whisper, his gaze on me.

I nod immediately, not even considering the idea of stopping now. I'm so ready for him, and I can't be reasonable at the moment. After everything I went through, I want to do something for myself for once in my life.

Even if it means I might end up falling in love with my kidnapper.

I'm already screwed anyway, so...

Angelo takes a second to assimilate my answer, then he pulls a condom out of his pants pocket.

"Do you always carry a condom with you?" A crooked smile pulls at one side of my mouth.

He laughs, ripping the package with his teeth. *Damn, that was sexy.* "No, I just hoped we might finish what we started at the gym, so I thought it'd be better to be prepared," he explains.

In no time, he is on top of me, teasing me with the tip of his dick at my entrance.

"This is your last chance to give up," he warns me, a grin playing on his lips. "It would kill me to stop now, but I don't want you to feel like you *have* to do this."

Is he worried that I might think he's forcing me to have sex with him?

"I told you I don't think that about you," I murmur, closing my eyes and tilting my head backward when he pushes himself in just slightly. Enough to make me gasp and buck my hips, begging for more. "Just please make me forget about everything."

Angelo grunts and finally thrusts inside of me. And for the next thirty minutes, he does exactly what I asked him to do—I forget about everything and everyone, except for *him*.

SIXTEEN
SHARING SECRETS

Tatiana

I LIE against Angelo's chest, staring blankly at the wall, his thumb circling gentle caresses on my back. The sun is setting outside, and I have lost track of how long we've been here. For all I care, we could just stay here forever. I wouldn't mind.

I wonder where the other guys are or if they know what we're doing in here, but I don't bother to ask Angelo about it. Not that I'm embarrassed about what we did, but we're supposed to be enemies, kidnapper and kidnapped. This isn't how things were supposed to evolve between us.

I bet they hate me for not giving them what they want, for wasting their time, and for fucking Angelo–something they're all probably aware of by now.

But what can I do? It's not like I forced him to sleep with me. I didn't even try that hard to seduce him.

"What are you thinking about?" he whispers against my head, placing a soft kiss on my temple.

"Not much," I reply with a shrug.

"I doubt that," he says, continuing his featherlight strokes on my skin.

His touch is so relaxing that I'm almost asleep, my eyes blinking lazily. I don't answer.

"Is everything okay?" he insists, his voice bordering on concerned.

I nod against his chest. "Yeah. I was just wondering if your colleagues hate me," I admit.

"Why would you think that?" I can't see his face, but I can imagine his frown.

"Well, you were supposed to be getting answers out of me, not fucking me senseless."

"Who says I can't do both?" he jokes, and I raise my chin to look at him. He smirks down at me. "They don't hate you. It's not the first or last time that one of us has gotten involved with an asset."

I crease my brows at him. "Is that what I am?" I narrow one eye at him, wondering if he can tell I'm teasing.

He studies my face to make sure he hasn't upset me. Then he shrugs slightly. "Yes? But not only that, at least not to me. Once they realize you're not an enemy or a threat, they'll be fine. Don't worry about it."

His words have me a little less worried. I normally wouldn't care what people think of me, but being trapped in this house twenty-four/seven, and not having seen one single man other than Angelo until now, I can't ignore the idea that they are avoiding me.

"I guess I need to tell you the truth so they can believe me. So *you* can believe me," I add, resting my head back on his chest.

His muscles stiffen under me, but he doesn't say a word.

I close my eyes for a second and take a deep breath. There's no way I can keep postponing telling my story. I don't need to trust any of them. It's not like I have anything left to lose. My life is already at stake here, so I'd better get this over with.

"What do you want to know?" I ask, unsure of where to start.

"Who you are..." he whispers. "No matter how hard we searched, there's nothing about you anywhere."

I bet. "I was supposed to be dead. My adoptive parents hid me away. I don't know how Oleg found out I'm alive." I take another deep breath, gathering the courage to pour my heart out to him. "My father, Petr, was the head of the Romina Empire decades ago, and Oleg's older brother. He had a mistress, Natya, and she had just given birth to me when Oleg found out about the affair."

Tears burn my eyes, but I ignore them. I shouldn't feel so emotional while telling this story since I don't even remember any of this, but the mere thought of all the injustice my parents suffered, everything that was robbed from me when I was just a baby, still haunts me to this day.

As if sensing my despair, Angelo kisses the top of my head, encouraging me to continue.

"Lev was the capo my father trusted the most, and when he sensed that Oleg was planning something, he asked Lev and his wife, Ilya, to take me away from there. He made them promise that they'd protect me and raise me outside of the life, away from all the terror belonging to a mafia family would bring me."

I appreciate the fact that Angelo is listening so intently to me. I'm even more grateful that I can't see his face. I couldn't bear seeing the pity in his eyes.

"My life was pretty normal growing up in Russia, but Lev insisted on teaching me how to fight and protect myself just in case. It wasn't enough to escape Oleg when I got here, though. Or to escape your men either." I chuckle darkly. When put into perspective, I realize how weak I actually am.

He says nothing but holds me a little closer.

"After years away from here, Oleg suddenly ordered my parents to return to the US. I freaked out. I couldn't let them come here by themselves. I'd die not knowing if they were okay, not knowing what Oleg was doing to them. After losing both my birth parents, I couldn't lose them too."

"What happened?" Angelo whispers.

I close my eyes, reliving the worst memory I have imprinted in my brain. I can still hear the echo of the gunshots in that living room, see the blood pooling under their bodies, their heads hanging to the side, lifeless.

"His men got to us at the airport. We didn't have a chance to escape. I still don't know how they knew who I was or even that I was with them. We planned everything carefully, but it was all in vain in the end. My adoptive parents were murdered in—in front of my eyes," I explain. Tears fall freely down my cheeks now, but I don't care. It's the first time I've cried since they were killed, and I realize I'm still mourning them. I don't think I'll ever stop. "They died because of me. To protect me. And even so, Oleg got what he wanted."

"I'm so sorry," he murmurs into my hair.

I shake my head, taking a deep breath and pressing on. "Oleg was going to kill me, too. But then he decided I'd be better off as his son's wife. He is so fucking repulsive that he wanted to marry me to my cousin just so he could keep his legacy within the family."

"You were being forced to marry Yakov then? That's what it was?" he asks in disbelief. "Fuck, I knew that bastard was a monster, but that idea never crossed my mind. I should have known."

I lean on my elbow to look him in the eyes. "You knew something was off. You have a good heart, Angelo, I can tell. That's why you didn't kill me right away or torture me," I point out softly.

His dark eyes are soft, scanning my face, but something lingers deep within them, an emotion I know all too well. Sadness. Loss. He must be able to identify with me, though he's not telling me what happened.

He lifts a finger to wipe away the tears on my cheek with a gentle touch. "I didn't think I could hate Oleg any more than I already do for what he did to me and my family, but you just proved me wrong," he grumbles, his jaw clenched.

I don't want to pry, but since we're having this intimate conversation and putting all the cards on the table, I feel like it's only fair to ask. He can keep his secrets to himself if he wants. I would never force a painful memory out of someone if they're not willing to share. I told him. Not because he forced me to, but because I needed to share this with someone–and he deserves to know the truth.

I've been rotting away on the inside, carrying all this weight by myself. Weirdly, I feel lighter somehow, now that I've told him, although I doubt I'll ever be at peace with myself. "What happened?" I whisper.

"The Saints had a run-in with the Rominas," Angelo begins, a shadow passing over his face. His voice is deeper, colder. Lethal. "I had no family, just my little brother, who was just a kid at the time. Somehow, Oleg got to our safe house where he was staying before we got there."

He takes a deep breath, and I notice a slight tremble in his arm. and I reach for his hand, squeezing it in a reassuring gesture.

"It was all such a macabre... mess," he carries on. "Corpses littered the ground everywhere, but I didn't even bother to look to see who they were. Lots of them were my friends, but I could only focus on finding my brother. I located Oleg in the alley.... He had Luca." His voice cracks slightly. Angelo takes a deep breath and I wait until he can continue. "Oleg had him in his clutches. He forced him to kneel and put a bullet to his head before I had the chance to stop him."

My skin crawls with the mere thought of a kid being murdered in cold blood like that. I watch that fucking coward kill my parents, but a *kid*... that's even more fucked up. I can't even put into words how fucked up that is, let alone imagine having to watch it happen.

Looking at how distraught and broken Angelo is, my heart quivers in my chest, his pain mingling with mine. The hatred I see burning in his eyes all makes sense now. When I look at him, I see my own raw emotions mirrored right back at me

Angelo had his family taken from him by the same fucker who

took mine. Now, more than ever, I want to be able to help them take down Oleg and his whole goddamn empire.

"I don't even know what to say," I murmur, my voice raspy from crying. "It's not fair that he gets to walk around without a fucking care in the world after all the cruelty and suffering he's caused."

"He will pay for all he's done," Angelo states firmly, gritting his teeth. "Even if it's the last thing I do in this life. I'll make sure he pays for taking Luca away from me and for putting you through this hell. I promise you." He leans forward, placing a gentle kiss on my lips and tucking a loose strand of hair behind my ear.

I take comfort in his touch, his words a balm to my shattered heart. It feels so good not to be alone anymore. He has no idea how much it means to me to have someone else with the same goal as me.

Angelo won't leave me to do this by myself, and if I have to die to help him keep his promise, I'll gladly do it.

As long as I bring Oleg and everything he stole from me down with me when I go.

SEVENTEEN
BONDING OVER BREAKFAST

TATIANA and I spend the rest of the day in her room, only leaving for dinner, and we're back in bed before midnight. The house is empty because the rest of the team had to go to a meeting with Tony and left me here watching her—since, in their words, I already know how to deal with her.

I wanted to punch the smirks off their faces, but they weren't wrong.

I also don't want them near Tatiana while they're still so suspicious of her. That would only scare her. And now that she's shared everything with me, I'm more convinced than ever that I was right all along—she was never a threat.

There's no way she could be such a good actor and lie about her past. I saw the pain in her eyes, the hatred, and the guilt she carries. It's the exact same look I see in the mirror when I stare at myself.

I told her I didn't think I could hate Oleg any more than I already did, but now that I know what he put her through... God, rage boils inside me to the point I can barely control it.

Luca, Tatiana's family... not to mention the other members of our cartel who lost family members and friends at Oleg's hand. The fact that he's still out there, unpunished—it's so fucking infuriating.

At least Tatiana is here with me. She won't have to suffer at his hand again. I'll do everything in my power to keep her safe and far away from him. Now that I know the whole story, I'm sure Tony will want to keep her safe, too.

Falling asleep with her in my arms and waking up with her hair spread across my chest is incredible. It's a feeling I've never experienced before—this need to be close to her, to protect her from all the evil in the world, to make her smile, and to feel her body next to mine every morning when I open my eyes. I have to admit, it feels amazing. Of course, we're not a typical couple, and we haven't known one another that long, but this isn't just lust, a fascination I have with a beautiful prisoner. Not for me anymore.

No, for me, it's rapidly becoming something much deeper than that.

"Good morning," I whisper in her ear, pulling her close and tightening my embrace.

"Morning," she replies in a soft, low voice.

"Did you sleep well?"

"Like I haven't in a long time," she says with the most endearing smile on her lips.

I hug her tightly and kiss her forehead.

"Why don't you get ready, and then we'll go down to breakfast together? I need to check on everyone. They should already be here," I tell her, releasing her so she can get up. I wish I could stay in bed with her all day, but that's a luxury I can't afford.

In half an hour, we've both showered and gotten dressed. When we step into the kitchen, Sal and Dice are at the table, watching us with curious looks.

I clench my teeth, ignoring them, and head to the counter to pour Tatiana and me some coffee.

When I turn to hand her the mug, I realize she's still in the doorway, staring at the guys with wide eyes, her face pale like she's not sure what to make of them.

"Hello, again, miss," Sal greets her with a playful smile.

"You... I remember you," Tatiana whispers.

I frown, but then I realize what she's saying—at the same time Sal chuckles and lifts his arm, revealing the bandage covering his arm—where she sliced him.

"Yeah, I'm sure you do remember me," he says, but there's no grudge in his voice. "I remember you, too, sweetheart. Gonna have a way to remember you for a long time."

"I—I didn't know.... I thought you were with Oleg," she explains hurriedly, like she's desperate to convince him she didn't mean to hurt him.

"Hey, it's fine. No hard feelings. You were protecting yourself. I should've handled the whole situation differently. Had I known you were trying to get away from Oleg, I would've told you we were the good guys." Sal shrugs and goes back to his plate of bacon and eggs.

I'm grateful he didn't give her a hard time over it. Things are already tense and awkward enough.

Dice, on the other hand, stays stoic. He doesn't say anything, but I've known him long enough to understand he's not exactly thrilled about this.

"Tatiana, this is Sal," I say, pointing at him. "And this is Dice."

Sal smiles at her—even though they just talked—but Dice only nods without lifting his head from his plate.

"Come on in, Tatiana." I offer her the coffee. She walks over cautiously, like she's expecting one of them to jump at her if she lets her guard down.

I fix us both a plate, and the kitchen stays silent. It pisses me off, but I don't say anything. They need time to get used to the situation, and I don't want to push them. Neither Sal nor Dice likes to be pushed. They are cautious people by nature. That's why they're so damn good at their jobs.

Tatiana's defensive—and I can't blame her. She's eating with only a glance at her plate now and again, stabbing eggs with precision despite having her head on a swivel. I hate seeing her like this. Maybe we should've eaten in the bedroom.

Sitting across from them at the table gives them plenty of opportunities to speak to her. I want them to see what I see in her. And if she's willing to share what she told me yesterday, I won't have to be the one relaying it, trying to explain the raw emotion I heard in her voice and saw in her eyes when she told me about her parents.

Dice finishes his food and leans back in his chair, studying Tatiana like he's sizing her up. "So, Tony wants us to check on you and see where your loyalty stands," he reveals, his eyes locked on her.

She turns her attention to him, realizing he's talking to her. She puts her fork down, swallows, and gives him a steady gaze. He hasn't rattled her yet. Even though she's nervous, she's bold as hell—and I love that about her.

"What do you want to know? You don't have to torture me to get answers," she says with a slight shrug. "Just ask."

Sal stifles a laugh, hiding it behind his hand.

Dice shoots him a look before turning back to her. "Angelo might've fallen for your charms, but I'm not that easy," he says.

Tatiana doesn't flinch. Neither do I. I just roll my eyes and let them go at it. She's holding her own just fine. Might as well sit back and enjoy the show.

"Then ask me whatever you want," Tatiana presses, sipping her coffee.

"Who are you, exactly?" he asks, leaning toward her a bit.

She takes a deep breath and stares him straight in the eye before she starts spilling everything she told me last night.

Sal and Dice stay silent the entire time, just like I did when she was telling me. Her voice is steady while she speaks, but I've learned to read the emotion beneath the surface. Her fists are clenched in her lap, her lips trembling slightly, and her eyes are glossy as she fights back tears.

She looks so strong—yet so fragile. I wish I could take that pain away. I wish I knew how to deal with these feelings myself.

But I don't think it's possible. Guilt and grief stay with us, no matter what we do. We just have to learn how to carry them—and maybe find some peace in each other.

"That fucker is a monster," Sal mutters when she finishes. "So, if I got that right, you should be the one running the Romina Empire now. You're the rightful heir."

I hadn't thought of that—but he's right.

Dice is still quiet, but I can see the rage burning in his eyes.

"I don't give a shit about any of that," Tatiana says bitterly. "I know it was my father's, but all it brought me was pain. It can all burn with Oleg. I don't want any of it."

I want to tell her she doesn't know what she's walking away from —but I can't blame her. If I were her, I wouldn't want it either.

"He's taken too much from all of us," Dice finally says, his jaw clenched. "It's past time we ended this."

"Any news on his whereabouts?" I ask, eager for an update.

"The boss says Oleg's back at the Romina estate," Dice answers. "The bastard doesn't seem to know where we are, or he would've sent someone after her." He gestures toward Tatiana beside me. "If he's even figured out we have her yet."

"I don't think he'll bother coming after me anyway," she says, surprising all of us.

"Why not?" Sal asks, frowning.

"I'm not worth the trouble. I don't have anything on him, and honestly, I think he only kept me around to punish me for fooling him all these years," she says. "He doesn't need me, and he doesn't see me as a threat. But I'll prove him wrong. I'll find shit on him. Lev must've had something."

We all go quiet, thinking about what needs to happen next.

"Until we've got something solid, the boss said to stick to the original plan," Dice says. "We'll take him down. For everyone we've lost." He looks into my eyes. "For Luca."

I swallow the lump in my throat and nod.

For Luca.

EIGHTEEN
NOSTALGIA

Tatiana

GETTING to finally meet two other members of the Saints feels somewhat... exciting. I was shocked to see the one I had cut while running away from the wedding was part of their gang. This whole time, I'd just assumed that he had been working for Oleg. At least he doesn't seem to be holding a grudge against me, which is a relief.

The other one, though—Dice—was harder to convince that he can trust me, but in the end, I think they both believed me and my story.

I still don't know the plans they have for me, and I assume they need to tell their boss what I've disclosed first, but surprisingly, I'm not *that* worried about my future anymore. I know Angelo won't leave me on the street by myself. He'll find a way to keep me protected, even if his boss tells him I'm of no use to them anymore.

Maybe I can return to Russia and start again somehow.

The mere thought of leaving Angelo behind hurts my heart, but if that's what it comes to in the end, I'll have to find a way. It's a bit alarming that I'm already so attached to him.

Fucking Stockholm Syndrome much?

After breakfast, Angelo tells me to leave the room because he needs to have a private meeting with the guys. I agree immediately, not wanting to prevent them from doing whatever it is they need to do, even though I am aware that they will discuss everything I just shared with them.

It feels like I'm walking away so they can decide my future *without* me, but to be completely honest with myself, I don't want to be a part of it. Insisting on being included in their discussion won't help me, so I excuse myself, heading up to the second floor.

I don't want to go to my room, though. I'm feeling suffocated inside those walls. And since Angelo didn't specifically tell me what I couldn't do—except leave the house, of course—I decide to walk around and find something more interesting to do with my time.

I haven't had the chance to explore the house, so I walk through the halls, peeking inside some rooms where the doors are already open, and eventually I find a large library.

It's a huge room, the walls covered with shelves filled with books, two comfortable couches, a wooden desk, and a window that has a view of a forest and a lake make it a perfect place to read. It's beautiful, but it stirs a memory deep inside me of a similar room in the home I grew up in. I lose myself in it for a minute, wondering what it would be like if I had stayed in Russia.

Would Lev and Ilya still have been murdered if I hadn't come? Did Oleg already know about me before we arrived here? He must have to intercept us at the airport like that. Was that his plan the whole time? That I come here so he could get rid of them and marry me off to his bastard son?

I have so many questions, but I can't find answers to any of them.

Shaking my head, I focus my attention on the books around me, taking in the scent of old paper and remembering the times when my parents used to read to me by the fire back in Russia. Those cold days were always so filled with warmth. They raised me with so much love, dedication.... How is it fair that they had to die to keep me alive?

I randomly grab a book with a Russian title and a green leather cover and sit down on the floor, close to the fireplace. I skim through the pages, trying to understand what the book is about, but my head is not in the right place. I'm not able to focus on anything right now.

I'm exhausted. My brain and body are heavy, weighed down with the activities of the past few weeks but mostly, my emotions are all over the place. With everything that I went through, and getting involved with Angelo, I can't keep my mind on one topic long enough to breathe, let alone read a book.

I need to reach the end of this nightmare. Soon.

I want to live my life. I want to at least have a chance of having one. I had a nice childhood, but I was constantly looking over my shoulder. That era of my life needs to end.

I stare blankly at the pages for God knows how long, until I hear a shuffling sound by the door.

"Didn't take you for a bookworm," Angelo muses.

In my peripheral vision, I see him leaning against the doorframe, his hands in his pockets.

I smirk to myself, not looking up. I'm not really sure what to say, and frankly, I wanted to be alone. But I can't tell him that. Besides, he's seen me at my worst already. I feel like, right now, I can show him my weak side without fear.

"I'm sorry about all of that. I know it's not easy for you to talk about," he murmurs when I don't reply.

I finally look at him, not sure what to say. All I can do is nod.

He nods toward the book in my hands. "You miss it, don't you? Russia?"

I hesitate. *Do I?* Do I miss the place or what it means to me? Do I miss the happy memories I have from there, or do I belong in Russia?

Shrugging, I try to put my thoughts into a coherent sentence. "Honestly, I don't know what I miss. When I lived in Russia, I used to dream of one day living a normal life. It was as normal as it could be, and I know Lev and Ilya did their best to keep their promises to my father, but…" I sigh. "I still wonder what my life could've been like. If my parents hadn't been murdered, if I had stayed and been raised here. Would it be a regular life, with no hiding, no violence? Or would I have become a part of the mafia? It makes me wonder, you know?"

"I do." Angelo walks into the room and sits down on the couch, keeping a small distance from us, allowing me to have my personal space for a little longer. I like that he is thoughtful that way. "And now? What do you dream of?"

Great question.

I wish I could say I have good dreams whenever my head hits the pillow, but nightmares have become a nightly routine these days. The only night I can think of recently when I didn't have one was last night, when I slept with him. Angelo managed to clear my mind of any bad memories.

All I dreamed about was building a life with *him*.

And I was happy.

Still, I don't want to tell him that. I have no idea *what* we are at this point, and it's not like I can expect him to be on the same page as me, no matter how much he expresses his feelings are mutual through his gestures and words.

My future is uncertain, and so is our relationship.

I close the book and put it aside, shifting so I can face him completely. The silence stretches between us for longer than I intended, and it leaves me slightly on edge.

For once, neither of us is talking about Oleg or tragic pasts.

We're talking about something that feels way scarier than any of those things—our future. Together or separated, whatever it is, it freaks me out to not have a plan. Not to know what to do or expect.

"It's hard to have dreams when every day could be my last," I finally confess, doing my best not to sound like a victim. I don't want him to pity me or think I'm saying that just so he will release me. But it's the truth, and he is the one who asked.

He stares at me for another second before leaning down and picking up the book from the floor. He glances at the title and frowns slightly. "This one's got a bad ending," he tells me, his tone a bit more cheerful now. He's changing the subject, and I appreciate that he didn't insist on pushing me. Until we know how this is going to play out, it's best that we don't talk about any plans for the future. There's no point for either of us.

Looking at the book in his hands, something strange occurs to me. I raise a brow. "You read it? In Russian?"

He laughs, shaking his head. "I read the translation. I don't speak Russian, and I sure the hell don't read it." He sets the book beside him on the couch. "And well, I didn't like the ending."

That piques my curiosity. I didn't take him for a reader. It's... *sexy*. He's not just magnetically attractive, but he's also intelligent.

"What would you have changed?" I ask, tilting my head as I watch him.

His eyes darken, a mysterious expression shadowing his features. The way he stares at me makes my chest tighten and my core begin to heat. The effect he has on me is addictive.

"I'd give the protagonists a way out," he tells me, his voice serious and firm.

Since I don't know what the story is about, I have no idea what he is referring to. But for some reason, I feel he isn't just talking about the protagonists of that novel. Is this his way of saying he hopes I find a way to win?

I really hope he is talking about us because I have to believe there is a way out of this for me—this house, this life, this nightmare.

All I want is to have a chance to be happy. Hopefully, in my happy ending, Angelo will be by my side. But until Oleg is dead, that ending will stay unwritten.

NINETEEN
MAKING UP

The morning sun warms my skin, stirring me gently from sleep. I stretch my arms above my head, my muscles loosening as a sense of peace settles over me. It's strange how a good night's sleep can reset everything—my mood, my resolve, even my sense of purpose. Today, I feel new. Whole.

Turning to my side, I gaze at Angelo. He's still asleep, facing me, his features relaxed and soft in the quiet light. I take him in—the curve of his lips, the strong line of his jaw, those unruly dark curls that slip over closed eyes, guarded by lashes so long they could make any woman jealous.

He looks like a different man when he's asleep—unbothered, weightless. Awake, he carries the world like it's chained to his back.

A part of me wants to believe I'm the reason for that peace. That I'm helping him, in the way he's helped me—just by being here, by seeing him, really seeing him, the way that no one else has. Just as he's able to see me differently.

My heart pounds as flashes of the past two weeks flicker through my mind. These two weeks have changed everything. I've felt more, lived more, than I did in the twenty-four years before I met him.

If I could go back and rewrite my story, there are a hundred things I'd do differently—but not meeting Angelo, not having this relationship with him–whatever it is.

That's the one thing I'd never change.

Everything about him is perfect.

But I'm not ready to say I love him. It's not that love scares me. It's the thought of losing him. The risk we live in every day is suffocating. And Angelo's always at the center of it—more exposed, more hunted than I'll ever be.

I try to picture a future with him, something peaceful, something real. But as long as Oleg breathes, peace is a fantasy. That man is a shadow over our lives.

And then it hits me.

The only way forward is through him.

Oleg has to die.

I know Angelo and his team have been planning, watching, waiting for the right opportunity. But I'm done waiting. I know what I need to do.

"Good morning, baby," Angelo murmurs, stirring beside me. I hadn't even realized he was awake.

"I have to kill Oleg," I blurt, the words slipping out like a secret too heavy to keep.

His eyes snap wide open. Confusion creases his brow as he shifts to face me. "What did you just say?" His voice is rough, laced with sleep and disbelief.

"I have to kill him," I repeat, firmer this time. "Oleg."

He watches me closely, the fog of sleep fading as he processes what I'm saying.

"That would be suicide," he says, his tone calm, almost gentle, like he's trying to protect me from myself.

Maybe he is. But I don't care. I sit up, a wave of rage rising through me, pushing logic to the background. "I'm the only one who can get close enough. Maybe he still thinks I'm useful. I could pretend I was taken, not that I escaped. Pretend I want back in on his twisted plan."

Angelo is already sitting up, shaking his head hard. "That's crazy, baby. He'd kill you the second you walk through the door."

I hate how his words make my stomach turn, not because they're harsh—but because they might be true. "Then help me," I plead, grabbing his arm. "Help me end this. Help me end *him*."

He sighs deeply. "We're already on it. I have people tracking him right now. Why would I risk letting you, knowing how dangerous this is?"

Let me? The word scrapes against my pride. I bite back the ugly retort already forming in my mind. He doesn't own me. I'm not one of his soldiers. And I'm certainly not helpless.

"If we're not smart about this," he says softly, "you'll lose more than your chance at revenge. You'll lose your life. And he'll win."

"It's not revenge," I reply, my voice trembling with fury. "It's justice. And you, of all people, should understand that."

His expression shifts—less guarded, more vulnerable. "I do," he says. "Trust me. But I can't let you walk into a situation where you might get hurt. We're close–closer than we've ever been."

His reassurance feels like a leash.

"I can't sit still while you handle all of it. If you won't help me, I'll do it myself."

The truth is, I have no plan. No clear path. But I will find one.

Angelo stares at me like he wants to say more, but instead, he shakes his head and stands without another word. He slips on his pants and walks out of the room.

I fall back onto the mattress with a groan, glaring at the ceiling. Fuck. Why did I corner him like that? Why now, with no strategy, no backup?

I'm still drowning in regret when the door clicks open again. Angelo steps back inside, calm, quiet. He climbs onto the bed, scanning my face with something softer in his eyes than before.

Relief floods me.

"I'm sorry," he says, brushing hair from my cheek, his thumb trailing warmth across my skin.

"I'm the one who should be sorry," I whisper. "I'm just... I don't know. A fucking mess."

He cradles my face. "I'm just trying to protect you. All of this—it's not just dangerous. It's deadly."

I nod, but I'm done with this argument. Until I know what to say—what to do—I'll keep my mouth shut. Instead, I inch closer, wrapping my arms around his neck and pressing my forehead to his. "Let's talk about something else," I murmur, then I raise a teasing brow. "Or do something else."

His eyes darken in an instant. His hands grip my waist with urgency. "I have work to do," he says, though he makes no move to leave.

"Right..." I say innocently, starting to pull away.

But his grip tightens, yanking me back onto his lap. "It can wait," he growls as his hands slip under my shirt, trailing fire along my back.

"I hope they're not counting on you," I tease, kissing his neck, biting his ear.

"They'll be just fine for a little bit longer," he groans.

The rest blurs into heat, skin, and breath. His hands, his mouth, the way he touches me like he's trying to memorize every inch—I lose myself in it, forget the world outside this room, forget everything but us.

And when we collapse, tangled and breathless, I feel more alive than I have in days.

"I really do have to go now," he says after a moment, regret etched in his voice.

I nod, already plotting. Already thinking.

Because I might not have a plan yet.

But I will.

TWENTY
DISAGREEMENTS

Angelo

I pull myself from the bed and get dressed, still feeling the rush from my quick encounter with Tatiana. As much as I want to spend more time with her, I know I can't afford to linger. Work's been piling up, and I've been slacking lately—ever since things started getting heated between us. The Saints need me, and I can't ignore them.

Keeping an eye on Tatiana, as per Tony's orders, has also taken a lot of my focus. I haven't had a chance to personally discuss with him yet what Tatiana shared with me about her past and her involvement with the Rominas, but I know that Sal and Dice have already filled him in. I just hope Tony doesn't see her as a liability or a potential threat, but instead, as an ally.

"Can I ask you something?" Tatiana's voice pulls me from my thoughts. She's lying there, looking up at me, her lashes fluttering in that way I know always gets me.

"Sure," I reply, trying to sound casual. I walk back toward her but keep my distance so we don't end up going for round two and delaying my work further.

She hesitates, and I can already feel it—the tension. I know what's coming, and I don't think I'm ready for it. Maybe it's another argument about Oleg or her obsession with bringing him down. Frankly, I'm not in the mood for that today.

I stepped out earlier, trying not to say the wrong thing and wreck what we have. But I can't just stand here and watch her try to fix everything on her own. The idea of Oleg or Yakov laying a hand on her makes my blood boil. There's no way in hell I'm letting her out of my sight, even if it means being the bad guy and keeping her locked in this house for her own safety.

She's still staring at me. Her voice is quieter this time. "Do you think you could lend me a laptop or maybe a phone?"

I raise an eyebrow. That's not what I expected.

She seems so unsure, like she's testing the waters. "I just... I can't stand being in this room anymore. I feel useless. If I had a device, maybe I could do some research. Try to remember something–anything."

I pause. It makes sense—she wants to piece together her past, maybe jog some memories she's lost or overlooked. But letting her access the outside world? That's a tricky move.

My mind races. Would she really call for help? Would she try to escape? Am I overthinking this, or am I being cautious for the right reasons?

She doesn't have anyone else. She doesn't even know this city. She's not going anywhere. And right now, I'm the only person she can trust. I just hope she sees it the same way.

"I promise I won't do anything drastic," she adds, almost pleading. "If I find something useful, I'll tell you. Remember when I mentioned Chinatown? Maybe I can uncover something else online."

I take a deep breath, trying to stay rational. "Where would you even start?"

She shrugs, her fingers playing with the edge of the blanket. "I don't know... I can look up maps of the city, check Oleg's name. Maybe something will come up that triggers a memory. I just need to do something, Angelo. I can't sit here all day. It's driving me fucking insane."

Her frustration is palpable. I can see it in her eyes, hear it in her voice. If I'm feeling like this, she probably is really losing her mind.

I sigh, knowing there's no perfect solution here. It won't hurt to let her do some research. Besides, anything in this house can't be traced. Oleg won't know if she's looking up his name or diving into his business.

"All right," I finally say, stepping away. "I'll get you a laptop, but you need to promise me you won't do anything without running it by me first." I look into her eyes, trying to be firm.

"I promise," she says, and for once, there's no hesitation in her voice.

Her determination is almost admirable. I can't blame her for wanting justice—hell, I want the same thing for Luca. But I can't let her act on impulse, not after everything she's been through.

"I'll grab it in a little bit," I tell her, moving toward the bathroom. I have time for a quick shower after all, and I need one. "Sal and Dice are downstairs. If you're hungry, go eat. I'll be down in a minute."

I turn on the shower, letting the warm water heat up as I strip and step inside. The warmth rushes over me. I lather up, trying to wash away the stress and the lingering tension. My head's a mess right now, and my heart's no better. I need to talk to Tony soon, to figure out what to do about Tatiana. If I betray her trust, I don't know if I can live with that. But I can't risk everything for her—no matter how much she intrigues me. I need to stay focused. There's too much at stake for me to lose concentration, even for a moment.

After my shower, I throw on some black slacks and a white button down, deciding to forego the jacket since I won't be leaving the house. I have a video call with Tony soon, but there's no need to be dressed to the nines.

I head downstairs, finding Tatiana in the kitchen with Sal, Dice, and Kian, who looks like he's just walked in from the cold. He's holding car keys in one hand and rubbing his red cheeks with the other.

"Hey," I greet him.

"Hey, man! Good to see you." He grins, glancing toward Tatiana. "You've been keeping her all to yourself, huh?"

I grunt in response, not in the mood for Kian's teasing. "Any updates?" I ask, moving to the counter for a cup of coffee.

Sal and Dice shake their heads, equally frustrated.

"Nothing in Chinatown?" I press, glancing at Tatiana.

Her eyes widen, and she shifts in her seat, clearly interested in what Kian has to say.

"We've got some establishments under surveillance," he says, grabbing a piece of bacon from the plate in the middle of the table. He shakes out of his coat, hanging it on the back of his chair before sitting down. "We're almost sure they belong to the Rominas. We can't go in guns blazing yet. We're planning something more subtle—hit them where it hurts without tipping our hand. Take enough to hurt them."

"Stealing from them?" I ask, raising an eyebrow. "What's the point of that?"

Sal chuckles. "It's not as satisfying as killing them, but it's a start. At least we'll hit them where it hurts."

I feel the familiar weight of frustration building. I want more. I want blood. But I don't want to risk Tatiana's safety.

"That's fucking ridiculous," Tatiana mutters, her fists clenched. Her voice is low but filled with fire. I can't blame her—she's as pissed as I am. "Are we just going to sit here and do nothing while Oleg does whatever the hell he wants?" she adds, looking from me to the others. "He's got to pay for what he did. To me. To us."

I feel her pain, I do. But I also understand the importance of keeping her safe. "We've talked about this," I say softly, not wanting to argue.

"But I want to help," she insists, her eyes desperate for my approval. "I can't just sit here."

"You will help when the time is right. For now, let us do our job," I reply, my tone brokering no further discussion.

Tatiana opens her mouth but then closes it, looking away from me. She crosses her arms, clearly disappointed and angry.

I run a hand through my hair, exhausted. I hate this. I hate seeing her upset, but I won't let her jeopardize everything we've worked for. Sal, Dice, and Kian are watching us, judging, no doubt, but I don't care anymore. The truth is out in the open now, and there's no going back.

TWENTY-ONE
CONFLICTS

Tatiana

I GRIT my teeth and force myself not to roll my eyes. Throwing a tantrum won't help—but that doesn't stop the anger simmering just beneath my skin. I don't like the way Angelo drew that line between us. Cold. Sharp. Final.

It's not just that he's shutting me out. It's *how* he's doing it—like I'm still some piece on his chessboard, a liability to manage. A prisoner, technically. But from him? That's a slap in the face.

He's across the kitchen, his body rigid, watching me. I ignore him. If he wants distance, fine. I've had worse from men with half his brain and twice his ego.

I focus on the window, my jaw tight. I *will* find a way to be useful, whether he lets me or not. I didn't survive this long just to be benched.

"Give me a cigarette," Angelo mutters, moving toward Sal and snatching the pack from the table.

My gaze flicks over in time to see the tension in his shoulders, the anger in his hands.

He doesn't smoke. Hasn't since I got here.

"Sure you wanna do that?" Kian asks, brows raised.

"Just give me one," Angelo growls without looking at him. He lights up and walks out, letting the screen door slam behind him.

I don't follow. If he wants to sulk, he can do it without an audience. He's the one who pulled away.

Whatever.

I push my plate around and force myself to eat. I'll need my strength, even if the food tastes like ash.

The guys start talking sports—something I care less than nothing about. I tune them out, my thoughts drifting back to Russia, to Lev's office, to the files he used to keep locked up. *There* might be something—anything—about Oleg I could use. But I doubt Oleg left anything behind. He probably burned the whole house down the second I went missing.

The thought makes my throat tighten, but I swallow it down. Grief is a luxury I can't afford right now.

My hatred for Oleg isn't new. It's a slow-burning thing, etched into every memory. But now that Lev and Ilya are gone—murdered—there's nothing holding it back. I don't want revenge. I want *justice*. And if no one else will put an end to that bastard, I will.

I glance at the men around me. The Saints hate him too. That much is clear. But waiting around, hoping they handle it? No chance in hell.

Sal gets up, rinsing his plate. "We're heading into the office. Need anything?"

He's trying to play nice—probably feeling awkward after my clash with Angelo. I don't care about his guilt, but I *will* use it.

"Actually," I say, voice steady, "I asked Angelo for a laptop earlier. Thought some digging might jog my memory. Maybe it will help me find something useful about Oleg."

I pause, then shrug. "But since he's in a mood, I figured I'd ask someone more reasonable."

Sal looks at Dice and Kian. A silent conversation passes between them.

"I don't see a problem," Dice finally says. "Tablets are clean. But you screw with us, and we'll know."

He looks me dead in the eye, and I match it without flinching. "I'm not stupid. I know what side I'm on."

He studies me a second longer, then disappears into the living room and returns with a sleek black tablet. He holds it out—but doesn't let go right away.

"Everything you do, I'll see," he warns.

"Fine by me," I say. "I've got nothing to hide."

He lets go.

Once they're gone, I dive in. First stop: maps, locations, anything that might stir a memory. Nothing. My mind draws blanks. Just a dull ache forming behind my eyes.

I switch tactics and search Oleg's name, the Romina family. Old news articles pop up—most of it garbage. Sanitized, vague reports about my father's murder. Lev told me the truth. These headlines? They're fairy tales.

After a couple of hours, Kian drops a bag of food in front of me. "Grab what you want. We'll eat later."

I nod and mutter, "Thanks," not looking up.

Eventually, hunger wins. I shove the tablet aside, rip into the food, then get back to it. But by six, I've hit a wall. No leads. No sparks of memory. Just frustration.

I shower, trying to rinse off the disappointment. It doesn't help, so I head outside.

The two guards on the porch tense when I step out.

"Hey," I say coolly. "Just getting some air. Don't worry—I'm not dumb enough to run."

They nod but don't respond. That's fine. I'm not here to make friends.

I settle on a bench, breathing in the crisp air. It's the first time I've been outside since I was dragged here—and as much as I hate to admit it, it feels good—the quiet, the space, no walls closing in.

"Can we talk?"

His voice slices through the air like a blade.

I turn. Angelo's standing near the porch, hands in his pockets, looking casual—but I can see the heat in his eyes. He's trying to mask it. He's failing.

"Sure," I say. Short. Controlled.

"I talked to my boss," he says. "He believes you."

My brows lift. That's unexpected. "Didn't think he would."

"He did." He pauses. "But you're still not free to leave."

I stare at him. "That supposed to be a favor?"

"It's protection," he says tightly. "Oleg might come after you. We're not taking that risk."

"Shouldn't that be *my* call?"

His jaw tightens. "Not in this situation."

I shake my head, letting out a low, bitter laugh. "So I'm not a prisoner—but I'm not allowed to walk out the front door. Sounds like a technicality."

He exhales and runs a hand through his hair, finally coming to sit next to me. He reaches for my hand—hesitates, then takes it. His touch is warm, steady, too damn gentle for someone playing warden.

"Be mad if you want," he says. "But I meant what I said. I'm not letting you go. I won't lose you too."

It should piss me off more than it does. And yeah, part of me *is* mad. But another part—the part that's been alone, hunted, haunted— wants to believe him.

Still, I keep my voice cool. "You don't get to make that decision."

"I already did."

I look away, my jaw tight. He's infuriating, controlling, and overbearing. And I hate how much I want him anyway.

TWENTY-TWO
LETTER FROM THE PAST

Tatiana

ANGELO and I ended up in bed after our talk on the porch. Not because we reached an understanding—we didn't. We're still standing on opposite sides of a line neither of us is willing to cross. But I knew pushing him harder would only cause more damage.

So, I hold my tongue.

For now, keeping the peace means swallowing my pride, locking my thoughts away, and playing the role of someone willing to wait.

It's after midnight. Rain pounds against the windows like a warning—fierce, unrelenting. Angelo lies asleep beside me, peaceful, unaware of the storm brewing right here in this bed.

I watch him for a long moment, memorizing the shape of him, the warmth of him, just in case this is the last time.

Sleep won't come, so I reach for the tablet on my nightstand. I browse for a while—news, maps, dead ends. Then, on impulse, I check my old email. I haven't opened it since I left Russia. I expect spam, junk, maybe nothing at all.

What I *don't* expect is a message from Lev.

Dated the night we left.

My stomach drops. I cover my mouth to keep the sharp inhale from waking Angelo. Everything about it screams "trap" at first glance. But I open it anyway.

And I break.

Dear Tatiana,

I hope I'm with you when you read this. If not... it means Oleg found out what we did—that we hid you from him all these years.

I never once regretted it, not for a second. You were the best thing that ever happened to Ilya and me.

I'm sorry we kept you hidden. I'm sorry you had to live like that. I only pray we gave you a small chance at happiness.

We're catching a flight soon. But if something happens... I've rented an apartment in New York City (the address is at the bottom). Some of our things are there. You'll know what to look for.

If you're reading this alone, then you're in this fight without us now. Be smart. Oleg is dangerous. He'll stop at nothing to get what he wants.

I know your heart. I know what you're thinking. But please, if you can—let it go. Live. Find peace. Don't chase vengeance. It doesn't suit someone with a heart like yours.

I love you. Always.

Lev

I read it twice. Then a third time. Tears stream down my face before I even notice. I slip out of bed, careful not to disturb Angelo, and lock myself in the bathroom. The moment I turn on the shower to drown the sound, I fall apart.

The grief I've buried for weeks rips its way to the surface—the loss, the helplessness, the rage.

It takes time to steady my breathing, but when I finally lift my head and look in the mirror, I don't recognize the woman staring back.

Eyes bloodshot. Face streaked. But it's not the pain that stuns me —it's the fury. Burning. Alive.

Lev said I wasn't made for revenge, as did Angelo. But they're wrong. That version of me—the soft, sheltered girl—is gone. Oleg saw to that. So did Yakov.

I can't live in limbo, waiting for someone else to save me. I'm already slipping away from the one person who might love me, and I can't let this rot inside me any longer.

I have to end it.

Not for closure. Not for peace.

For justice.

If I can get close to Oleg or Yakov—if I can convince them I was dragged from that wedding against my will—I'll find my way back inside their walls. And then I'll kill them.

My hands.

My bullet.

No Saints. No Angelo.

Just me.

I walk back into the bedroom and glance at Angelo. He's turned away, his breathing deep and steady. I linger for a moment. A part of me wants to curl beside him, take one last night of comfort.

But I can't.

This ends now.

I grab the coat from the wardrobe and slip it on. My eyes fall on the nightstand. Keys. Wallet. Gun.

My heart pounds as I approach. One wrong move and he'll wake, and it'll be over.

I move slowly, my fingers closing around the smart key first, then the wallet. The gun is heavier than I expected, and colder too.

I take one last look at him.

If I fail, I probably won't survive it. And if I succeed... Angelo will never look at me the same way again.

But I still walk out.

The hallway is dark and quiet. I don't know where the guards are, and I'm not going to wait around to find out. I move silently, hugging the walls. No shadows. No movement.

I make it to the first floor without incident.

I can't use the front door. I already know the guards stationed outside would stop me. Instead, I slip through the back door into the garage.

The door creaks. I freeze, holding my breath. No footsteps. No voices.

I'm still good.

The cold hits me hard when I step out, but I keep going. My coat flaps in the wind, and I press the key, scanning for the car.

A black vehicle beeps to the right. Too loud.

I dart toward it, nerves on fire, adrenaline crashing through me. My hands tremble as I get in. For a second, I can't remember how to breathe.

"Fuck," I whisper, trying to start the engine. "Come on, come on—"

The car roars to life.

I'm shaking.

This is it.

I drive slowly toward the gate, the tinted windows hiding me. The guard looks at the car, then nods and hits the button.

The gates open.

I keep driving. I don't look back.

Because if I do, I might turn around.

And I can't afford to stop.

Not now.

TWENTY-THREE
SHE'S GONE

Angelo

A SHARP BEEP echoes from the garage downstairs and jerks me out of sleep. For a second, I think it's part of a dream. I lie still, blinking at the ceiling. But something feels off—too quiet, too empty.

I don't need to look to my side to know she's gone. I *feel* it. The air is colder. The silence is heavier.

I sit up, scanning the room. The door is open. The lights are off. There's no one in my room at all—including Tatiana.

Then I notice another problem—my gun, keys, and wallet are missing from the spot where I usually keep them on my nightstand.

"Fuck," I growl, bolting out of bed. I yank on my pants and shove my arms through my shirt like I'm racing death itself. My chest tightens, adrenaline slamming through my veins like a freight train. I shove my feet into my shoes as fast as possible.

She took my car, my weapon, and my goddamn trust.

"You can't do this to me, Tatiana," I mutter, storming into the hallway. My voice is hoarse, laced with anger and something far worse—fear.

"She's gone!" I shout down the corridor, pounding on Dice's door without waiting. "Get the fuck up—we've got a problem."

Dice swings the door open already half dressed, his eyes blazing. "You sleeping on the job now?" he barks, grabbing his belt and weapon.

I ignore him, even though I know I'm going to hear about this later. I can't fucking explain what I was thinking, letting her in. My feelings will have to wait, though. She's acting impulsively, and she's going to get herself hurt–if not killed. "She took my keys. My gun. Everything," I say through clenched teeth. "She's driving my fucking car."

Sal, Kian, Max—they all file out, alert and confused, their jaws tight.

"Give me your keys," I snap at Max. He tosses them over without a word.

"Where would she even go?" Sal asks, jogging beside me down the stairs.

"She doesn't know the city," Kian adds, following behind him alongside Max.

"She's not thinking. She's feeling. She wants revenge." I stop, turning to face them all. "You heard her. She's not gonna sit around and wait. If she thinks she has a shot at getting to Oleg or Yakov— she'll take it, even if it's suicide."

Everyone goes still. We all know it's true.

"I'll hit the ceremony location," I continue. "Kian—check the mansion. If they're not there, loop back. Keep looking for her until one of us finds her."

We're halfway to the garage when a thought slams into me. "The GPS," I say. "Check the car."

Sal's already sprinting to grab his laptop.

"I'm not waiting," I mutter. "Call me the second you get something."

"I'm riding with you," Dice says, jumping into the passenger seat before I can argue.

Without another word, I floor it, tires screeching as we tear out of the driveway. "She fucking lied to me," I mutter, white-knuckling the wheel. "I trusted her."

"She didn't lie. Not exactly, anyway," Dice replies calmly. "She just couldn't wait. You know how that feels."

I glare out at the highway, biting back the answer I don't want to admit: Yeah, I *do* know how that feels–that hunger to fix what's broken with your own hands, to make someone *pay for what they've done to you, to your family.*

"She's gonna get herself killed," I grind out. Thoughts of losing Tatiana make my stomach tighten into a fist. Even if everything she said to me was a lie, I can't think about her dying.

Dice is quiet for a beat, then says, "Or she's gonna do what you wouldn't let her."

I don't answer. I can't. The possibility of her getting into the mansion and killing Oleg and Yakov without getting hurt is so slim, it seems impossible. Every second that ticks by tightens the noose around my neck.

The phone rings. I press a button, putting it on speaker. "Yeah?"

"She's headed toward the city," Sal says. "She's just a few miles ahead of you–still moving."

"She knows how to drive in this city?" Dice asks, skeptical.

"No idea," I mutter, switching lanes. "But that won't matter if she runs into the wrong people." Taking a deep breath, I say, "Thanks, Sal. Stay on the line, and tell me exactly where she's going."

We drive in tense silence, Sal's voice giving us turn-by-turn directions until we hit the neighborhood where we found her after the wedding.

"She's near the deli," Sal finally says. "Where we picked her up."

What? That doesn't track. Not if she's trying to get to Oleg.

"Why the hell would she go there?" Dice asks, voicing the thought before I can.

"She's not thinking like us," I say, turning sharply at the next light. "She's not trying to find the mansion. She's trying to find a *way in*. Maybe she thinks the estate will give her access."

"Or maybe she's got her own plan," Dice murmurs.

The next words from Sal freeze my blood.

"The car stopped," he says.

"Where?" I demand.

"Near the park—behind the estate where the wedding was supposed to happen."

That whole property belongs to the Rominas. If she's trying to get in...

She's walking into hell.

"I just lost her signal," Sal adds, cursing under his breath.

"Fuck," I snarl. "We're close. We'll find her."

I punch the gas, and the car lurches forward. Traffic is light this time of night, thank God, and Sal said we were close to her. If she doesn't know we're chasing her, there's a possibility we could catch up to her. I know I can run faster than her. I've got to catch her before it's too late.

If anything happens to her—if I find her too late—I don't care what it costs. I will burn the Rominas to the ground.

TWENTY-FOUR
AMBUSHED

Tatiana

I REGRET LEAVING the house the moment I reach the city. The buildings are monstrous, and I'm not used to a place as overwhelmingly chaotic as New York.

At first, I was determined to head straight to the apartment Lev had rented—curious, optimistic, convinced that whatever he'd left there might hold answers about Oleg. I had hoped to find something, anything, that could help the Saints in their mission to dismantle the Romina Empire.

I type the address Lev sent via email into the GPS, but I start recognizing the street names—familiar turns, shops and signs. Then I see it— the corner deli where Angelo kidnapped me that day. My stomach turns over and the blood in my veins turns to ice. I'm too close to the place where the wedding ceremony took place. Where I ran from. Where it all began.

Emotionally, I begin to unravel and as if that's not enough, I realize the car behind me has been changing lanes immediately after I merge for long enough that I know I'm being followed.

Panic claws at my chest and my palms start to sweat. I can't breathe.

At first, I think it might be Angelo and the others, having noticed I slipped out. Maybe they've come to bring me back. But when headlights blaze behind me, tires shrieking over the pavement, I know instantly—these aren't the Saints.

This has to be Oleg's men. How the fuck did they find me? Were they watching the house? Tracking the car? Is it possible they've been staking out the streets near where I vanished, hoping I'd return? That would be insane! And yet... here they are!

A suffocating weight presses down on me as my mind spins, trying to make sense of it all. I glance in the rearview mirror and catch a glimpse of one of their faces—a man I saw in the mansion, standing silently behind Oleg. A shadow, just like then, but now in pursuit.

I need to escape, but I don't know this city, not well. I don't know where to go. I can't go back to Angelo's. I won't risk giving away their location. I won't lead an ambush to their doorstep. I'm on my own— left to face the fallout of my reckless decision.

Why didn't I just wait for Angelo to wake up? Why didn't I ask him to come with me? He probably would have. I'd have been safe with him. But it's too late now.

A scream rips from me when their car slams into the back of the car I'm driving, jolting me into the wall of a closed restaurant.

The impact isn't strong enough to deploy the airbag, but I fly sideways, hitting my head on the window. Hot liquid trickles down my forehead. I blink, dazed. The sharp tangy scent of copper confirms it—I'm bleeding. I don't have time to assess the injury. I have to run. My body aches, but I can still move. That's something. If I can get out of this car, I might still have a chance.

I fumble with the seatbelt, my shoulder screaming in protest as I force the driver's door open. Once out of the car, I crawl into the shadows and hold my breath, listening for voices or footsteps before deciding which way to run.

One of the men barks frantic orders at the others. "Her car crashed! She's running away!" he shouts. "Get to the other side and circle the park!" At least I know not to go into the park.

Running is my only option. I bolt, weaving through unfamiliar streets, turning left, then right, searching for anything—anywhere I could hide or call for help. But if I run into a store, someone there will call the police. And what then? How do I explain this without dragging the Saints into it?

Still—am I willing to die in order to keep from ratting them out?

I barely have time to think about it before chaos explodes behind me. Gunshots crack in the air, so I dive behind a dumpster in a narrow alley, my lungs burning, my heart threatening to burst.

As I wonder whether it was one of Oleg's men or if the Saints are here and are firing at the enemy, I try to breathe, to steady myself. I stupidly left Angelo's gun behind in the car. If I'd taken it, I'd at least have some way to defend myself.

The footsteps grow louder—closer. Voices echo. I brace for the end. This is how I die—in a filthy alley–because I thought I could handle things on my own. I'm disappointed in myself. Tears threaten at the corners of my eyes. I'm such a fucking idiot!

"On your left!" someone yells—a voice I recognize, but I'm too frozen with fear to peek out. Was that Dice? Two more gunshots. A grunt. A body drops. I don't need to look—I know someone's been hit. What the hell is happening? Was that really Dice? How did he know where I am?

"Take their car and call the others. Get rid of the bodies," another voice commands.

Angelo.

I know that voice. I'd know it anywhere.

"I'll get Tatiana and take her home."

And just like that, I see him. His shoes appear in my vision first, and I break. A sob escapes me as I stand and fling my arms around him, burying my face in his neck. His scent calms the storm inside me instantly.

"I'm so sorry," I whisper against his skin, and he wraps his arms around me. He breathes in deep, his chest rising against mine, then gently pushes me back to examine me. His eyes widen at the sight of my bloody forehead.

"Fuck! Are you okay?" he asks, his voice tight with fear—no anger, no judgment, only concern. And that makes my guilt even worse. "Let's get your head checked right now." His hand moves toward the wound, hesitating in midair.

"I'm fine," I say, though the motion makes nausea roll through me. Maybe I'm not fine. Angelo lifts me into his arms without another word and carries me back to his car.

Under the dim streetlight, I see the damage. The car's in bad shape. "I wrecked your car. I'm sorry," I sob, covering my mouth with both hands.

"I don't give a damn about the fucking car," he growls, his voice a low rumble vibrating through his chest. "You could've died. Do you even understand what you did?" His words hit hard—but they're true. I know I messed up. I know I let desperation get the better of me. I wanted justice for what Oleg did. I just couldn't accept the way Angelo wanted to do it.

I stay silent as he opens the passenger door for me. He buckles my seatbelt then brushes a blood-soaked strand of hair from my face. Even now, when he is furious with my actions, he still cares for me enough to make sure I am safe. His brows are furrowed, his jaw clenched, and his eyes are dark with worry.

Even after all of this—especially after all of this—he's everything.

"Thank you for coming after me," I whisper.

He meets my gaze, and something inside me shatters. Maybe it's the adrenaline fading, but I grip his collar and pull him down for a kiss. I don't care that I'm bleeding. Don't care that I'm likely smearing it on him. I just need to feel him, to know he's real.

Angelo is cautious, gentle—like he's afraid I'll break in his hands.

This isn't the time or place, and we both know it. I pull away slowly, my eyes still closed. "I'll take you home," he murmurs, brushing his lips against mine once more before moving to the driver's side. The dented door creaks as it shuts behind him.

The windshield's cracked, but we make it onto the highway. A few minutes pass before Angelo breaks the uncomfortably empty silence. "Will you tell me what the hell you were thinking, sneaking off on me like that?" I stare out the window, ashamed and embarrassed. There's no point lying now.

"I wasn't thinking," I admit. "I saw an email from Lev—the day we left Russia. He said he'd rented an apartment in New York, left some stuff there. I thought..." I take a breath. "I thought I could find something useful. Something that would help. But I realized how stupid it was as soon as I got there. They were following me—or maybe waiting. I honestly don't know how they found me."

Angelo doesn't respond. His jaw tenses, his focus locked on the road or maybe on trying not to chew me out.

"I was heading to the apartment," I continue, cautiously. "I didn't realize I'd pass by that neighborhood. I didn't mean to go near it."

"That area belongs to them," he says quietly. "If you'd asked, I would've told you to take another route. But you went behind my back. You stole my gun, Tatiana. Do you even know how to use one?"

The empty silence fills the gap between us again for so long I fear I might burst. I can feel the tension reverberating throughout the car, and most of it is coming from Angelo's tight jaw and even tighter grip on the steering wheel.

Just as I am about to open my mouth to say whatever comes to mind first, just to kill the quiet, Angelo speaks. "You heard the gunfire, right? You know you could have gotten any one of us killed? You—Tatiana! You could've been killed! What were you thinking?!"

He's right.

What was I thinking?

TWENTY-FIVE
STRINGS ATTACHED

Angelo

THE RIDE back to Staten Island is cloaked in silence, thick and suffocating. After scolding Tatiana for what she did, I can't trust myself to speak again without unloading everything I'm feeling—rage, fear, confusion. My hands grip the steering wheel like a lifeline, my knuckles bone-white under the overhead glow of passing streetlights.

Tatiana's forehead is still streaked with dried blood. Just glancing at it sends a sickening twist through my gut. I don't know what I would do if I lost Tatiana.

I stare hard at the dark stretch of highway ahead, trying to piece it together. Trying to understand how the hell we got ambushed. The Rominas—how did they find her? We hadn't been followed, I was sure of that. No one knew where she went. She'd been driving alone, off the grid. So why did they show up in the exact spot she chose?

Coincidence? No. Too perfect.

Were they watching her all along? Waiting for an opening?

That's the only thing that makes any sense. The idea makes my jaw clench so hard it aches. I'd convinced myself we were being careful, that we were two steps ahead. But if this was a sneak attack, it was executed flawlessly. And Tatiana—goddamn it, Tatiana—walked straight into it alone.

As we cross the bridge and roll onto the familiar streets of Staten Island, my phone buzzes on the dashboard. Dice.

I jab the screen and put him on speaker. "Yeah?"

"Where are you?" he asks, all business.

"Pulling into the mansion now. What's going on?"

"We handled the bodies and torched the car," he says. "But Oleg's not an idiot. He'll know something went down soon enough."

"Then make sure no one followed you," I snap. "We can't afford another slip."

"We're good. And Sal called Tony. He's not thrilled, but we calmed him. You might want to call him yourself, explain everything before he spirals."

"I will, after I take care of her wound." I pause at the gate, waiting for it to open. "She might've given us something. Something important. If this pans out, it could be the lead we've been waiting for."

"Hope it's not another dead end. Keep me posted."

He hangs up without waiting for a response. Classic Dice.

I pull into the garage and kill the engine. For a moment, I just sit there. Breathe. Try to swallow the panic still rising in my throat like bile. Then I look over at Tatiana. Her face is pale, blood crusted along her temple, but her eyes are alert.

"You need me to carry you?" I ask, voice softer now.

"I can walk," she replies, already opening the door.

I step out and move around the car, placing a steady hand on the small of her back as we head inside. Her steps are stronger than I expect, but I don't remove my hand. I won't. Not until I'm sure she's okay.

When we get to her room, I guide her to the chair by the window. "Sit. I'll get the first aid kit."

She grunts something under her breath, but I ignore it. She can hate me later. Right now, I'm treating her, whether she likes it or not.

The water runs cold as I wash my hands in the bathroom sink, trying to steady myself. Then I return with the kit, set it down on the table, and start pulling out supplies. Gauze. Antiseptic. Wipes. Bandages.

She's sitting stiffly, arms crossed, glaring at me like a sulky teenager. But I don't flinch. I part her hair gently and examine the cut.

"It's not as bad as it looked," I tell her. "Lots of blood, but not deep. You got lucky. A little further left and you'd have lost an eye."

Tatiana doesn't flinch, but I see her jaw tighten.

"This'll sting," I warn her. "Try not to slap me."

She nods, putting a brave face on, but I see the tension in her shoulders.

I press the gauze against the wound. She hisses, and her eyes flutter shut, face twisting. I hate this—hurting her to help her. But she stays still, lets me work, even as her breath hitches.

She's tougher than anyone gives her credit for. Tougher than me, maybe.

I finish cleaning the wound and wipe the blood from the rest of her face, then seal it with a bandage. My hands linger longer than they should. I'm not ready to stop touching her.

"You might have a concussion," I say, stepping back. "Want me to call a doctor?"

"No," she says quickly. "I'm fine."

"Tatiana—"

"I'm sure."

I run a hand through my hair, finally letting out the breath I've been holding. The adrenaline that carried me here is fading, leaving only exhaustion—and fear.

I turn away before she can see my hands shake.

"Angelo?" Her voice is soft, almost shy. Like she knows she cracked something open in me.

I don't answer.

A moment later, her arms are around my waist, her cheek pressed to my back. I close my eyes, gritting my teeth. Her touch feels like absolution and punishment all at once.

"I'm sorry," she whispers. "I won't do that again. I'll tell you everything next time. We can plan it together."

I turn, facing her. My hands find her hips without thinking.

"You can't act on impulse," I tell her. "Not with the Rominas. Not with Oleg. You could've died tonight."

"I know." Her voice is small. "But let me help you. I'm not fragile, Angelo. I can do this. I just need you to teach me how."

Her words hit harder than I expect. I see it in her eyes—the same fire I first saw when she stared me down.

I almost lost her tonight. That thought alone makes my stomach flip.

"I don't want to lose you," I murmur.

Her lips part, and I see it—hope. Need. Fear.

I pull her close and kiss her, and the world falls away. Her mouth opens beneath mine, hot and hungry. Her fingers thread through my hair as I grip her waist tighter, pressing her to me. I can't get close enough. She moans when I push her gently toward the bed, and I pause, grounding myself.

"You're still hurt," I say against her lips.

"I'm fine," she insists, climbing into my lap and grinding down. "And if I'm not, I'll tell you." She smirks, wicked and beautiful, and I groan when she presses herself harder against me.

"You're evil," I breathe.

"I'm persuasive." Her hand reaches between us, stroking me through my jeans, and my restraint shatters.

"If you want me, you'll have to let me... you'll have to let me shower you off first," I murmur into her ear. She sighs and relaxes into me, letting me help her out of her clothes. We slowly make our way into the bathroom and I turn the shower on.

The room fills with steam and I undress, following Tatiana into the shower. She presses her body to mine and we kiss so passionately I feel her hiss in pleasure. I nibble her lower lip and gently move the hair away from her face.

Next, I turn her away from me so I can shampoo the blood from her hair. I softly caress her scalp and wash every strand. We have the water temperature set to as high as we can stand it, but the way Tatiana melts into me is so much hotter.

To think, just hours ago, I was furious with Tatiana for running off and making me chase her into the city. And now I'm rubbing body wash all over her every curve.

I want to pamper Tatiana and protect her. But I also want to fully understand her, and in order to do that, I have to listen to her. She is definitely a free-spirited, passionate woman.

Tatiana blissfully moans as I run my hands down her spine, down her sweet ass, and give it a squeeze. She turns around, looks me in the eye and says, "Angelo, please take me to bed now."

I don't need to be asked twice. I almost don't even remember to shut the water off before scooping Tatiana up and laying her carefully on the bed. As she lowers herself onto me, slow and deliberate, I bury my face in her neck, trying not to lose it completely. She moves with confidence, with intention. Every movement tells me she wants this, needs this—needs me.

And I give it all to her. Because tonight isn't just about lust or adrenaline or fear.

Tonight is about everything we almost lost.

Tatiana

FEELING ANGELO inside me is everything I need after the night I've had—after the fear, the blood, the chaos.

It's not just sex. It's an anchor, a reassurance, a reclamation of power over my own body. The moment he touches me, all the trauma begins to unravel, thread by painful thread. He doesn't just make me feel alive—he makes me feel wanted, needed, like I'm something precious he refuses to lose.

The way he looks at me right now... like I'm the only thing that exists in his world. It makes me ache in places far deeper than the physical. I rock against him, my rhythm desperate, as if the faster I move, the further I can run from the horror of earlier tonight.

"You're driving me insane," Angelo groans, his fingers digging into my thighs, holding me firmly in place. He's trying not to lose control, and I can see it in the tension of his jaw, the restraint in his eyes.

I smirk, breathless. "Glad to know it's mutual."

My pace quickens, fueled by the growing fire low in my belly. Every stroke, every press of his body inside mine, invigorates me. I'm chasing release like it's my only salvation. My head falls back, eyes fluttering shut as the coil inside me tightens, heat flooding my veins.

His hands roam my sides, up my waist, grounding me in this moment. He leans forward, his mouth wrapping around my nipple, and the shock of it sends a tremor straight through me.

"Fuck," I whimper, my body trembling.

He sucks gently, flicking his tongue just enough to make me cry out. And when his thumb finds my clit and starts tracing tight circles, I know I won't last another second.

My release crashes over me with devastating force. I gasp, my muscles tightening, my entire body going rigid as pleasure rips through me like a tidal wave. A cry escapes my lips—raw, unfiltered, real. My vision blurs. My body quakes.

When it finally subsides, I'm left panting, completely undone. My limbs feel weightless, my mind floating in the aftermath.

Beneath me, Angelo is still breathing hard, sweat glistening across his chest. His hands stay on my hips as if to make sure I don't disappear. There's a look in his eyes—something tender, something I don't quite know how to name.

I blink, trying to recover. "Wait... did you—?"

He nods with a lazy smile. "Oh, I definitely did."

A breathy laugh slips from me. I slide off him and collapse onto the bed beside him, completely spent. My heart is still hammering in my chest.

He pulls me close, wrapping his arm around me protectively. I melt into him without resistance.

"You okay?" he asks, his lips brushing my cheek.

"I'm fine," I whisper. "I'll tell you if I'm not. But right now, I'm just... grateful. For this. For you." My voice cracks a little on that last word, and I hate how vulnerable it makes me sound. But it's the truth. This man has turned my world inside out.

For days, I've been trying to untangle my feelings. Do I love him?

Or is it the trauma, the high-stakes survival bonding? Is it possible to feel this intensely for someone I've known for such a short time?

Focusing on running from Oleg's men who are hunting me down seems easier than sorting out my emotions right now.

"What's going on in that head of yours?" he asks, tucking a strand of hair behind my ear. His touch is so gentle, it makes my chest ache. Angelo's eyes roam over my face with curiosity. He brushes a strand of hair behind my ear and stares at the bandage he applied over my wound.

"I don't know," I murmur, avoiding his gaze. "I think I'm trying to understand too many things at once." He nods as if he understands. Maybe he does.

I shift onto my back, staring up at the ceiling. "I know I messed up. Going out alone was reckless. I probably made things harder for everyone. They probably all hate me now."

"No one hates you," Angelo says softly. "They're just worried. So am I."

"Well," I exhale, trying to change the subject, "do you think we can go to the apartment? The one Lev rented?"

His brows lift, amused. "You're finally including me in your plans?"

I roll my eyes. "I always included you. I just wanted to be included, too."

"Touché," he mutters. "Yeah, I think we can figure something out."

Hope flickers in my chest. "Really?"

"Really," he confirms, a small smile tugging at the corners of his mouth. "We'll need a solid plan. No more surprises. No more solo missions."

"Agreed," I say quickly. "Do you think the guys will help? What about your boss—Tony? Is he pissed?"

Angelo's expression darkens slightly. "He's not thrilled. But I'll call him, explain what happened. He's a reasonable guy when he's got all the facts."

He leans in and kisses my forehead before standing and grabbing his phone. "You should get some sleep. We'll need rest if we're checking out the apartment in the morning."

I nod, though the idea of sleeping without him leaves a sudden, unexpected emptiness in my chest.

"Angelo?" I call as he reaches the door.

He pauses, glancing over his shoulder. "Yeah?"

"Do you really think we'll find something? I mean... what if there's nothing useful there?"

He considers that. "If Lev went through the trouble of renting a place and sending things there, it matters. We'll find something. I believe that."

That's enough to soothe me—for now. "Okay."

He gives me a final look, something unreadable in his eyes, and then slips out the door.

The silence left in his wake is louder than it should be.

I lie back and stare at the ceiling, everything from the night replaying in my head like a bad movie. The ambush. The car crash. The blood. The fear. The near-death moment that brought everything crashing down.

It's clearer now than ever that I can't afford to act impulsively again. I won't survive another mistake like that. And worse, I might not get lucky enough to have Angelo there to save me next time.

This is one of the things I should learn from the Saints. They probably have seen more evil and injustice than I have. They know what real life is like. They learned to control their feelings so they wouldn't get in the way when they had to get things done. Now I understand what Angelo was saying when he told me we needed a plan, that we needed to act carefully against someone like Oleg. I just wasn't ready to face that harsh reality.

This isn't some twisted fairytale where I'm rescued by the hero and everything magically gets fixed. This is real life. Harsh, violent, unforgiving. And I'm done being the victim.

The next time Oleg tries something, I'll be ready. I'll make him regret every second he spent hurting my family. I'll make him and his son pay for every ounce of blood they've spilled.

I'll use whatever Lev left behind. I'll build a case, a plan, a war. Whatever it takes.

I think back to that day on the street—when I was taken. Back then, I thought I'd fallen into the worst hell imaginable. But maybe... maybe it was fate, because that's the day Angelo came into my life. And somehow, this ruthless, dangerous man became the safest place I've ever known.

I don't know how or when it happened, but I can't imagine facing any of this without him. I don't want to.

I close my eyes and try to breathe. There's a lot ahead. A lot to fight through. But for the first time in a long time, I don't feel like I'm alone in the fight.

Angelo's with me. And that means everything.

Next time, I'll be ready. Next time, I'll make sure Oleg and his fucking allies pay for everything they took from me, from us.

They will get what they deserve.

I'm just grateful I have Angelo and his friends to help me. What would it be like for me if they had never kidnapped me? I'd be alone in this world, having to live with the man who killed my family and his monster of a son, having to see all kinds of atrocities and suffering only God knows what.

Turns out Angelo became my guardian angel the moment he took me from the street that day. And it's one of the many reasons why I can't see myself living without him any longer.

TWENTY-SEVEN
THE APARTMENT

Tatiana

I WAKE before the sun rises, my body still tense from a night of restless sleep. I'd tossed and turned for hours, unable to shake the vivid flashes of the ambush from my mind. Twice, I jolted awake, breathless, and each time Angelo pulled me into his arms, holding me tightly until I drifted off again.

It's frustrating—infuriating, really—to realize how fragile I still am when it comes to facing my trauma. Last night, all I wanted was to toughen up, to stop being so affected by memories I can't change. But how can I do that when the slightest trigger robs me of sleep and floods me with nightmares?

Angelo tells me I'm being too hard on myself, but I can't pretend it doesn't eat at me. I was not raised to be weak.

When I finally drag myself out of bed and into the shower, he's still asleep, probably exhausted from being woken up repeatedly. I let the warm water run over me, careful not to soak my bandage. For a few quiet minutes, I let myself relax—though it feels selfish to do so.

By the time I leave the bathroom wrapped in a towel, Angelo is awake, still lying in bed and scrolling through his phone.

"Morning," he says, voice rough, lips curled into a lazy smile. "I won't ask if you slept well. But can I change your bandage?"

I nod, grateful—though I hate to admit how much I need this moment of care.

He climbs out of bed, retrieves the first aid kit from the night before, and starts tending to my wound. I stay quiet, only flinching at the sting of the antiseptic. He tells me to stay still, and I roll my eyes —though I do as he says.

"So," I finally say, needing a distraction, "how'd the conversation with your boss go? Did he decide I'm a liability and he wants me out on the street?"

Angelo chuckles as he closes the kit. "He doesn't hate you, and no, you're not getting kicked out. Actually," he sits back down beside me, "he's pretty eager to see what we'll find in the apartment. So we'll eat, then head to the city."

Excitement flutters in my chest. "Great. I'll get dressed—we can leave right away. I'm not even hungry."

He shakes his head before I can get up. "Not so fast. You're eating something first. I don't want you passing out on me. We've got all day. Plus, we're waiting on Dice—he's bringing us a new car, something less flashy and harder to trace."

I blink, realizing I hadn't considered that. Just more proof I'm not as ready as I want to be.

"Oh. That makes sense. Are the guys coming with us?"

"No. Just us. But there'll be teams stationed around the city in case things go sideways. I don't think it will," he adds, getting up to take a shower. "Oleg doesn't know about the apartment. And I checked the address—Lev used a different name. It should be safe."

That's just like Lev. Always thinking ahead. No wonder he was my father's favorite. I'm just grateful I got to learn from someone like him.

"That's Lev..." I murmur to myself.

As Angelo showers, I get dressed—jeans and a T-shirt to stay low-profile. We're heading into New York, after all. I blow-dry my hair, grab a coat, and head downstairs, to try to force down some breakfast even though nerves have tied my stomach in knots.

The house is quiet, empty. I wonder if the others have already started their day. Angelo joins me a few minutes later, and we eat in silence, both of us tense with anticipation.

The drive into the city feels longer than usual. I do my best to keep calm—watching the scenery, flipping radio stations, making small talk with Angelo. He doesn't seem to mind, even if I'm probably annoying him. He must know it's helping me hold it together.

When we finally reach Manhattan, Angelo takes a different route—avoiding Oleg's territory. Eventually, he parks in front of a modest red-brick building in a quiet neighborhood. We both study it from the car.

"Is this it?" I ask.

"Yep. It matches the address in your email. Come on."

He checks our surroundings once more before getting out. I follow, and we approach the front door together. "Want to do the honors?" he asks, gesturing to the keypad.

I enter the code Lev gave me. The lock clicks, and Angelo pushes the door open, letting me step inside first. The hallway smells musty and old, the air dim and still despite the sunlight outside.

"Apartment 301," he reminds me.

"I know," I whisper. I've been repeating the address and code nonstop in my head, terrified I'd forget them and lose this lead entirely.

At the top of the stairs, I pause. The door looms in front of me like a relic. I realize—too late—that I hadn't prepared myself for the emotional weight of this.

This might be my last real connection to Lev and Ilya. I don't know if I'm ready to face that.

"Let me go first," Angelo says, stepping ahead and pulling his gun from its holster. He enters the code and eases the door open. "Wait here while I check the place."

I nod, my fists clenched at my sides.

About a minute passes before he returns. "All clear," he says, swinging the door open wider.

I step inside, my hands trembling.

The apartment is small and unassuming—cozy, even. There's a couch, a TV, and a small table. A basic kitchen, bedroom, and a bathroom off to the side.

Then I see it: a blue suitcase under the window.

Tears sting my eyes. That suitcase was Lev's. He didn't have it when we left. Maybe he sent it ahead. Maybe someone brought it here for him.

"Do you recognize it?" Angelo asks.

"Yes. It's Lev's. He didn't bring it with him...."

"You said he had some allies here, right?" Angelo finishes my thought. "Maybe one of them brought it here," he suggests, and I nod, stepping forward in the direction of the case.

"Could be," I mutter under my breath, more curious about the contents of the case than how it got here.

I pull it toward the couch and sit down, laying it on the floor. It's not heavy, but it's definitely not empty either.

Angelo sits beside me as I open the familiar suitcase. Lots of papers, folders, and notebooks stare back at me, even some pictures and a couple of burner phones.

Blueprints. My breath catches.

"Oleg's mansion," I whisper. "The one we were taken to. The one my parents—" I cut myself off, shaking away the flood of memories. "Can we use this?"

Angelo meets my gaze, a fire in his eyes. "Yes. This changes everything."

Relief, grief, and hope all crash over me.

Each item from the suitcase feels like a clue, a breadcrumb leading us somewhere. But where? The plans, the blueprints—

they're a tangible connection to the past, but I can't help but wonder how many steps ahead Lev was in all of this. How much did he already know about what was coming?

I flip through the blueprints again, my fingers tracing the detailed lines of the mansion's layout. Each room, each hallway is meticulously outlined, as if Lev anticipated the day we'd need it. I can almost see the layout in my mind—every corner, every staircase. It's like a map to Oleg's stronghold.

"This..." I whisper, feeling the weight of its significance. "This is everything we need. If we can get inside, we'll know exactly where to go, what to avoid. We'll be prepared."

Angelo nods, his expression hardening. "With this, we have the advantage. We just have to play it right."

I pull out one of the phones, turning it over in my hands. The screen is cracked, but it flickers to life when I press a button. No signal at first, but I keep trying. I can't stop myself from feeling a tinge of hope. Maybe there's something on here—something Lev left for us. As the device finally connects, a flood of messages pour in, too many to read in one go. I scroll quickly through them, eyes scanning for anything relevant.

"Anything?" Angelo asks, his voice low, filled with a quiet urgency.

I glance at him, a mix of frustration and excitement creeping through me. "I don't know yet. But this is big. There's something here —something that could tie all of this together. Oleg's mansion, the blueprint.... It's all leading somewhere."

My mind races. This could be the break we've been waiting for, the edge we need to finally put an end to all of this. But there's still so much we don't know, so much that could go wrong. I look at Angelo, trying to steady my breathing.

"We're not done yet," I say, more to myself than to him.

TWENTY-EIGHT
EVIDENCE AND ALLIES

I STARE AT THE SCREEN, my brow furrowing as I try to make sense of the name. Guskov. It feels familiar, but I can't quite place it. I'm sure I've heard it before, maybe from Lev. But there's something unsettling about the whole situation.

"Do you know him?" Angelo's voice cuts through the quiet, his tone curious but not without a hint of concern.

I shake my head slightly, feeling the weight of the unknown pressing down on me. "His name rings a bell. I think Lev mentioned him once or twice, but I don't really know him. Not personally, at least."

I begin scrolling through the messages, each one more concerned than the last. The words seem to echo with a sense of urgency, a beckoning for contact.

'Lev, did you arrive?'

'Man, where are you?'

'Fuck... Oleg knows about Tatiana.'

'Tatiana?'

'Are you okay? Please call me when you get this message.'

'Where are you?'

Angelo leans forward, his eyes scanning the screen over my shoulder. "Looks like he's been trying to get in touch with you for a while. Do you think he knows about Lev's death? Could be he's worried. Maybe he's trying to figure out where you stand in all of this." He pauses. "Do you think he's one of Oleg's men? A double agent?"

I don't answer right away. My mind races through the possibilities. I wasn't in the mansion long enough to remember names or faces, but I certainly never heard the name Guskov before. None of Oleg's men seemed to recognize me, but that could be a tactic in itself. Still, my gut tells me something's not quite right here.

"I'm not sure," I say after a moment, my voice tinged with uncertainty. "Lev told me that there were some men loyal to my father, people who didn't want Oleg running the gang. He had allies, you know? So maybe Guskov is one of them. But I really don't know."

Angelo is still studying me, his gaze intense. "Well, he's clearly trying to reach you, and he seems worried. You could call him, find out what's really going on."

I hesitate, my fingers hovering over the phone. The idea of calling him feels like a risk I'm not sure I'm ready to take. What if this is a test? What if Oleg has somehow gotten his hands on Lev's burner phone and is trying to lure me into a trap?

"What if it's a trick?" I ask, my voice tight with doubt. "What if Oleg is using Guskov to get to me?"

Angelo's hand gently rests on mine, steadying me. He gives me a reassuring smile, the kind that says, I'm with you. "This is a burner phone. No way for them to track it. And we've got ways to verify if Guskov is who he says he is before you make any moves."

I take a deep breath, feeling the tension in my chest. I don't have the luxury of second-guessing every move. With everything that's happened, I can't afford to stay on the sidelines anymore. If

Guskov is really on our side, then he could be an ally. But if he's not...

I press the call button, my heart hammering in my chest. My hands are shaking, and Angelo notices. He takes my hand in his, squeezing it gently as if to anchor me.

"Tatiana?" A voice answers on the other end, deep and gravelly, but unmistakably genuine.

My stomach tightens at the sound of his voice. I glance at Angelo, who gives me a subtle nod. It's time to face this.

"Who is this?" I ask, trying to sound calm, though I'm sure the uncertainty is evident in my tone. I don't want to give anything away.

"It's Guskov," the man replies, his voice tinged with an emotion I can't quite place. "I'm a friend of your father's. Was," he corrects himself, his voice dropping at the last word. "I've been trying to reach you. Are you all right?"

His words send a shiver down my spine. There's something in his voice—concern, empathy—but can I trust him? I don't know this man, not really.

"I..." I hesitate, not sure how to respond. My mind flashes back to Lev, to the conversations we'd had about loyalty, betrayal, and the people who had once been close to my father. "I don't know if I should trust you. Everything's... everything's a mess right now."

"I understand," Guskov says quickly, his voice softening. "But I swear to you, Tatiana, I'm not with Oleg. I haven't been for a long time. When I heard about Lev... about what Oleg did to him and Ilya, I knew I had to find you. I had no way of knowing if you were alive, but I couldn't just sit back and do nothing."

I don't respond right away. His words make sense—too much sense—but there's a part of me that's reluctant to fully believe him. Lev had trusted him, but then again, everyone had trusted Lev. And look where that has gotten us.

"What did Lev tell you?" I ask, my voice barely above a whisper. "Why is your name on his phone?"

"I've been on your side all along, Tatiana," Guskov answers

without hesitation. "I've never betrayed your father. Oleg and I, we've been at odds for years. I stayed close to him to gather information, to try and bring him down. Lev and I, we had a plan... but we didn't get the time we needed."

I swallow hard, a lump forming in my throat as I listen. A plan. Had they really been working to take down Oleg this whole time? Had I just stumbled into something much bigger than I'd imagined?

"What was the plan?" I ask, almost afraid to hear the answer, but unable to stop myself.

There's a long pause before Guskov speaks again, his voice filled with a quiet resolve. "We were going to hit him hard. A two-pronged attack. A team would go after Oleg's most profitable businesses, and the other would take the mansion. We were going to kill him. Lev knew that if he didn't make it, he'd need someone to take over. That's why he wanted me to reach out to you."

I sit back, stunned. The weight of his words settles over me like a heavy blanket. The plan had always been to kill Oleg, but hearing it out loud makes it all feel so much more... real. Tangible.

I glance at Angelo, my thoughts racing. "Can I tell him I'm with you? With the Saints?" I ask, my voice lower now, as if I'm afraid someone might overhear.

Angelo thinks for a moment, his eyes flicking to mine before he nods.

"Guskov," I say, my voice growing firmer. "I think we need to meet in person. But before that, there's one thing you should know."

"What's that?" Guskov asks, his tone steady, waiting for me to speak.

"I'm with the Saints now," I say it plainly, no hesitation. "They're helping me get justice for what happened to my parents. If we're going to work together, you need to understand that I won't turn my back on them. I won't leave them behind. That's the only condition."

There's a long silence on the other end, and for a moment, I wonder if I've made a mistake. But then Guskov speaks again, his voice low but resolute.

"I understand," he says finally. "I'll talk to my men. I'll get back to you."

Before he can say anything else, I end the call. I don't want to drag this out any longer. My heart is pounding in my chest, my mind a blur of emotions—relief, fear, anticipation.

Angelo is still sitting beside me, his hand firmly holding mine. He glances over at me, his lips curving into a small grin. "You know, that was pretty hot," he teases, his voice playful despite the tension that still lingers in the air.

I let out a shaky laugh, trying to keep my composure. "And scary as hell," I reply, feeling the weight of everything finally crashing down on me.

Angelo's thumb traces soothing circles over my palm, his touch sending a shiver up my spine. I close my eyes for a moment, letting the sensation ground me, even as everything around us feels like it's spinning out of control.

In that moment, all I can think about is him. Just him.

I shift, feeling the familiar heat between us flare up again. Before I even realize what's happening, I'm straddling him on the couch, his hands instinctively going to my hips, but he doesn't move, he just waits.

"Thank you," I whisper, my breath hitching as I lean closer, our faces barely an inch apart. "Thank you for being here. I don't know what I'd do without you."

TWENTY-NINE
CALM BEFORE THE STORM

Tatiana

"YOU'RE KILLING ME, ANGELO," I whisper, my voice breathless as I squirm beneath him, trying to find the perfect angle, the perfect moment. The heat radiating from his body pressed against mine, but it's not enough. I want more. I need more.

Angelo's lips curl into a grin, a wicked expression that makes my pulse quicken. He's fully aware of the effect he has on me—always has been. His hands slip under me to grab my legs, shifting me until I'm lying back against the couch, my head sinking into the cushion.

"This couch seems a bit small for both of us, don't you think?" I ask, the playful tone in my voice belying the tension simmering underneath. I struggle with his shirt, trying to peel it off, but my hands are trembling too much.

He glances around, his gaze flicking over to the bedroom door behind us. "Come here," he commands, his voice low, dark.

Before I can even process it, he's standing, lifting me in his arms with an effortless strength that leaves me breathless. I wrap my legs around his waist, my arms instinctively curling around his neck, clinging to him as he carries me across the room. The moonlight spilling in from the window casts a soft glow over everything, making the atmosphere feel both intimate and electric.

In seconds, I'm on the bed, the soft mattress beneath me a contrast to the sharp need building inside. Angelo's gaze roams over my body, and I catch the hunger in his eyes—the hunger that always ignites something deep inside me. I finally manage to strip him of his shirt, tossing it aside, my fingers grazing over his chest as I admire him. He's all muscle, smooth skin, and sharp angles. My heart beats faster as I study him, the anticipation so thick it almost chokes me.

"When and where did you get these?" Angelo's voice is hoarse, his eyes narrowing as they take in the lingerie I've worn specifically for this moment. He looks both surprised and... delighted.

I smirk, already knowing what he's thinking. "I ordered it online. And no need to worry about me being discovered. I used the credit card you gave me for emergencies." I pause, letting the tension build. "It wasn't really an emergency, but I needed some new clothes, so...."

He lets out a low chuckle, his gaze darkening. "You never cease to surprise me." With that, he leans in, kissing the nape of my neck, his lips moving slowly along my skin. His breath is warm, making me shiver as I lean into him, desperate for more of his touch.

His hands trail down my body, and I gasp when I feel him press against me, his hardness undeniable even through the fabric of his boxers. My breath hitches as I reach down, my fingers grazing over him, feeling the throb beneath my touch. His eyes flare with raw desire as I begin to stroke him, slowly, teasingly, feeling him grow harder with each motion.

"Fuck, baby. This is so fucking good," he groans, his breath ragged. I smirk, my pulse thumping wildly at the sight of him so vulnerable, so completely undone.

I love watching him like this—when he's so close to losing control. "You have to stop now, or I'll..." He cuts off, his voice trembling. His body trembles, and I know I'm pushing him to the edge, but I'm just as desperate. I want more, and I want it now.

I speed up, feeling him throb beneath my touch. "Come on, Angelo," I tease, my voice a breathless whisper. "Let go."

A strangled sound escapes him, and with one final, powerful release, he comes undone. His release coats my hand, and I can't help but smirk at how hard it is for him to contain himself. I lean forward, placing a soft kiss on his lips as he breathes heavily, trying to regain some semblance of control.

"Good boy," I tease, grinning as I watch him. His chest rises and falls with each deep breath, his skin slick with sweat.

But there's no time to rest. Before I can fully enjoy the sight of him recovering, he's already making his move. Without saying a word, Angelo slides off the bed, and my heart pounds in anticipation as he grabs my thighs, pulling me toward him. I gasp as he places my knees over his shoulders, spreading me open in the most deliciously vulnerable position.

"Angelo..." I breathe, my body already humming with the need for him. My mind can't focus on anything else but the feeling of his hands on my skin, his lips leaving soft, burning kisses all over my legs, up my inner thighs. The trail of his mouth feels like fire, and when he reaches my most sensitive area, my body jerks with a gasp, unable to control the need building inside me.

His tongue flicks against me, teasing, then delving deeper. My body arches in response, my fingers gripping the sheets as I try to hold on, desperate for more of him. "Angelo, please," I beg, my voice trembling. He doesn't answer with words. Instead, his tongue pushes deeper, and I feel my body begin to unravel under him, pleasure coursing through me like electricity.

I try to hold back, but the pressure builds, and before I know it, I'm clenching around him, my body trembling as waves of pleasure wash over me. My vision blurs as I gasp for air, trying to steady myself, but I can't stop. I don't want to.

He finally pulls back, leaving me breathless and needy, his eyes smoldering as he watches me. "So fucking beautiful," he murmurs, and his voice is almost a growl.

But just as I think he'll give me a moment to breathe, Angelo is already removing his boxers, his movements quick and sure. He climbs back onto the bed, positioning himself over me, his eyes locked on mine as he pushes himself inside me.

The way he enters me is slow, measured, but I can feel every inch of him, every movement sending shockwaves of pleasure through my body. My nails dig into his back as he thrusts deeper, harder, each movement making the heat inside me burn brighter. I can't think anymore. All I can feel is him.

With each thrust, he gets deeper, his body slamming against mine, and I clutch the sheets, desperate for release. My breath catches as I feel the familiar tension building once again, the edge so close I can almost taste it. I let go, letting the pleasure consume me, my body quaking as I moan his name.

"Angelo..." I whisper, my voice breaking.

He doesn't stop. With one final, powerful thrust, I come undone. My body locks up, and for a moment, nothing exists but the wave of pleasure crashing over me, leaving me breathless and gasping. Angelo's body stills, and I feel him throbbing inside me as he comes as well.

We lie there for a moment, both of us trying to steady our breathing. His chest rises and falls with each deep breath, and I can't help but marvel at how beautiful he looks, how real this all feels. But even in the aftermath, the weight of our mission hangs over us. I can't forget what we need to do. Not yet.

"What are we going to do now?" I ask, my voice shaky as I sit up, needing to break the silence.

Angelo turns to look at me, his expression shifting from passion to something much more serious. He reaches for my hand, squeezing it tightly. "We'll get those documents back to the mansion and study them. Maybe we can follow Guskov's plan with your dad. It's a good strategy. We'll gather what we can before going after Oleg directly."

His words are a reminder that we're not done. Not by a long shot. The revenge we've both been waiting for is within reach, but I know it won't be as simple as just taking down Oleg. There will be consequences, emotions I'm not ready to face.

I nod, my fingers tightening around his. "Let's finish this. Together."

THIRTY
PROMISES

Angelo

THE FILES and blueprints that Lev had left for Tatiana turned out to be far more invaluable than any of us could have anticipated. Thanks to his meticulous planning, we managed to track several of Oleg's and the Romina family's businesses, as well as uncover key bank accounts that Guskov had mentioned during our last conversation. If it weren't for Lev's foresight, we would have been blind, groping in the dark, still searching for threads to pull. But now, we have the tools we need to make our move.

Speaking of Guskov, after Tatiana and I had returned to the safe house, I made the call. Tony needed to come in for a meeting. I wasn't going to make any major decisions without his input, and I knew he'd appreciate having a hand in plotting the next steps. He showed up about an hour later, and the three of us gathered around the table, all of us tense, but ready.

Even Tatiana joined the meeting, which—while expected—wasn't something I had been eager for. I knew she was going to want to come with us. She didn't have to ask me, not really; she had already made up her mind. But when she asked Tony for permission instead of mine, something in me snapped. I'd been prepared to give her space to make her own choices, but the fact that she went to Tony first made me feel like a part of the decision-making process had been stolen from me.

I hate the idea of her being in danger. More than anything, I hate how much she wanted to be part of it. But she is a grown woman, and I can't make her follow orders like a child. If she wants to risk her life with us, there is nothing I can do except to be furious and protective —feelings that don't always align.

For the next two days, we spent every waking hour planning and preparing. Sal and a few others had managed to hack into some of the Romina accounts, which was great, but our plan was to act quickly— catch Oleg off guard and dismantle everything before he had time to react. We couldn't afford to give him a head start, and with all the moving pieces, we hadn't had the time to drain his accounts yet. If we did it now, he'd notice. It would be a clear signal that we were closing in.

We got lucky in a way—Guskov and his men, despite their past with the Rominas, agreed to join forces with us. While some of his men were rough around the edges, their insider knowledge of Oleg and the Romina empire gave us leverage we desperately needed. We weren't operating in the dark anymore. Now, we had the right people in place. With their help, we stand a chance at ending this for good.

Hours pass, and the evening is fast approaching. I'm dressed in my combat gear, my body fully equipped for the mission ahead— every knife, every gun in place, tucked away so that they're both concealed and easily accessible.

"Are the cars loaded?" I ask Dice, my voice firm, as we go over one last check on everything we need to bring.

Kian, Max, and Sal are already in one vehicle, with Tony.

Guskov is in another vehicle, with a couple of his men rounding out the third. It was going to be a big operation, but we can't afford any mistakes. Oleg has eyes everywhere.

"All set over here," Dice calls back from the other side of the SUV we'd just finished packing.

"Good. I'll let Tatiana know," I said, turning toward the house. But before I can take more than a couple of steps, Dice's voice stops me.

"Hey, man," he said.

I turn back, a knot tightening in my gut. The look on his face is serious, more than I'd ever seen it before.

"Listen, I know we talked about this already," he began. "And I know it's not our choice but hers... I just want you to know that, no matter what, I'll be there to protect her. She's one of us now, and we're all in this together. So, do us all a favor—keep your head in the game. This isn't just about you and her. It's about all of us."

The sincerity in his words hit me harder than I expected. In a world where loyalty was often a fleeting concept, Dice's commitment to her was as solid as the steel in my chest. I nod at him, my throat tight.

"Thanks, man," I mutter.

No more words were necessary. We both knew the drill. I knew what he meant: Don't lose sight of what we are here to do. Don't let personal emotions cloud judgment, because in this line of work, that was a quick way to get people killed.

If I'm honest with myself, though, I can't shake the nagging feeling that no matter what happens tonight, there is a piece of me that won't come back the same. I'm not afraid of dying, not really— but I can't bear the thought of losing her. She has come to mean so much more to me than I'd ever expected.

But that is a thought I won't dwell on. Not right now.

I step into the house and find Tatiana in the room we've been sharing. She looks every bit the warrior tonight—her long hair braided tightly, black leather pants hugging her figure, a plain shirt covering her torso, but it is the bulletproof vest she wears underneath that catches my eye. I had insisted she wear it, and though she didn't argue, I could see the weight of it on her.

But she understood. She knew the stakes.

"Everything okay?" I ask, walking over to her and inspecting her gear. Tony had given her a gun and a couple of knives, which she wore with the confidence of someone who had long ago learned the language of violence. A compact pistol rests in a holster at her hip, a tactical knife is strapped to her right thigh, and a smaller folding blade is hidden in her boot.

Her eyes meet mine—steady, focused—but I can tell she is scared. No matter how hard she tries to hide it, I can see the fear flickering beneath the surface. And I share that fear, though I'd never admit it aloud.

"Yes, readier than ever," she replies, her voice calm but tight. "This will finally end tonight, right?"

I nod, my jaw clenched. "This ends tonight."

No hesitation. No second chances. Oleg has taken everything from her, and it is time for him to pay.

I step closer, gently cupping her face in my hands. "Promise me you'll be careful," I say, my voice almost pleading.

She leans into my touch, closing her eyes for a moment, then opening them to look at me again. "I promise. I just need this to end. So we can move on with our lives. So I can finally dream of a real future... with you."

Her words slice through me like a blade. The future—our future —was something I had never allowed myself to imagine until now. But there it is, sitting in front of me, bright and beautiful.

"Stay alive, and I'll give you everything you deserve," I whisper, my heart a heavy weight in my chest at the mere thought of anything happening to her.

Her eyes soften, her lips curving into the faintest of smiles. "You better keep that promise. You're not allowed to die on me tonight either."

She wraps her arms around me, holding me tight, and for a

moment, I feel the world fade away. It's just us, together in this space, and nothing else matters.

I kiss her, tender but intense, pouring everything I feel into that one kiss. It's a promise. A vow. A final goodbye to the man I used to be.

She pulls away, her eyes searching mine one last time. "We have a deal. Now let's go."

The drive to Manhattan feels like an eternity. The car is thick with silence, none of us willing to speak, our nerves churning in the pit of our stomachs. Dice, Tatiana, and Andy sit in the back, their faces etched with resolve, but I can tell they are all just as tense as I am. Everyone is thinking the same thing: Tonight, one way or another, this is going to end.

I can't keep my mind from wandering to Luca. His face, his voice —it's all here, a constant shadow in my thoughts. This isn't just for me. It is for him, too. Oleg took his life, and I am going to make sure the bastard pays for it.

When we finally reach the mansion, I park a safe distance away, surrounded by trees and shadows. The place is enormous, sprawling out in front of us like a fortress. From the outside, it doesn't seem as heavily guarded as I'd feared—at least not at first glance. But I know better. If I had to guess, all of the guards are inside, waiting. And if I'm wrong, if they're spread out across the grounds, we will be walking into a potential ambush.

But tonight isn't about making predictions—it's about executing the plan. Oleg will not walk away from this.

I turn to Dice and Andy, both of them nodding at me, their eyes as cold and determined as mine. They're ready. They know what needs to be done.

I give Tatiana one last look, squeezing her hand before she steps out of the car.

"Be careful. Stay close to me and the guys. We're a team. Stick together," I say, even though I've already said it a hundred times.

"I will," she replies, her voice steady, but there is a trace of something unspoken between us. "And you stay alive. You promised me a good life."

Her words cut through me, but I don't let it show. "I'll keep that promise," I say, though a small part of me doubts whether I will make it through the night.

Outside the car, the air is crisp with the chill of the night. The cold wind whips at my face, but my focus is on the mansion, the target that has haunted my thoughts for so long.

There is no turning back now.

This is it: the end of Oleg Romina's reign of terror. And the beginning of something new for all of us.

THIRTY-ONE
THE DEVIL'S LAIR

Tatiana

ALL I CAN HEAR as I follow Angelo and the others are our muffled footsteps on the forest floor and the relentless pounding of my heartbeat. I'm already out of breath—even though we're not running—because the bulletproof vest Angelo made me wear is dragging me down like a weight.

I've already drawn my pistol and cocked it, holding it steady in front of me, my arms extended and ready for whatever's ahead. Adrenaline floods my system, sharpening my vision, heightening every sound, every shift in the shadows.

I expected guards—men stationed outside like before, guarding the gates and the main house like when I was kept here. But there's no one. Where the hell is everyone? Are they inside, waiting for us?

Angelo was certain they weren't expecting us tonight. So what's going on?

As if answering my thoughts, he signals for us to keep moving.

We trail him to the back of the house. The plan is to enter through the kitchen and then split into teams to deal with anyone in our path.

My team is assigned to Oleg.

When I asked Tony to join the mission, Angelo was furious—but he still managed to secure the right to handle Oleg himself. His boss didn't hesitate to agree.

At the back door, Angelo pulls a small pick from his boot. His fingers work fast but precisely, and I can barely see what he's doing before we hear a faint click. At that exact moment, Tony and Sal's groups emerge from different sides of the property. I hadn't even noticed them arrive.

Angelo eases the door open.

"You know what to do," Tony says with a sharp nod before stepping into the house.

We all file inside, but the moment the door closes behind us, one of Oleg's men rounds the corner. His eyes widen—and then he shouts.

Too late to stop him.

In seconds, the house erupts. The Rominas swarm like ants from a kicked nest—armed, yelling, scrambling. Our first attacks are clumsy, blind with panic, but we're quick to recover.

The absence of guards at the gate hadn't been a coincidence—it was a calculated trap. Oleg must have known someone was coming, despite Angelo's confidence in the element of surprise. Instead of posting men outside, he pulled them in, consolidating his forces where he had the advantage: inside the house. It was a tactical shift, turning the mansion into a kill box, forcing us into tight hallways and blind corners where his men could strike from cover. By leaving the gate unguarded, he invited us in—then sealed us inside with nowhere to run. We hadn't walked in undetected; we'd walked into an ambush.

"Split up!" Tony shouts, dropping two men with effortless shots. Instantly, teams scatter in every direction.

"Stay behind me," Angelo barks without looking back.

He and Dice veer left. I follow close, head down, knees bent. Bullets fly. It's more terrifying than I imagined.

We push into the mansion's grand foyer—no cover, no time. Gunfire rains from above and at ground level. We're exposed. The marble tiles are slick under my boots, but I stay on Angelo's heels.

Once the shock wears off, I snap into action. I didn't come here to freeze. It's been years since I held a gun, but I force myself to focus. A man rushes down the stairs to my right—I aim for his chest.

The recoil jolts my arms. He tumbles down the steps, dead before he hits the ground.

I don't have time to process what I've done. My first kill—but I knew what I signed up for when I asked Tony to let me come. The psychological damage will have to wait.

First, I have to survive.

Angelo glances over his shoulder. His eyes say it all—pride and regret, tangled together. I get it, and I appreciate it.

Tonight is also about proving something to him—that I can handle myself, that I'm not someone he has to shield from this world. I can stand on my own.

Once we've taken out the men in the foyer, we rush upstairs. I avoid looking at the body I step over—my kill. Gunshots echo everywhere, my ears ringing. Sight is my only dependable sense now.

"Wanna take the right and I go left?" Dice asks as we hit the landing. Angelo hesitates.

Why is it so quiet up here?

The rooms on the right are all closed. To the left, the hallway that leads to the library and Oleg's office is empty. Doors are slightly ajar, but there's no movement.

"I think we should stay together," Angelo finally says, his gaze flicking back and forth. "We might be outnumbered until the others catch up."

He's right.

We're only three—well, two and a half, if we count my questionable skill level.

My hands tremble around my gun. We haven't seen Oleg or Yakov, but I can feel them nearby.

"What do you think?" Angelo turns to me. Dice scans the hallway ahead while Angelo studies my face. "Any guess where he could be?"

I want to snap that he's putting too much pressure on me, but I get why he's asking. Out of everyone, I know Oleg best.

Back when I was held here, he was rarely home—but when he was, he stayed in the living room or the office. He's clearly not in the living room now. So... the office?

"Isn't the office too obvious?" I ask, doing my best to hide my nerves. "He must have a hidden room or something—"

The thought hits me.

"Remember that unlabeled space on the blueprint? Near his bedroom? What if that's a secret room?"

"That's a good hunch," Dice says, shifting on his feet, uncomfortable staying so exposed. "We'd cover more ground if we split—"

"I said we stick together," Angelo snaps, cutting him off, his eyes darting downstairs, searching for reinforcements.

No one's coming.

Whatever's happening below, the Saints haven't reached the foyer. I just hope we're not losing.

"Fine. Let's just fucking move," Dice mutters, taking the lead toward the right.

My palms sweat against my pistol grip, but I don't dare wipe them.

We advance slowly. Dice and Angelo clear each room while I watch our backs. Every noise makes my nerves spike.

Gunfire erupts from the last door on the left. I duck instinctively, crawling back to cover as bullets fly past.

Angelo and Dice take position, pressed against the wall. Two men charge out, and a brutal fight erupts.

I don't have time to think. I turn and bolt down the hallway toward Oleg's office, trusting that no one sees me. Angelo's too busy. I don't want to distract him.

I just need to confirm my theory.

I sprint past the library and TV room, almost reaching the office —then I freeze.

A voice behind me, cold and familiar:

"We thought you might try this."

I turn slowly. One of Oleg's men steps out of the TV room, gun aimed at my chest. My body locks up, my brain scrambling for a plan.

What the hell did I expect? I thought I was being brave—proving something—but all I've done is walk straight into danger without backup.

My heartbeat thrums louder than the gunfire in the distance, and regret claws its way up my throat. I should've stayed with Angelo and Dice.

"Really stupid move," he sneers, head tilted, eyes scanning me. "Colluding with the Saints? What a traitor."

His venom rolls right off me. If I knew I'd hit him, I'd shoot him now. To hell with consequences.

"I'm supposed to feel guilty?" I scoff. "After you kidnapped me and tried to force me to marry that bastard? Yeah, no."

I gather every ounce of courage and smirk. This was my call. I came here. I can't wait for Angelo to save me—he's fighting for his life. This mess is mine to clean up.

The guy laughs—and I see an opening.

I aim for his shoulder—but before I can shoot, a second voice cuts through the air. It comes from behind me, from inside Oleg's office.

"And here I thought I was being generous when I offered you to marry my son."

THIRTY-TWO

MAZE

Angelo

ONE SECOND.

That's all it takes to lose sight of Tatiana.

One second she's right behind me—then gunfire erupts, men come charging out of a room, and just like that, she's gone.

A surge of dread hits me the moment I realize she's no longer at my side, but there's no time to panic. If I stop now, I'll end up with a bullet—or several—lodged in my chest.

Dice and I press against the wall, ducking as bullets scream past us. Rominas pour out of the room, weapons raised—but somehow, we're faster.

One. Two. Three. Four.

My shots hit their marks, and four bodies hit the ground before I even register how many there were to begin with.

Dice handles another group of three, but we don't have time to think about our next moves before footsteps on the stairs tell us that more men are coming. I don't need to wait and see if they are ours or not.

"We need to get out of this hallway. We're easy targets here," Dice snarls at me, already heading toward the door. I follow him, even though my entire body protests.

"I need to find Tatiana," I hiss, locking the door behind us and taking in our surroundings.

It's a big room, but I only register the details in flashes. A poker table in the middle—stained, cluttered with cards and chips, chairs knocked over like whoever was playing ran fast. To the left, a bar packed with bottles—glass glinting under dim lights, some already shattered from stray bullets. Two large couches sit low to the ground, one flipped halfway over like it had been used for cover before. There's a side door to the right—narrow, dark, maybe an exit. I don't have time to study more. Just enough to clock potential cover, escape routes, and threats.

There's a door to my right and I rack my brain, trying to remember where it leads. I studied the blueprint for hours, but with fear threatening to eat me alive now, I can't focus.

Where is Tatiana? Did someone take her, or did she step away from me on purpose? She wouldn't do that to me, though, would she? She promised me she'd stay close, no matter the situation.

A voice in the back of my mind whispers what I already know: if the roles were reversed—if I had the chance to take justice into my own hands for what was done to my family—I wouldn't think twice. Promise or not, I'd go. Just like she did.

"Shit, she must've gone after him," I mutter, mostly to myself. Dice is already moving toward the side door, not waiting for confirmation.

A deafening bang erupts behind me, yanking me back into the chaos. We're still being hunted, and I don't have the luxury of spiraling into what-ifs. I need to move. I need to get out of this room —and I need to reach Tatiana before Oleg does.

I'm right on Dice's heels as he crosses through the side door, and we find ourselves in some kind of narrow tunnel, stretching toward another black door at the far end. This place is a fucking maze. Studying the blueprints was one thing—looking at lines and markings on paper, all neat and orderly—but being here, inside this goddamn labyrinth, is a whole different story. Every corner feels like it could lead to another trap, another dead end. My mind races, trying to piece together the layout, but nothing feels familiar. We're blind, and we're not alone.

Not to mention these motherfuckers come out of every corner, and it doesn't help that they know this place like the backs of their hands and we don't.

"They are fucking everywhere," Dice mutters as he leads the way, his gun in hand and pointing ahead, prepared for another ambush.

I grunt in response, not able to give him an answer. I can't stop thinking about where Tatiana might be. I can only hope she's handling herself well enough until I get to her. I know she can do it, but it's not her I don't trust. It's the Rominas. They don't play fair, and the idea of losing her just like I lost Luca is overwhelming.

I'll never forgive myself if I lose her too.

I still can't remember where this tunnel lets out—there are too many overlapping corridors in this fucking mansion—but I don't have time to ask either before Dice opens the door and we end up inside another shadowed room, lined with cabinets and crates.

"This room looks like an old depository, but I don't remember it being labeled on the blueprint," I whisper to Dice. The walls here are even more narrow, the ceiling is lower, and it smells like dust and mold here, making my nose itch.

"Goddamn, what the hell is this room for? It looks like no one's been here for decades," Dice murmurs with impatience.

"Looks like an escape route," I grunt, eyeing the narrow walls and low ceiling. "I can't remember where this leads to."

"Maybe the blueprints were outdated?" Dice mutters, scanning the shadows ahead with his gun raised.

I shrug, the weight of uncertainty pressing down on me. "Maybe..." The truth is, nothing about this place feels predictable.

"Where the fuck do you think she went?" Dice asks, not bothering to look at me as he continues moving forward, his steps slow and cautious. "Do you think she was taken?"

"I—" My words are stuck in my throat as I watch his right hand move up, his fist clenched as he signals me to hold.

A guard rounds the corner directly in front of us, armed to his teeth, but Dice is faster, dropping him with a clean shot to the chest. The man crashes backward, a loud thud echoing through the walls as his body collapses to the floor.

"You were saying?" Dice encourages me to continue, but the sound of the man's body falling to the floor drew the attention of more.

Another Romina capo lunges from a hidden door close to me, bumping against me and catching me off guard. We crash down, my gun falls out of my hand, and he elbows me in the jaw. I grunt, ignoring the pain, and throw a punch to his ribs. I look to the side, searching for my gun, which is just out of reach. Dice is fighting another guy down the hallway, so I'm on my own here.

Reaching for the knife strapped to my right thigh, I grab it, slamming it into the side of the guy's neck. Hot blood spurts across my hand and arm, and I shove him off me, getting to my feet in an instant.

I head for the exit just as Dice shows up in the doorway, sweating, his face smeared with blood. We're both breathing hard and my heart slams against my chest. But there's no time to speak—the capos who'd been tracking us from the main house finally catch up, boots thundering down the corridor like a warning shot we can't outrun.

There are only five of them. We bring two down right away with two shots in the head. Dice grabs the third one by the collar and slams him into a wall, stabbing him a couple of times. I shift my focus to the fourth, driving my knife behind his knee, then slashing his throat. I dive to the floor and grab my gun, rolling over and jumping up just in time to see that there's only one of them left now.

He lifts his gun toward me, but I beat him to it.

However, the hollow click that follows makes my blood turn to ice.

Fuck.

It's empty.

I move to reload, darting to the side, but I'm too slow. The shot echoes through the dimly lit room, and pain erupts in my left arm, throwing me sideways against the wall.

Gritting my teeth, I don't bother putting pressure on the wound, or even checking the extent of it. I need to reload my gun before this motherfucker finishes me off.

"I got you, man," Dice murmurs before showing up beside me and filling the guy with holes.

I take a deep breath, finally clamping my hand over my wound, feeling blood soak through my fingers. "Fuck," I hiss, standing straight and examining the hallway we're in.

Dice steps forward to check on my arm, and I move my hand just slightly so he can examine it. "It doesn't look too bad," he tells me, shaking his head.

"It certainly hurts like it," I wince, forcing the pain to the back of my head to finish reloading my gun.

"You good to go?" he asks, looking me in the eyes.

I nod sharply, cocking the gun. "Yeah. We need to get to Tatiana. Do you think it's safe for us to return from that tunnel? It'll be faster that way. She might have gone to Oleg's office."

"Yeah, you're probably right. I think it's worth a try," Dice encourages me, moving back to the dark room.

My vision blurs as I take a step forward and lean against the wall once more to steady myself.

"Shit, man!" he hisses, returning to my side and holding me by my elbow. "Are you sure you're okay?"

"How the fuck can getting shot hurt this much? I don't remember it hurting like this," I mutter through clenched teeth.

"That's because you fainted last time," he jokes, chuckling but helping me get to my feet. "Now, take deep breaths and push it aside. Adrenaline will kick in, and you'll forget about the pain for a while."

Easier said than done, I want to retort. But I don't, focusing on doing what he suggested instead and following him back to the tunnel.

Tatiana needs me.

My arm can hurt all it wants later, but for now, I need to make sure she is safe.

That she is alive.

Tatiana

FEAR AND ANGER consume me as I turn to look at the face of the man who murdered my parents. Twice.

Oleg's icy blue eyes pierce through my soul and keep me rooted to the floor. He's not making a single move, the grin on his face widening into an evil smile as he sizes me up and down.

"You'd make a hell of a wife to my son if you weren't so stupid," he carries on, still not moving. My mind is working a million miles per hour to figure out what to do. Running is not an option. But attacking Oleg while one of his goons is watching me like a guard dog would be a reckless move, and I don't have the luxury of making another one.

My gun is aimed at him anyway, just in case he decides to pull something cute. I wouldn't be able to fight the two of them, but I'd bring at least one down with me. It's not an option to leave Oleg off the hook, so I change my target and aim my pistol at his chest.

"I'd rather be buried alive than marry him," I snarl through gritted teeth. I hold his gaze, hoping the intensity in my eyes is enough to distract him from my shaky hands. I'm not shaking because I'm scared. I'm shaking because I'm enraged. Staring at this man makes all the emotions I have been trying to control boil to the surface. He took everything from me. From Angelo. And God knows how many more. And yet, here he is, standing in front of me as if the entire world bends to his will. He carries himself as if nothing and no one can touch him here.

Oleg thinks he's invincible, and I'm willing to risk my life to prove him wrong.

"This is over, Oleg," I challenge him, my defensive posture never wavering.

"Is that right?" He chuckles, tilting his head. "Does it look like this is over to you, Rocco?"

"Certainly not. Not for us anyway." The bastard laughs behind me, but I don't dare look. I keep my eyes on Oleg the entire time, barely even breathing, prepared for whatever he throws my way.

My heart is beating frantically against my rib cage, and my mouth is dry as if I have swallowed a mouthful of sand, but I force myself to be strong, to keep going. This is the moment I've been waiting for, and even though these are different, unfair, and unexpected circumstances, I still have a chance to kill him.

"The Saints will end you. You and your fucking empire. It will all turn to dust before your eyes." I have no idea where this courage is coming from, but I'm sure the anger I'm feeling is helping fuel it. "You'll see your precious legacy crumble to the ground." Oleg's expression doesn't change, but I see his left eye twitch, and that is enough for me to know I hit a nerve.

"You've got fire, I'll give you that much," he says. It should sound like a compliment, and he probably thinks it is, but I don't give a damn about what he thinks of me. He seems too amused for my taste, but I'm still at a disadvantage here. I need to consider my next move very carefully, or I'll get a bullet in my head before I have the chance to take a breath.

"Why don't we talk somewhere more... private?" he suggests, nodding at Rocco over my shoulder.

"Don't you fucking touch me!" I yell when I feel Rocco's fingers digging into my arms like iron clamps, forcing them down. I don't drop my gun, but there's no way I can shoot anyone now without risking hurting myself in the process. Rocco's pistol isn't visible, so I can only assume he put it away at some point after Oleg showed up. He probably thinks he has it all handled now that the boss has arrived.

Well, I won't make it this easy for him.

I struggle to fight Rocco, but he is strong. Oleg watches everything with amusement, just moving to the side when Rocco drags me inside the office. I kick and scream, trying to escape from his grasp, but he's holding my wrists tightly. I slam my heel into his shin, but he only grunts, not loosening his grip on me.

"Stop moving, bitch," he hisses against my ear, causing shivers to run up my skin.

"Let me fucking... go." I slam my head backward, hard and fast. The cracking sound of my skull hitting his nose is sickeningly satisfying. Rocco curses and stumbles back, and I take the opportunity to finally release myself. I spin to see his bloodied face, his eyes widening as I lift my arm and pull the trigger, not hesitating at the slightest. It was him or me.

His body falls, lifeless, hitting the wall behind him. I'm not sure if he is dead or just unconscious, but it doesn't really matter now.

Oleg's applause pulls my attention back to him. He's leaning against his desk, watching as if it's simply a fucking movie scene. There's not even a glimpse of emotion in his eyes as he glances at the body of his man on the floor.

This guy is really the devil. He smirks at me, moving away from the desk and starting to circle me like a predator.

"That was a nice act, but seriously, girl.... Do you really think this will end well for you?" he asks, his voice calm and firm, as if this is nothing but a game for him. His eyes are locked on me, and I can't pretend he doesn't give me the creeps, especially when I remember my parents being murdered in cold blood before my eyes. Oleg didn't even flinch back then, as if they were a simple nuisance to him instead of two innocent human beings.

"You are a monster," I murmur, feeling the taste of blood in my mouth. Tears threaten to pool in my eyes, but I shove them away with a shake of my head. "I might not be the one to end you, but the Saints certainly will. And this will end tonight." I smile at him, hoping I can convey confidence in my tone and expression.

Oleg chuckles, his shoulders moving slightly. That's when I notice the knife in his hand. I frown, wondering what he is planning on doing with a knife, considering I'm holding a gun. I could shoot him before he even got near me. In fact, I don't even know why I'm fucking waiting.

I should just shoot him and end this, once and for all.

I pull the trigger, but there is no bullet. I hear a faint pop that makes my heart stop beating in my chest. Oleg laughs loudly this time, his head falling backward before he looks back at me, his eyes now darkened and narrowed.

He is no longer amused. He is fucking pissed that I didn't even hesitate at trying to kill him. Luckily for him, it didn't work. But now he's aiming his fury at me.

"You fucking fool." With two strides, he crosses the space between us and punches me in the face. My jaw cracks at the impact, and I fall to the floor, holding my chin. Pain shoots through my head, but I can only stare at him in shock. Of all the things I expected him to do to me, this was not on my list.

"That was for daring to try to kill me," he says, as if I need an explanation as to why he hit me. "And this," he adds through clenched teeth, squatting in front of me and holding the sharp knife against my throat. The cold blade touches my skin, and I go rigid, unwilling to make a single move, afraid that he will cut my neck. "Is for betraying your fucking family and colluding with the enemy."

He doesn't need to say it for me to know he is referring to the

Saints. Fear washes over me as I stare into his evil eyes, but I still force myself to remain strong. I might die now, but I won't die as a coward. If I have to leave this world, I'll do it proudly, just like my family. Just like Petr, Natya, Lev, and Ilya. I will keep my head high until the end. For them. For all they did for me, so I could live a happy life. So I could stand a chance of even having one.

"I'd do it a thousand times more if it meant I got to see you go down and pay for everything you did to my family," I spit out, ignoring the blade pressing against my skin. There's a sharp sting as he forces his hand on my throat, and a hot liquid starts pouring down my neck. But still, I don't back away. "The Romina Empire will die with you today. And no one will remember you or your legacy. This is all you ever cared about, isn't it?"

Oleg's hand retreats, only to come crashing back with full force against my face. My head snaps sideways, and my vision blurs for a moment, pain blooming across my cheek. I stare up at him, showing him my best smile.

"Petr and Lev are probably laughing at you right now," I carry on, boldness taking control of me. My chest fills with pride and a strange sense of peace as I remind myself I would die for them. Everything else fades, but the weight of knowing that I'll be leaving Angelo behind tugs at my heart. And that's the only regret I have as I spit blood on his face and add, "You'll never be as great as they were. Never."

THIRTY-FOUR
COWARD

Tatiana

THE HATRED in Oleg's gaze cuts through me, his nostrils flaring as he rubs his hands over his face, and it's enough to make my stomach lurch. But I don't regret a single thing I said to him. I'd do it all again if I knew I'd hit a nerve. He can look all untouchable and arrogant if he wants, but even monsters have a weakness. Oleg's ego is his.

He's always thought he was superior to everyone else. That he got where he is today because of his skills and talent. But the truth is that he is where he is because he's evil. He never cared about anyone or anything, as long as he could achieve his goals. If he had to step over people, kill them to get them out of his way, he wouldn't even hesitate.

He deserves what's coming to him.

It's a shame I won't be here to witness it, but Angelo will get revenge for Luca, and that's enough for me.

"You stupid bitch," Oleg hisses through gritted teeth, his jaw tense as he stares down at me.

I brace myself for another hit, or maybe even a shot, but it never comes.

The next thing I know, the door to the office bursts open, and shots fly everywhere around me. I drop to the floor, crawling to hide behind the couch, protecting my head with my arms.

I don't see where Oleg went, but right now, I'm more concerned about protecting myself. I scramble to find my gun, but then it hits me. It's empty and I didn't have the chance to reload. I need to crawl back over the couch to do so, but as I peak over, I'm astonished by the scene unfolding in front of my eyes.

Angelo is here, with Dice, Sal, and Kian, but there are other Romina men as well. I don't even know when they arrived or how they are all still standing. Oleg is nowhere in sight. I can't tell if he's hidden behind a piece of furniture or if he managed to flee the room without anyone noticing.

I frown as I realize they are all engaged in a physical fight now, punches and kicks being thrown instead of bullets. Why aren't they shooting each other?

Angelo is dodging hits from three different men who have him surrounded, and Dice and Kian are occupied with another group of Rominas. They're outnumbered, but so far, they're holding their own surprisingly well.

I'm about to dive for my gun when I notice someone escaping through the door, unnoticed.

My heart jumps to my throat and my skin crawls as I realize it is Oleg, being the fucking coward that he is and running away from a fight.

Son of a bitch.

Determination and rage boil inside me, and my hand reaches for the knife on my thigh.

No one seems to realize I'm still here, so I have a chance to get out of the room and go after Oleg without anyone stopping me.

Someone must have kicked my gun away, and I don't have time to search for it.

Keeping my head low and hiding behind the furniture, I head for the exit. A gunshot echoes near me, and my ears ring, but I don't turn back to see what happened and if someone was hit.

I only pray it's not Angelo as I cross the doorway and get to the hallway.

There's only one way out from here, so I head toward the stairs, constantly scanning my surroundings so I'm not blindsided by the enemy lurking around.

As I get to the top of the stairs, my stomach sinks to my feet as my eyes fall downstairs, on the foyer floor, covered with the corpses of men.

A movement to my left piques my attention, and I turn just in time to see Oleg escaping into the garden. I rush forward, doing my best not to stumble over the bodies lying on the marble floor, and chase after him.

I force air into my lungs, inhaling sharply as I turn my gaze away from the faces of those already dead. I know none of them is Angelo, but it's still sad to see so many people losing their lives over... what? Greed? Money? Power?

Besides, my emotions are threatening to overwhelm me. Not only is Oleg escaping, but I also have no idea what happened to Angelo after I left the office. All I can do now is pray that he's safe—at least as safe as anyone can be under these circumstances.

The night air hits my face as soon as I step out of the mansion through the side door. Fury consumes me as I spot Oleg heading for a car parked a few meters ahead. There's no fucking way he's getting away! Not if I can do anything about it.

I wish I had my gun with me now so I could at least try and shoot him from this distance.

"Oleg, you fucking coward!" I yell, my throat burning. I keep running, forcing my body to obey. He doesn't look back, and I push harder, my legs screaming in protest beneath me.

I'm so close....

Just a couple more steps, and I throw myself at him as he reaches for the car door, slamming us both into the side of the vehicle. He stumbles, and before he can recover, I stick the small blade into his side.

He grunts in pain, lashing out with his elbow and catching me hard in the ribs. The impact is enough to steal the air from my lungs, and I stumble backward, bending down slightly and gasping for air.

Oleg hisses as he stares at me while pulling the knife from his torso. It doesn't seem to have done much damage, but it gives me some satisfaction to know I have hurt him, even if just a little.

He tosses the bloodied knife to the ground and stares back at me, his eyes burning with fury.

"You shouldn't have done that," he spits, pulling a gun from behind his back and pointing at me.

Damn.

Now I'm done.

The gaze he throws at me is deadly. There's no way he's letting me off the hook this time.

I must look terrified because a wide grin shows up on his face as he stares at me, evolving to a loud laugh that makes bile rise up to my throat.

I'm paralyzed, my feet stuck to the ground as if I'm glued to it.

"Scared?" he taunts me, raising his brows at me in defiance. "You should've stayed by my side." He takes a step forward, pressing the cold barrel of the gun against my forehead. My legs and hands are trembling aggressively, but I clench my teeth, unwilling to prove him right and show how scared I am.

"Any last words, sweetie, before I send you to meet your parents?" he adds, putting pressure on the gun to my head.

Panic climbs up my body, but I push it away, forcing a smile to curl up my lips as I stare back at his evil face.

"Yeah. Burn in hell," I say in a low but firm voice.

Oleg smirks, cocking his gun. His breathing is heavy, but his gaze is calm.

I close my eyes, waiting for him to shoot me dead. Angelo's face is the only thing I see as realization washes over me.

I'm about to die, and all I wish is that I could see his face one last time. It's a bittersweet feeling knowing I'll meet my family soon, but I'll lose him in the process.

Having met him made me think it was possible for me to have a happy life. For the first time in my life, I could see a future where I could actually be happy with someone.

But God has a different plan for me.

It was good while it lasted, but now it's time for us to part ways.

My only regret is that I never told him I loved him.

And now this amazing feeling will be taken to the grave with me.

Bang!

THIRTY-FIVE
SAINTS AND ROMINAS

Angelo

THE STING in my arm is distracting as Dice and I walk back through the tunnel that leads to the main house. I don't think it did permanent damage. However, I can't move my left arm much without feeling like I'm about to vomit or pass out.

Our boots echo in this enclosed space, and my breathing is coming out in sharp exhales as I struggle to keep my shoulder from swinging.

"All good there, man?" Dice asks over his shoulder, a few feet ahead of me, leading the way back to chaos.

"Yeah," I grunt in response.

My right arm is stretched in front of me, the gun firmly in my hand. My injured arm is glued to my torso, the bloodied knife still in hand. Just in case.

We reach the main house again and carefully step inside the room, studying our surroundings to guarantee no one is lurking around, waiting for us.

The place seems empty, so Dice and I head to the hallway.

I'm desperate to get to the other wing of the mansion. Whether Tatiana went there by herself or was taken—which I doubt—I'm positive that's where she is.

The house is surprisingly quieter this time, and my insides churn when I imagine what could've happened downstairs while we were away.

"How the fuck do we know what's going on now?" I grumble. Just then, three figures appear in the foyer downstairs. Sal, Kian, and Max look up at us, weapons at the ready, their faces and vests splattered with blood.

"You guys good?" I ask, my eyes darting from left to right instinctively.

"Max, can you get some backup? I think Oleg has Tatiana," I add. He halts halfway up the stairs, and with a quick nod, pivots and heads back the way he came.

Kian and Sal join Dice and me, and we finally head toward Oleg's office. Dread courses through me as I approach the end of the hallway, fear threatening to paralyze my every limb.

What if Tatiana is already dead? What if I'm too late?

Shaking my head and pushing the thoughts aside, I lead the way. When we get to the door and I hear her voice, I don't even hesitate before kicking it open. It takes me only a split second to see Oleg holding his knife against her throat, and rage blinds me.

I pull the trigger before I even realize it. But with Oleg so close to Tatiana and the risk of hitting her too, at the last second, I aim for his feet. The shot buys her a moment, just long enough to scramble away.

But then, before any of us can make another move, the sound of footsteps fills the hallway. We're surrounded by Oleg's men forcing their way inside the room. Oleg manages to hide somewhere, and I can't see Tatiana anymore, but I have other things to worry about now. The fact she is still alive is enough for me to focus on disarming the motherfuckers coming at me.

Dice and Kian are engaged in a fight, but I can't see Sal.

A bullet swooshes close to my ear and I squat down, dodging the shots aimed at me. I kick the hand of one of the Rominas, and his pistol flies across the room, landing close to the big desk.

I shoot his leg and repeat my movements with the other two who have me surrounded. But the last one slaps my good arm, sending my gun to the other side of the room. Adrenaline pumps through my veins and, for a moment, I forget about the hole in my shoulder.

No matter how much faith I have in myself and my men, we went into the enemy's den unsure of what we would encounter, and there is nothing more dangerous than enemy territory.

And this doesn't seem to have an end in sight.

Dice grunts beside me when he is kicked in the face, and the noise of a bone cracking tells me his nose is broken. Kian jumps in, grabbing the guy who hurt Dice and putting him in a sleeper hold.

Just when I think we have everything handled and all of them knocked out, five more burst into the room, giving us no room to catch a break. The Saints put the Rominas down in record time.

My eyes scan the room, looking for my gun and two people I can't see anywhere.

"Oleg and Tatiana are gone," I say, still out of breath. My heart is pounding against my chest so hard that it hurts, but the dread that's settled deep inside me begins to rise again, preventing me from thinking straight.

I managed to find her, only to lose her again.

"Fuck," I hiss, already heading for the door.

"Angelo," Dice calls. When I turn, he tosses my gun. I grab it midair and nod sharply in appreciation, darting down the hallway.

Fear paralyzes me, and I hesitate. There's no sign of Tatiana anywhere. Now, I only have my instincts left to guide me, and my past has proven that can be a risky move. But I can't accept a different outcome other than finding Tatiana and bringing her home with me tonight, so I hold onto it with all my might and dart down the stairs, diverting from the bodies spread on the floor.

From the window to my left, I see movement in the garden, and my heart jumps to my throat when I spot Tatiana and Oleg engaged in a struggle.

She plunges a knife into his side. He shoves her backward, removing the weapon.

Time seems to slow down as I watch him grab his gun and aim for her head while muttering something to her.

I force my legs to move forward, but no matter how fast I run, it doesn't seem to be fast enough.

He is going to shoot her.

And I'm about to watch her die in front of my eyes, just like what happened to my little brother years ago.

I can't let that happen, but I'm not fast enough.

I cross the doorway, my boots crushing the grass beneath them. The night air is cool against my skin as I speed up.

If I get close enough, maybe I can try to stop him.

"Any last words, sweetie, before I send you to meet your parents?" he is saying to her, his eyes filled with fury and pure evilness.

This motherfucker....

"Yeah. Burn in hell," Tatiana replies. Her voice is firm, but I can tell she's frightened, her fists clenched at her side and her jaw tense as she stares at the man who ruined both our lives.

She is right about that. Oleg is going to burn in hell because that's where I'm sending him tonight.

He cocks his gun, and the sound has my knees trembling beneath me. But I don't stop until I have a clear line of sight for him.

I come to a stop, aiming my gun at him. I curse under my breath when I notice my hands are shaking slightly, but this is my only chance to save Tatiana.

With one sharp inhale, I aim for his heart and shoot.

The loud bang echoes throughout the entire property, and for a second, it's the only sound I hear until the ringing in my ears dissipates.

Oleg stumbles backward, his eyes moving from Tatiana to his blood stained chest.

I give myself a split second to smile before I continue in their direction, more than ready to end this. But Tatiana is faster, squatting to grab her folding blade from her boot and sinking it into Oleg's heart, inches above my shot.

He gasps, dropping his gun to the ground.

"This is for my family," Tatiana says, twisting the knife inside him. "And this is for Angelo's brother," she adds, pushing him backward against the car, deepening the blade into his body.

The horrified look in Oleg's eyes as he stares back at her is enough to fill my heart with pride.

This is over.

Justice, at last.

THIRTY-SIX
END OF A FIGHT

Tatiana

I WAIT for death when I hear the bang.

What is it supposed to feel like?

Should I see my whole life pass before my eyes? Is a light supposed to appear at the end of a dark tunnel or something of that sort? Should I be feeling any kind of pain, or is it supposed to be smooth and peaceful?

Whatever it is, none of it happens.

I can still feel my body, and my senses are sharpened, as if I'm simply closing my eyes to sleep but adrenaline is keeping me from relaxing.

What is going on?

Cautiously, I force my eyes open again. I'm still alive. And apparently, I wasn't the one who got shot.

It was Oleg.

He has stumbled backward, and his eyes are on his chest where a huge blood stain is covering his shirt.

My brain is struggling to understand what happened, but I push these intrusive thoughts aside. He was hit, but he is not dead yet. And considering this is the devil incarnate, I doubt he will go down with a simple shot to the chest.

My hand is already moving to my feet before I can even make sense of what I'm doing. Grabbing my folded blade from my boot, I open and stick it into his heart, a few inches above the hole the bullet made.

"This is for my family!" I grunt, using all my strength to twist the knife in his chest. Bile threatens to climb up my throat, but I force it back down. My wrist hurts with all the pressure I'm putting, but I ignore it.

My emotions are all over the place now, but I need to remind myself that this is indeed for my family... for everything that Oleg took from me, all he prevented me from having.

He took my biological parents from me while I was still a baby. I never got to see their faces. I never got to hear their voices. I was only left with stories of who they used to be and what-ifs.

For years, I wondered what my life would've been like if I got to be raised by them. Having them by my side through my first steps, school, college...

And then there were Lev and Ilya, two angels who took me in and accepted the burden of raising me as their own child. They gave me so much love and attention, giving up on their own lives to keep me protected.

And Oleg took them from me, too.

It is true that I wouldn't have met Angelo if it weren't for him, but I'm not willing to give Oleg any credit.

He also took the only important thing Angelo had in his life.

We're two broken souls because of *him*.

"And this is for Angelo's brother," I add, pushing Oleg against the car and sinking the blade deeper into his heart.

The horrified look on his face is so satisfying. He deserves to suffer way more than this, but I'm tired. Physically and mentally.

When blood sputters from Oleg's mouth, I let go of the knife and take a few steps back as I realize what I've done.

He slides down the side of the car and collapses to the ground, his widened eyes still on me.

Oleg gurgles something, but I can't understand what he's saying. I'm torn between turning my gaze away from him, afraid to have this memory haunt me for life, and watching him die, committing to memory this moment, so I never forget he is finally gone.

I watch as his head tilts back and his body goes limp against the car. His eyes are still open, but there's no more soul in his body.

If there ever was one....

Oleg is gone.

Dead.

Beyond redemption.

He is no longer walking this Earth, taking people's families from them. There's one less evil person on this planet tonight.

My whole body starts shaking aggressively as realization washes over me, and I feel like I'm about to faint. My legs give out under me, but before I hit the ground, strong arms hold me from behind and pull me up.

The scent of something musky and familiar hits me, and I start crying, unable to control my sobs.

"Shhh, it's okay, baby. It's over." Angelo's voice soothes me, his arms strongly holding me close to his chest.

I'm numb, exhausted, sad. It's a mix of emotions I can't quite interpret. The only feeling I want to acknowledge right now is how safe Angelo makes me feel in his arms.

There's movement around us, men surrounding us, but I'm not afraid anymore. Angelo is here. And considering he is not tensing up, I can only assume these guys are from the Saints.

My eyes are still fixed on Oleg's body as Angelo walks away from him, taking me to a car parked close to the front gate. Staring into his lifeless eyes is strange. It's like I'm waiting for him to blink at any time, revealing that he is actually alive.

Angelo sets me down in the car, but when he moves to close the door, I grab him by the wrist, still shaking and crying compulsively.

"Where are you going?" I ask, my voice cracking. I look at him, my eyes pleading. I don't want to be alone. I can't stand the idea of him being away from me right now.

He looks back at me, his brows creasing slightly as he takes me in. I know he is worried about me, but I can see he is also distracted by everything happening around us. The Saints are everywhere, probably checking the mansion and making sure all is taken care of.

I have no idea how they are going to handle all those bodies, but I can't find it in me to ask, or care.

I just want to get away from this place and never come back.

"I'll let the guys know I'm taking you home," he explains, his voice calm and soft. He lowers to place a kiss on my forehead and brings our noses together, his gaze held on me. "I'm not going anywhere. Don't worry."

I nod, the lump in my throat still present. But I force it down, willing myself to be strong so he can do his duty without having to worry about me.

Angelo closes the passenger door softly and walks away from the car. I watch out of the window as he pulls Dice aside and says something to him. He nods in return. Then Angelo comes back and sits beside me in the driver's seat.

No words leave our mouths as we drive out of the Rominas' property.

We're close to the highway when something occurs to me, and I speak for the first time after minutes in silence.

"What about Yakov? What happened to him?" I ask, my eyes widening in shock as I realize I haven't seen him the entire time I was at the mansion.

Angelo's jaw clenches, his face darkening as he shakes his head.

"We couldn't find him anywhere," he informs me angrily, not giving me much information.

That feeling of dread comes back to me, and a shiver runs down my spine.

It isn't over, is it?

Oleg is gone, but what if Yakov decides to come back to haunt us, wanting revenge for his father?

"Shit," I murmur, more to myself than to him.

"We'll get to him. It's just a matter of time," he tries to reassure me, but it doesn't work much.

We remain a few more minutes in silence until Angelo glances sideways at me and clears his throat. "Are you okay? Did he hurt you?"

His voice is filled with concern, and my heart shrinks in my chest. My jaw hurts from the punch I got, and the small wound in my neck stings, but it's nothing compared to what the others had to go through, I'm sure. I've suffered more psychologically than physically.

"It's not a big deal." I shrug, not wanting to worry him further.

"What did he do?" Angelo asks through clenched teeth, shifting uncomfortably in his seat.

"I'm fi—"

"What did he do?" He cuts me off, repeating his question.

I take a deep breath and lean my head against the leather seat.

"He punched me in the face, and his blade sort of cut my neck, but it's nothing deep," I add quickly when his head snaps in my direction to check the extent of my injuries. I run my fingers over the cut on my neck and hiss when it stings, but the blood must have dried because my hand is clean when I pull it back.

"Son of a bitch," Angelo snarls under his breath. His brows are creased, and the muscles in his jaw are tensed.

"I'm really fine," I repeat, firmer this time. "I'm just mentally exhausted, and I can't bring myself to think about everything that happened tonight. But I'll be okay, as long as you're with me." I reach for his hand and squeeze it, hoping my touch will reassure him since my words don't seem to be enough.

"I'm never going anywhere," he states firmly, gripping my hand tighter. I run my thumb across his palm that's on my thigh, comforting him just as he is doing with me. "I love you. I figured out tonight that I never got to say that to you. And I know this is not the right moment to do it, but I was so afraid to lose you. I—" His voice cracks and the hand on the wheel clenches, his knuckles turning white from the pressure.

His words echo in my ears, and my heart swells at his confession.

"I felt the same thing. I almost died tonight. Twice," I add, remembering the two times I faced Oleg. And somehow, I managed to survive. "I could only think about how I never got to say I love you and how we didn't really have a chance to build something together."

Tears pool in my eyes again, but Angelo pulls my hand to his mouth and places a kiss on it.

"I made you a promise, remember?" he reminds me. "I will give you the life you deserve. And that selfishly includes me. You're never getting away from me."

"Good." I smile at him, feeling a bit of the weight on my shoulders lift as I stare back at the man I have come to love.

THIRTY-SEVEN
COMFORT PLACE

Angelo

WATCHING Tatiana kill Oleg had me paralyzed for a moment, but when she stumbled backward, her legs wobbling, I noticed she was just about to faint. I rushed to grab her, pulling her into my arms and taking her away from his body.

Feeling her tremble, sobbing uncontrollably, made me aware of how hard tonight had been on her. She put on a brave face, and managed everything so well, that I could feel nothing more than pride. But once I got her away from the mansion and realized she had endured much more than I realized at first, I felt powerless.

I didn't manage to protect her like I wanted. And no matter how often I remind myself that she doesn't need my protection, that she can handle herself well enough, I still hate myself for allowing her to be put through all of this.

Getting beaten by Oleg, having to kill people to get justice for her family, and staining her soul makes me feel like shit.

The entire drive back to Staten Island, I debate with myself. I want to get home and take care of her, attend to her injuries, and shower her with love and affection in the way she deserves.

I also want to wait for a better moment to confess my love for her, but the words flow out of my mouth before I have the chance to stop myself. I just spent the whole night regretting not telling her how I felt before, so as soon as I took her away from that horror house, I had to make sure she knew how I felt.

Hearing those three words back is like a soothing balm to my shattered heart.

I never thought I would be able to love someone as much as I love Tatiana, nor did I think I was deserving of that kind of love.

But now that I have her, I'll make sure I never let go of her.

As soon as we get to the safe house, I help her out of the car and take her upstairs to her room.

I don't give my mind enough time or space to think about all that happened tonight. Not even the fact that Oleg is dead has settled in yet. I'm sure it will come to me once I relax, but there's still too much adrenaline running through my system at this moment for me to be able to focus on that reality.

"Do you want me to prepare a hot bath for you?" I offer quietly as soon as we step into the bedroom.

She sits down on the bed and looks up at me, and that's when I can finally see the wound in her neck, caused by Oleg's knife. It doesn't seem deep, but it could easily get infected if not treated properly. Her cheek is also reddened from the punch, and her lip is slightly split, with dry blood covering the wound.

I clench my fists beside me as I wait for her answer, not daring to say anything else. I'm on the edge of losing my control again after seeing her hurt like this, but there's nothing I can do now to vent it. Oleg is dead, and there's no one left for me to beat, or kill.

Yakov is in the back of my mind, but I need to force myself to focus on the here and now. The fact that he wasn't seen during our mission is pulling at my heart, leaving me uneasy. He's not anywhere close to his father in terms of evilness and skills, but it doesn't mean he's not powerful.

He can still get the Rominas after Tatiana and the Saints. I told her all is over, but it isn't—not completely, at least.

"I... yeah, I think that would be great," she finally answers me, and I head for the bathroom to fill the tub.

When I return, she has already removed most of her clothes and is standing in the middle of the room in nothing but her bra and panties. The dirty clothes tainted with blood and the bulletproof vest are set aside in the corner of the room, but there are no signs of her weapons anywhere.

I can only assume she left them back at the Romina mansion, but I don't bother to ask her. The last thing she needs to think of right now are the weapons she left behind.

"Do you need me to get you anything?" I ask, watching as she walks past me into the bathroom. As soon as she crosses the threshold, I notice some bruises on her back, and I have to swallow the lump in my throat and look away.

She turns to face me, and under the dim light, I notice her swollen eyes from crying.

I wish I could take all the pain away from her and suffer it all by myself because it kills me to have to see her like this. But I can't do that.

"Can you stay here with me? I don't want to be alone," she pleads in a whisper.

I nod, closing the door behind me and following her. She removes the rest of her clothes and steps into the tub, and I pull a small stool from under the sink and place it close to her.

"What will happen now?" she asks as she starts washing her arms, rubbing her skin to get rid of all the dirt and blood. I hand her a sponge, and after she pours some liquid soap on it, she returns to her task.

"I don't know yet," I tell her honestly. "We need to wait for the others to hear the complete report. I don't know what else happened after I found you, and they stayed behind to... check on everything."

Tatiana nods but remains silent, moving the sponge to her neck and face. She is careful so as not to touch her wound. I get up, moving to grab the first aid kit from the bathroom cabinet.

"Let me clean that for you," I offer, gesturing to her neck.

My adrenaline is starting to wear off, and my body is beginning to show signs of exhaustion. When I move my arm in a particular angle, pain shoots through me, and I'm reminded I was shot. Unconsciously, I move my hand to hold my shoulder. Tatiana's eyes follow my action, and they widen as she realizes I'm hurt.

"Angelo!" she shrieks in shock, kneeling in the tub so she can get closer to me. Her soft fingers touch my shoulder, and I wince, but I don't move away from her. I let her check the damage that has been done, unwilling to do it myself.

I don't even know if the bullet is still inside me or not, but I can't force myself to think about it now.

"Oh my God! You were shot," she declares, her voice cracking with concern.

"It's fine." But when I try to shrug, another wave of pain washes over me, and I hiss. "Okay, it hurts like hell, but I won't die. I'll get it treated as soon as the guys get here. Don't worry," I assure her, offering a small smile as I wait for the sting to go away.

It feels like my entire arm is burning and being pulled out of its socket, but I hang in there, not wanting to worry her anymore.

Tears well in her eyes again as she looks at me, her chin trembling. I'm not in so much pain that I don't find her absolutely adorable.

"Hey, come on. Let's finish this bath and get us both something to eat. I'm starving."

I'm not, really, but I just want her to think about something else for a change.

She seems about to refuse me but ends up sitting back in the tub and finishing her bath. A few minutes later, I help her out, wrapping her in a robe, and once we're back in the bedroom, I pull her into my arms, hugging her close to me.

Her scent invades my senses, and I allow myself to close my eyes for a minute, giving my body the comfort it so desperately needs.

She is here. She is safe. She is mine.

That's all the reassurance I need after tonight.

"Listen," I begin, pulling her away just enough for me to look into her beautiful blue eyes, "I know a lot is going through your mind right now, but I want you to promise me one thing. When you feel like it is too much for you to handle, come talk to me. I know how dark and deep our minds can go in this kind of business, but I don't want you to feel like you're alone. I'll be here to share the pain with you."

Tatiana swallows hard and nods, her eyes roaming my face. "I promise. I just..." She stammers but composes herself almost immediately. "I just don't know what to do now. The last weeks have been all about going after justice, or vengeance, or whatever you want to call it. I fear I might feel like it wasn't worth it at some point, or even struggle to find out who I am without this fight, you know?"

"I do," I agree, squeezing her shoulders lightly. "I really do. But you shouldn't let your mind go there. You did what you had to do, and now it's time to figure out what you want your life to be like. And I'll be here to help you find your way whenever you get lost."

A sob escapes her as she leans her head against my chest once more. I run my fingers through her wet hair, hoping to calm her heart and mind with that simple gesture.

"We'll figure it out together," I add in a murmur, placing a soft kiss on her head.

Even though my entire body is sore, and my shoulder feels like I'm being stabbed over and over, holding Tatiana like this makes it all feel worth it.

THIRTY-EIGHT
LEGACY

Tatiana

I NEED a couple of days to get my mind out of a fog after I killed Oleg.

Angelo and the others don't think it's safe for me to leave yet while Yakov is still out there, so we stay at the Saints' safe house. I was hoping to reclaim my life, but maybe taking these days to rest first is what I actually need.

I don't think I'm in the right frame of mind to make important decisions, especially important decisions that can affect the rest of my life.

I feel so indecisive. Moving back to Russia would mean leaving Angelo behind, and that is out of the question for me.

But up until a couple of months ago, Russia was the only place I ever called home. If I stay in the United States, what will I do here? Do I really want to be part of the mafia world?

I don't think Angelo will ever give up on that part of himself, and

I wouldn't dare ask him to for me. But do *I* want to be involved? Would I be ready to let go of him to leave it all behind? Or am I willing to accept the mafia life as part of him?

It is something I was born into, after all.

My mind is swirling with possibilities, but no matter how hard I think about it, I can't come to a decision.

As if sensing my despair, when the night falls, Angelo comes to me while I'm sipping tea and reading a book in the living room.

"Hey, I hate to bother you, but there's someone here who wants to speak with you," he informs me.

I frown. "Who?"

He steps aside, revealing Guskov, who seems to have recovered from the fight. Most of us have recovered, physically. The wounds and injuries we sustained are healing.

The dark circles under Guskov's eyes are gone, and he even has a smile on his face as he steps into the room, nodding at me.

"Good evening, Miss. Good to see you in one piece," he tells me, and I gesture for him to take a seat on the couch in front of me.

Angelo doesn't join us, but he also doesn't leave, leaning against the banister and crossing his arms in front of his chest while he watches us in silence.

"I can say the same about you," I reply, offering him a small smile and setting my book aside. "To what do I owe the honor of your visit? Is everything okay?"

Guskov proved to be a great ally during the mission, and he was also an old friend to both of my fathers, so I feel a special connection to him.

"Well, I came to check on you, but also..." He adjusts himself on the couch, shifting uncomfortably before clearing his throat. "I have something important to talk to you about." His voice is firm and serious, and I brace myself for what he's about to say. I have no idea what could be so important. Could it be related to Yakov? But if it is, he wouldn't talk directly to me. He would get the others involved too. Right?

"Okay...." I trail off, encouraging him to continue. I straighten my posture, swallowing hard and glancing at Angelo, who nods at me in reassurance.

If I were to guess, I'd say he already knows what this is about and is giving me the space to handle it by myself, which I appreciate.

"As you know, the Romina Empire suffered great loss during the mission, and many were not actually on Oleg's side. Now that he's dead, and his son is missing, we had a meeting to discuss and vote for the future, and the consensus is that it's yours if you want it."

My ears ring, and I stare at Guskov, numb and unsure I heard him correctly. I couldn't have. I clench my teeth so I don't drop my jaw and show how shocked I am as I replay his words in my head.

They voted for me to take over?

"It is rightfully yours anyway, since it is Petr's legacy," he adds as if I need some incentive to consider his offer. "Although it was stained for decades by Oleg."

He is not wrong about that, but what do I know about leading a mob?

I glance at Angelo, who is still watching me carefully, his dark eyes stuck on me as he awaits my answer.

"What about Yakov?" I manage to mutter.

Guskov rolls his eyes, leans back against the couch, and crosses his legs. His tone and body language are nonchalant.

"Even if it was his right to inherit it, the motherfucker doesn't have what it takes to lead us," he explains with a shrug. "He'd get us all killed before we could even understand what hit us. He's just a playboy who got used to having everything he wanted because his father made him believe he could."

I can't argue with that. Yakov is nothing but a repulsive, cruel, spoiled brat.

"But do you think I have what it takes? I know nothing about leading an empire," I argue, not confident enough to accept such responsibility.

"You are your father's daughter. Both Petr and Lev. I don't doubt your ability to lead us the way they did." I shake the tears that pool in my eyes with his words. "I know this is a lot to take in and consider, but I want you to know that you won't be alone. I will help you get through everything, and you have more allies than you can possibly imagine. Most of us are still loyal to Petr, even after all these years," he states firmly, holding my gaze.

There's so much honesty and intensity in them that I don't think he is lying. I can feel his loyalty, and he has proven it to me by agreeing to work with the Saints to take Oleg down and for reaching out to me, even after Lev was murdered.

Silence surrounds us as I consider what to do.

After a moment, Angelo clears his throat by the door, speaking for the first time in a while.

"I know this is your decision to make, and I don't want to influence you, but I just feel like I should tell you that I'll stand by whatever you choose. You just need to think about all that it entails. And if this is really what you want, I'll be by your side, no matter what."

I nod at him and stare at my lap, fidgeting nervously.

Would my father want this for me? If I had had the chance to live with him and be raised by him, would he teach me how to rule his empire one day? Would he want that for me? Would he support me if *I* wanted it?

I would be lying if I said that I know all that it entails, but I also can't pretend it doesn't feel somewhat... right. Of course, I have a lot to learn, especially how to toughen up, because this is no easy thing. I've grown up seeing Lev work for the Rominas, even from afar, and I heard stories too. I also got to see the Saints in action, and even got in the middle of it several times.

Is this the life I want?

It won't be peaceful, that's for sure.

Will I be able to build a true relationship with Angelo if I accept it?

And if I don't, what is it going to be like for us? He won't back away from the Saints. They are his family, and I would never ask him to turn his back on them to stay with me.

But we also never got the chance to discuss any of this. He just said he'll support me no matter what.

But will he, really?

THIRTY-NINE

UNDER NEW MANAGEMENT

Tatiana

"I DON'T WANT to rush you into making a decision." Guskov breaks the silence. "But we can't run without a leader for too long. It's been a couple of days already, and we have urgent business to attend to."

I look at him, doing my best not to look overwhelmed.

"I understand," I mutter. "Do you have any news on Yakov?" I change the topic slightly, needing more information before I make a life-changing decision.

He shakes his head at me, his lips a thin line. I can tell Yakov's disappearance bothers him as much as it bothers me. Where the hell is he, and what is he planning? Did he simply escape so he wasn't killed, or is he waiting for a chance to catch us off guard?

If I don't accept the position, it will be open for Yakov to claim, which is something we definitely don't need. He might not be fit to rule, but I would bet my life he is certainly capable of causing permanent damage.

"What about the ones who are faithful to Oleg?" I ask.

"We're getting rid of them," Guskov tells me simply. "Many were killed during the mission, some escaped, and the ones who stayed are being questioned so we can attest how loyal they are, or if they are simply scared to change sides."

"Makes sense," I agree with a nod. "Can I really trust you?" I don't mean to sound doubtful or ungrateful after everything he did for me, but I need to be sure before I do something this big.

Guskov's gaze never leaves mine as he rises from his seat and then kneels before me, bowing his head.

"I, Guskov Petrovich, swear to be loyal to you, Tatiana Romina, and to the Romina Empire, for as long as I'm alive," he states, holding his hand against his chest. I'm sure this is a big deal in this world, even though I have never seen anyone do it before.

I glance sideways at Angelo, who is still by the door, in silence and with an unreadable expression. I try to read his face, try to interpret what he might be thinking, but he gives me nothing. I know he doesn't want to influence my decision, but it'd be nice to know what he thinks about it.

Sighing, I turn to Guskov again.

"It's fine. You don't have to do that. I accept the position of leader at the Romina Empire," I finally say, and it's like an invisible weight sets on my shoulders with my acceptance. I'm sure this is what it really is—the weight of being responsible for so much and so many.

But I will have real friends and allies beside me, so that makes it all more bearable.

Guskov looks up at me, a genuine smile forming on his lips.

"I'm pleased to hear it. And I mean it when I say, for all of us, that the Romina Empire capos are happy to have you lead us."

I doubt he really knows what he is saying, but I appreciate it either way.

"I will be counting on you to help me through it, Guskov," I tell him honestly, not afraid to show my vulnerability. It's better that I show my humanity from the start instead of pretending I'm someone

I'm not. "I can tell you hold a place in your heart for my father. I hope you can see me as an extension of who he was to you and the others."

Emotion crosses his eyes as he returns to his seat across from me.

"You can count on that, Boss," he replies, his voice slightly cracking.

"Now, I know you're all handling the mess at the mansion, and I honestly don't want anything to do with that place, so please get rid of it," I give my first order, feeling the bittersweet taste in my tongue. "As for Yakov, we need to find him and make sure he doesn't come after us. Ever."

I don't mean I want him killed, but I trust he will know what to do.

Guskov nods firmly at me. "Consider it done. And I'll keep you posted. I doubt he's made it very far."

"As for the ones remaining, please make sure only those who are truly faithful to my father and I are allowed to stay. Whoever wants to stick around is welcome, but I don't want any traitors amongst us," I continue, determination settling in my stomach, although fear remains in the back of my mind.

"Understood." Guskov glances at Angelo and back at me, before asking, "What about you? Do you know where you're going to live? The Rominas have some properties scattered around Manhattan, so I can get one of those ready for you to move into," he offers kindly.

I consider his offer. I do need to find a place to live, but I don't want to make any more decisions without talking to Angelo first. This involves him too, even if indirectly.

"I will think about it and let you know. Okay? You can send me the list of properties so I can take a look at them before I make a decision."

"I will get that done as soon as possible." Guskov stands to his feet again, bowing at me once more. "I'll get to work and report back."

"Thanks, Guskov," I say warmly. He exits the room, nodding to Angelo on his way out.

Without a single word, Angelo comes toward me and sits by my side, leaning in to place a kiss on my temple.

"Are you mad at me?" I ask after a moment. My eyes scan his face, looking for any sign of his displeasure.

He frowns at me. "Why would you think that?"

I shrug. "I just... I know we never discussed any of this, and I didn't want to decide anything without talking to you first, but—"

"Hey." He cuts me off, soothing my anxiety as he cups my face in his hands. His eyes are kind and warm, and his features soften as he stares at me. "You have nothing to worry about. It is your life, you don't need me to tell you what to do."

"I know, but still... we should be in this together, right? It doesn't feel right for me to make a big decision like this without consulting you first," I explain.

Angelo takes a deep breath, leaning his head against the couch. He closes his eyes for a moment, and I wait, anticipating the long, serious conversation I'm sure we're about to have.

Well, it is long overdue.

I should have talked to him as soon as we were back from the Romina mansion. But I was too afraid. I didn't want to address the big elephant in the room. I didn't want to have to decide anything, too afraid of what it might mean to our future together.

"I'm not mad at you," he finally says, looking at me. His dark eyes pierce through me, and my heart starts beating fast. It's funny how he still has this effect on me. I don't think I'll ever get used to the intensity with which he looks at me.

"Are you sure? Because you sort of seem to be mad at me," I argue, my voice low and cautious.

"Do you really want to talk about that now?" It doesn't sound like he wants to avoid it, but rather make sure I'm in the right state of mind to get into this topic in our relationship.

"I don't know. Maybe. I think we should address it before it gets too late, don't you? How long are we going to remain in this house, hidden from the world?" I adjust myself on the couch, pulling one leg up and turning to face him completely. "You said you'd support my decision, but it doesn't look like you are," I add, frustration getting the best of me.

He runs his hand through his hair, clearly as frustrated as I am.

"I am. And I will. I just... can we talk about this somewhere else?" His eyes dart to the door as if he is waiting for someone to show up at any time and interrupt us, or hear us.

"Fine," I blurt, standing from the couch. "We can talk in my bedroom then."

I don't wait for him, striding across the room and leading the way to the stairs. I can hear his footsteps behind me, but I'm trying to control my feelings before we have this conversation. I don't want to be unfair to him or say things I don't mean, so I need to pull myself together if I don't want to ruin our relationship because I can't handle my emotions properly.

I burst the door open, walking inside the bedroom and tossing myself on the bed. Angelo walks in calmly, his face stoic as usual, although I can see a hint of a crease between his brows as he heads for the window.

He doesn't sit on the chair, though, remaining on his feet and leaning against the wooden desk, his skin glowing under the moonlight coming from outside.

"Alright, here we are. Now, can you just tell me what's going through your mind?" I plead.

This is it.

Time for the truth.

FORTY
PERFECT TOGETHER

Angelo

TATIANA LOOKS AT ME EXPECTANTLY, waiting for me to say something about her new role as the boss of the Romina Empire.

I didn't want to influence her decision while she was talking to Guskov, since this is, after all, her life. But the truth is that I am not sure how I feel.

No matter how hard I think about it, I can't see an outcome that would make us both happy and together.

"Angelo, can you please say something?" she whispers, her pleading, beautiful eyes on me.

"I didn't lie when I said I'd support you," I repeat, hoping she at least understood that part. I'd hate myself if I made her feel anything but supported. "No matter what you want to do with your life, you'll have my support."

"But I don't want only your support. I want you," she states firmly.

I run my fingers through my hair once again, holding her gaze.

"I'm a Saint, Tatiana," I remind her simply, doing my best to sound calm and understanding. She nods, but remains silent, waiting for me to continue. "We belong to rival gangs." She already knows it, but for some reason, I feel like I need to bring it to her attention again. "And I know this has been a possibility the entire time, since the Romina Empire is indeed yours by birthright, but..."

"But...?" She encourages me to keep going.

I shrug, frustrated and upset—with myself, for making her feel like she doesn't deserve this, or that she made the wrong choice. I wasn't expecting to react this way to her decision, but I guess I wasn't considering my emotions in the equation. Not that it should matter, though, since this is her life.

"I don't know. I just... this is a dangerous life, as you're more than aware of by now. And I know you don't need my protection, but I still feel like I should be there for you—if you want me to be part of your life, that is," I explain, but I'm so confused with all the thoughts swirling in my head that I'm afraid I'm not being as clear as I want to.

"Listen, I know what I'm signing up for. I might not know the extent of it yet, but I do trust that Guskov and the others will help me adjust. And I would love it if you could still be a part of my life," she tells me, her voice soft but fearful. Her eyes are roaming over my face, and I can tell she is afraid of what will become of us. I can't say I'm not scared either. "As for us belonging to rival gangs, I was thinking..."

Hope rises within me, but I push it down, not wanting to create expectations.

I raise my brows at her. "What?"

"What if we merged the Romina Empire and the Saints? That way we could stay together," she suggests.

It doesn't sound like a bad decision; however, alarm bells ring in my head. This could lead to so many potentially horrible outcomes.

"This would make us stronger than ever. We could rule the entire city, if not the state of New York. We'd also have our own people in Russia. Think about all the possibilities..." she presses.

She is right about that. We would be stronger than any enemy, covering so much territory and so many businesses. We'd be invincible.

But...

"This is not a decision I can make. Tony is the Saints' boss. And even though he trusts me, his word is the final one," I remind her, my heart sinking.

"I know. I can talk to him and present a proposal," she says excitedly, her eyes glimmering under the light. "Maybe he will like it."

I ponder the idea of leaving the Saints for her, in case Tony refuses her idea. But as much as I love Tatiana, I owe my life to them. I don't think I'd be able to live with myself if I betrayed them like that.

If it ends up being a decision I have to make—choosing between them or her—what the fuck will I do? I'm definitely not ready to give up on Tatiana. I refuse to give up on us, and I don't think it's fair for her to either.

At the end of the day, even with Oleg gone, we've reached a dead end.

Why does it have to be so fucking difficult for us to be happy together?

"What if he doesn't?" I retort, not wanting to sound bitter, but grimacing when I realize that's exactly what I sound like.

Tatiana winces almost imperceptibly, but doesn't let it take away her hope.

"We can figure out what to do then. Together," she emphasizes, standing from the bed and heading toward me. "I'm not giving up on you." Her scent invades my senses as she wraps her arms around my waist, pulling me close and gluing our bodies together.

My entire being reacts to her, my muscles relaxing as I melt into her touch. My hands find her hip, and I keep her trapped to me, bringing our foreheads together.

"Good, because I'm not giving up on you either," I murmur, placing a kiss on her soft lips. "I love you," I add, this time making sure she understands what I mean and how much my feelings for her are real.

The first time I confessed to her, we were leaving the Romina mansion after she had just murdered Oleg. I didn't intend for it to be less meaningful, but I had to get it off my chest at that moment.

Right now, though, I hope to convey the intensity of what I feel for her with my eyes, my body, my words, and my actions.

I hope she can understand how much she has changed my life.

"I love you," I repeat, kissing her again.

"I love you too," she whispers against my lips, and I deepen our kiss, tired of this conversation.

Whatever we decide to do, I want to be positive that we'll figure it out. As long as we have each other, we'll find a way to make it work. There's gotta be a way, and I won't rest until I find it.

For her, I'm willing to hold onto hope as tightly as I can.

What starts as a warm, soft, and emotional kiss develops into a wild, desperate one. Ever since our mission, we have barely had time to be together. And when we were alone, I just wanted to make sure she was taken care of.

I've seen how she was affected by the whole mission, and I wanted to give her space for reality to settle in. But now, having her in my arms and feeling her soft skin against mine, her lips reciprocating my kiss with just as much need as I'm feeling, I can't stop.

I want her to feel how much I care for her. How much she means to me. And if my words were not enough to convince her, I'm about to show her exactly what I mean.

Blindly, I guide her backward toward the bed and sit her down on the mattress, spreading her legs apart as I kneel in front of her.

"What are you doing?" she asks, slightly breathless, her eyes widening as I pull her pants down her legs.

"Just showing how much I love you," I tell her with a smirk, shoving the piece of clothing aside and keeping my attention on her lacy underwear.

My fingers trail up her soft thighs until I find the hem of her panties and pull them down in a swift movement. A gasp escapes her lips as I place my head between her legs and kiss the inside of her thighs. Then I move up, and the first brush of my tongue across her clit is enough to have her squirm on the bed.

Shit, she tastes so good.

"Oh, damn..." she murmurs, letting her head fall backward, her fingers tangling in my hair.

I lick her wet folds, applying just enough pressure to have her begging me to claim her.

But I want to take my time—to give her the pleasure she deserves, to make her relax and enjoy, after all she has been through.

Her body shudders as I insert two fingers inside of her, my thumb circling her clit and making her moan my name over and over.

Her back arches, her hips lifting. She raises her head to look down at me, and I notice how her cheeks are flushed, her fingers gripping the sheets beside her.

God, she is so perfect.

I go back to lap and suck at her, drinking in her sweetness and teasing her until she is on the edge.

"Baby, I want you," Tatiana manages to say, her voice coming out in sharp breaths.

"Patience. We have the whole night," I tell her with a grin.

FORTY-ONE
PILLOW TALK

Tatiana

I REST my head on Angelo's chest as I try to steady my breath—and myself—after he just sent me to the moon with the most amazing sex. It's the first time we've been together without me having Oleg consuming my thoughts. It's also the first time I'm feeling the weight of being responsible for a mafia empire on my shoulders.

I'm trying very hard not to think about everything that it entails, so I don't freak out.

I know I can do it.

I know I can find the courage to follow in my father's footsteps. I just need to get into the right mindset first.

I appreciate Angelo wanting to distract me, getting me to relax and feel good for a change, but I can tell this is also eating away at him. He doesn't agree with me taking over the Romina Empire. But he is too respectful and understanding to say that to me.

He said he'll support me, and I believe he will. But I can't blame him for having the concerns he's having. I also don't know how to handle them yet.

I only had that one single idea of merging our gangs, and if it doesn't work, I don't know how we can stay together without causing conflicts of interest between the Saints and the Rominas.

It's a bold move, but I really hope I can convince Tony.

"What are you thinking about?" Angelo asks in a low voice, lazily caressing my hair.

I close my eyes and take a deep breath, wondering if I should share my concerns with him. If he knows I'm doubting my plan, he will get more worried about me. And I don't want to feel like a burden to him.

However, if I can't share my fears with him, who will I share them with?

I shrug slightly, adjusting myself in his arms. Our legs are intertwined under the sheets, and I wouldn't want to be anywhere other than here, with him.

"Honestly, there's so much going on in my mind right now that it's been hard for me to focus on one thing," I admit with a sigh. "Oleg, the Empire, where to live, how to rule, us... I don't know where to start."

Angelo remains silent for a few minutes, and I don't press him to say anything. I'm sure he must be having these same questions inside his mind. The caressing of my hair hasn't stopped, though, so at least I know he's not mad again.

"I can't even begin to imagine what that must feel like for you. I only have an idea of how hard all of this can get. I think you'll get the hang of it as you go, you know, hits and misses and all that. I won't lie to you and say it will be easy, baby, because with all the experience that I have, it's been nothing but easy. And I am not even the boss."

I nod, not daring to move.

He is right. He's seen so much more than I have, and now, I will be the one in charge of making tough decisions. Handling illegal businesses, living with fear of being killed by an enemy, ordering people to be murdered by my men....

Can I really do it?

Is this how I want my life to be?

But maybe that's an opportunity to change things. Maybe I can make the world a better place somehow. If I'm taking the power from people like Oleg to rule, it should be counted as a good thing, right?

"Yeah, I know," I murmur, looking up at him. "Can I ask you something, and do you promise to tell me the truth?"

His dark eyes narrow on me as he takes in my question, his jaw and shoulders tensing up.

"Yeah, of course," he replies firmly.

"Do you honestly think I have what it takes?" I insist, not shifting my gaze from his.

Angelo sits up and leans against the headboard, forcing me to do the same. I cross my legs, holding the sheet against my chest, and face him.

"I know you can do it," he finally tells me. His hair is falling over his eyes, disheveled from all the... exercises we just did, and his chest is bare, his sculpted abs almost making me lose my focus.

I force my eyes to remain on his face while I listen to him.

"You're the most determined, brave, and resilient woman I've ever met," he continues, his voice firm but also kind. "Like I said, it's not an easy life, but I'd be a hypocrite if I told you this is not for you. You're a damaged soul just like I am. If you were to ask me my honest opinion, I'd tell you to just turn your back on all of this and get a normal life for a change, but I'm too selfish to do that, because that'd mean I'd never get to see you again. And I can't even consider that possibility."

I swallow hard, forcing down the lump that has formed in my throat.

"Even if we're from rival gangs, I'm sure that after all we went through, with Guskov and the others joining us for the mission, even if Tony refuses to merge the Saints and the Rominas, I don't think we'll remain enemies. I don't know...." He sounds slightly unsure, but I understand it. We can't be sure of anything until I have a conversation with Tony and decide the future of our gangs. Until then, everything we discuss here is merely hypothetical.

"Yeah, I hope we at least avoid that—being enemies," I agree, pulling the sheets tighter, a cool breeze causing my entire body to shiver. I notice the window is open, the curtain whooshing gently against the glass.

"As for Oleg, and all that you experienced, I'm afraid that it will never stop haunting you. In your dreams, and sometimes even when you're awake.... The only good thing is that you can rest assured that he will never show up again," Angelo continues, his face serious and somewhat sad, his eyes falling to his hands. "But other than that, you'll have to learn to live with it. And bury it deep within your heart so you can try and get a glimpse of a normal life," he suggests, his voice carrying so much grief that it brings tears to my eyes.

The fact that Angelo is not coating the truth with false hopes and encouragement means a lot to me. He's not trying to make things easier for me, but rather showing me the ugly reality of the life I chose to live. It leaves a sour taste in my mouth, but it's the truth. And I'm thankful he is willing to give me that.

"Thank you." I smile at him, hoping to convey all my feelings with this simple gesture.

"And lastly, about us." He leans forward, grabbing my hands in his. "I'm not going anywhere. We will find a way to be together. No matter how hard it might be, I'm not letting you go."

My smile widens, and I lie down again, comfortably adjusting myself in his embrace.

"I love you," I tell him, letting the warm sensation of feeling safe spread through me.

"I love you more." Angelo cuddles me, his arms keeping me trapped against his hard chest. He places a kiss on my neck, and my entire body shivers, instantly reacting to his touch. His scent invades me, and if I wasn't too exhausted, I'd be all over him after the sweet words he just said to me.

But sleep gets the best of me, and I close my eyes, feeling his skin against mine and his arms keeping me close to him.

If this is what I get to have every night after a tough day, maybe life won't be as hard as I expect. Maybe I can find some common ground, some balance, some sense of safety.

I know Angelo is my safe harbor.

And if I am able to return to him every day, I should be able to find some happiness.

FORTY-TWO

FIRST DAY AS THE BOSS

Tatiana

THE NEXT MORNING, I wake up and Angelo is no longer in bed. I get up, take a shower, put on my most business appropriate suit, beige and tailored, and head downstairs, not sure what I'm going to find.

For the past few days, things have been a bit uneventful for the Saints, who are still at the mansion.

Angelo told me they were waiting for everything to be handled after Oleg's death before they can return to wherever it is they live, but I know he's been keeping everyone here just in case Yakov pulls something and tries to get at me.

I appreciate the gesture, but now that I have accepted my role as head of the Romina Empire, I need to start moving and getting the hang of it all. I can't be babysat forever. What kind of leader would I be if I were?

As soon as I get to the kitchen, I find Angelo leaning against the island, sipping a cup of coffee while talking to Dice, Sal, and Max, who are seated at the table.

"Morning, guys," I greet them, walking inside and heading for the counter to pour some coffee for myself.

Dice nods at me while the other two offer a warm smile. Sal leans back on his chair, drinking through a straw what looks to be iced coffee.

"Moooorning.... What should we call you now? Miss Romina, or maybe something more intimidating, like Boss of the Romina Empire?" he teases, a grin forming on his lips.

"Ha, ha, very funny." I roll my eyes, leaning beside Angelo on the island and facing the others. "You can still call me Tatiana. We can decide on something else if you become my enemy," I joke, glancing sideways at Angelo, who surprisingly seems to be enjoying the exchange between me and his friend. "Did you sleep well?" I ask him, lowering my voice so the others don't listen.

He nods sharply. "Like a baby."

"So, what are the plans now?" Max asks, his curious eyes darting from me to Angelo.

"Well," I begin, "I was thinking I should go see Guskov and the others to officially introduce myself. I also need to figure out where I'm living. I have to hand over the apartment Lev rented in Manhattan, and then I was wondering if I could schedule a meeting with Tony."

I was hoping to tell Angelo about my plans first, but since Max asked and we're all friends here, I don't think there's a problem sharing it with them all.

The three men at the table raise their heads to look at me, but Angelo barely reacts, slightly turning on his heel to face me.

"Sounds like you have a solid plan already," he points out, but there's no judgment in his voice, just maybe surprise. He raises one brow at me inquisitively.

"Yeah, well, unlike you, I didn't sleep very well last night," I inform him. I had so much going on in my head, that after a brief nap,

I woke up and couldn't sleep again. That's why I had time to figure out my next moves.

"Okay, so, does anyone want to update us?" Sal complains, leaning forward, his elbows resting on the table. He's looking at me and Angelo with a frown, clearly confused. Max and Dice are also staring at us, but they are a bit better at hiding their interest.

I clear my throat, glancing at Angelo, wondering if I should tell them or maybe wait for something more concrete. But he encourages me with a sharp nod as if knowing exactly what I'm thinking.

"It's up to you to tell them," he says.

Honestly, if I have made any friends here, they are the three guys looking expectantly at me right now. I think it is only fair that I tell them what is going on and what they can expect from the future.

I walk toward the table and sit opposite them. Angelo quietly joins me, pulling the chair beside me and sitting down in silence.

"I don't even know where to begin," I sigh, taking a deep breath. The coffee in my hand is getting cold, so I take a sip, wetting my mouth and throat that suddenly feel too dry.

"From the start would be nice," Sal adds in a teasing tone. I'm so glad he's so light-hearted and easy to deal with. I'll miss having him around.

"Fine, okay.... I am the new boss of the Romina Empire," I state simply, realizing this might be the hardest bomb I have to throw at them, even though some of them seemed to have already figured it out, so it's better to get that off my chest sooner.

Max chokes on his drink, Sal's jaw drops, and Dice widens his eyes, which is the most facial expression I've ever seen since I met him.

"You what now? For real?" Max asks between coughs.

"Guskov said they voted to have me inherit my father's legacy. It might sound like the worst choice ever. Believe me, I also think that, but it does belong to my family. And I don't want to risk another Oleg showing up and claiming my position," I explain.

They nod slowly, following my line of thought.

"Someone like Yakov, you mean," Dice mumbles, speaking for the first time.

"Exactly."

"Speaking of that motherfucker, do the Rominas have any news on him?" Sal asks.

"That's what I want to know. They didn't know anything last night, but things might have changed overnight. That's why I think we should go." I turn to Angelo. "I'll give Guskov a call and set up a meeting. Are you coming with me?"

"Of course," he agrees, finishing his coffee.

"Wait! What did you mean by having a meeting with our boss? What does he have to do with anything?" Max wants to know.

"I might have a proposition for him, and that's all I can tell you about it for now. Tony has done so much for me by letting me stay with you guys and saving me from Oleg and the Rominas. And you guys too. I feel like I owe you too much." My voice cracks slightly at the end, emotion getting the best of me as I stare at their faces. "I'll be forever grateful."

The three of them clear their throats, putting on a serious face, but I can tell the feelings are mutual.

"Now, come on. If you want to do all of the things you said you want to do today, we should be going," Angelo chimes in, standing from the chair.

An hour later, we're arriving at Manhattan, heading for the penthouse that Guskov said he'd be in. Apparently, it's one of the places he suggested that I live. It's in a great location, in the middle of Manhattan, and close to most of our businesses and our headquarters.

Guskov is waiting for us as soon as we step out of the elevator, right into the middle of the living room. The floor-to-ceiling windows have an amazing view of the city and the Hudson River, and I must confess I'm instantly mesmerized by it.

"Can I assume you like it?" he asks, coming to my side as I stare out the window, watching the city below. For a moment, it feels like I'm almost above the clouds.

"Let's just say I can definitely see myself living in a place like this. It's... so peaceful and beautiful from up here," I murmur, more to myself than anyone else.

Angelo is quiet behind me, but one look at him is enough to tell me he also thinks the place is great. He smiles at me, taking a step forward and placing his hand on my lower back.

"It suits you," he notes.

"I'll stay here," I state bluntly.

"Are you sure? There are at least ten more apartments and houses for you to see," Guskov informs, creasing his brows at me.

I fight the urge to widen my eyes. Of course the Rominas own so much. What was I expecting?

"I-I..." I stammer, clearing my throat and pulling myself together almost immediately. "I'll stay here for now. If I find somewhere I love more in the future, I can move then. There are more important things for me to handle now, other than going around the whole city checking the real estate we own."

"Okay, makes sense," Guskov agrees.

"So, do we have any news?" I change the subject, hoping to hear good news.

"We haven't found Yakov yet." He starts with the bad news. Okay, I guess it isn't today that I'll get *that* good news.

I grimace. "Great," I grunt. "What else?"

"Most of the Romina men decided to stay and have sworn loyalty to you," he carries on. My heart fills with hope and anticipation. Now *that's* good news. Finally. "But... a few have disappeared."

I frown. "Disappeared?"

"Yeah. We think they might have gone to meet Yakov," he explains.

"Let's make sure we find them before they are strong enough to attack us," I order bitterly.

"Yes, Boss."

"Anything else?" I cross my arms in front of my chest, and when I turn to look at the rest of the living room, I spot a portrait of Oleg hanging above the fireplace. The motherfucker who did this managed to paint his eyes so realistically that, for a moment, it's like I'm staring into them again.

I shiver and grab the gun I'm carrying around in my purse now. Before Guskov has the chance to continue with his report, I aim for the painting and shoot at it. Surprisingly, I hit exactly the middle of Oleg's head.

"Get rid of that immediately," I snarl under my breath. "And any other that might be around."

"Of course, Boss. Consider that done. I hadn't given it much attention. Sorry," Guskov apologizes, bowing to me.

"It's fine. You were saying...?" I encourage him to continue, turning my back on the portrait.

Glancing at Angelo, I see him smirking at me, but he doesn't say a word.

"We got rid of the mansion," Guskov continues.

"Good. I want to have a meeting with the men to introduce myself officially. You also need to update me on the deals and businesses we have, so we should schedule another meeting this week."

Guskov nods sharply. "Okay. I'll have all of that settled. And I'll get this penthouse ready for you to move in as soon as possible."

"Thank you, Guskov," I say warmly.

He exits the apartment, leaving Angelo and me alone.

"I sent a message to Tony, and he's in town for a meeting. He said he should be free in an hour to meet you," he informs me, raising his eyebrows at me. "Can I set up the meeting?"

"Absolutely."

FORTY-THREE
A BOLD PROPOSAL

Tatiana

AN HOUR LATER, Tony arrives at the apartment Lev rented. I decided to set up the meeting here since it's private, safer, and away from curious eyes. I also need to get my stuff from the apartment before I contact the landlord, so it'd be easier for me.

Tony shows up at the door, wearing a black, tailored suit, his dark hair styled backward with gel, and his blue eyes set on me. He's a fine man, but also intimidating. Or maybe I am just nervous about the conversation we're about to have. I wasn't afraid when I asked him to participate in the mission to Oleg's mansion, but now I suddenly feel unsure of myself.

"Miss Romina, it's good to see you," he greets me, offering me his hand.

I grab it, hoping he doesn't notice how nervous I am. At least I'm not shaking.

"Angelo," he adds with a nod, noticing his capo leaning against the window with his arms crossed.

"Good afternoon, Mr. Bellini," I reply, closing the door behind us once he steps inside the apartment.

"Let's drop the formalities," he suggests, turning on his heel to face me. "I think we've been through a lot together already."

I smile at him. "Yeah, sure. I agree. Take a seat, please. I'll get us some coffee."

I head for the kitchen, which is basically in the same room since this apartment is so small, and Tony and Angelo engage in a discussion about whatever it is the Saints have going on in Staten Island. I focus on the task at hand, not wanting to eavesdrop or invade their privacy, even though they are not being very subtle with the volume of their voices.

After pouring three mugs of black coffee, I return to the living room and set their drinks on the coffee table. Tony is already seated on the couch, Angelo is in the same place as before, and I sit on the armchair across from them.

"All right, I must admit I'm intrigued with this conversation, Tatiana," he starts with a smile, leaning forward and grabbing one of the mugs. "Of course, I've already heard about the news and I assume I should congratulate you?" It comes out more as a question than a statement. He seems curious, his brows raised, and I understand why he's unsure of how I feel. He doesn't know the details of how I became the new leader of the Romina Empire, so he can't know this was my decision, even if it was voted by the capos.

"Yeah, well, I can't say it was in my plans, but..." I shrug, sipping from my coffee. The hot liquid spreads through my chest as I swallow, wrapping me in a cozy and comfortable feeling. "The Rominas voted for their new leader, and surprisingly, they wanted me. I wasn't sure I should accept it, but it is my father's legacy after all. And to be honest, I couldn't imagine someone like Yakov putting his hands on so much power."

Tony nods sharply. "I couldn't agree more. It was a clever choice. And I think you'll be fine. It certainly runs in the family, and if what

I saw back at the mansion was any indication of what you're capable of, I can tell the Romina Empire is finally in good hands."

I wasn't expecting to feel emotional today, but Tony's words hit somewhere deep in my heart. Maybe that's what I've been needing–some validation, someone like him, who runs the biggest mob in New York, to acknowledge my potential.

"Thank you. So..." I shift in my seat, anxiety creeping up on me. "I was talking to Angelo, and I wanted to propose something to you."

He leans backward on the couch, stretching his arm along the backrest, and crossing one leg over his knee. "I'm listening," he encourages me to proceed.

"I know the Saints and the Romina Empire have been enemies for decades, but I was thinking... how would you feel about a merger?"

"A merger?" Tony repeats, clearly intrigued now. He has straightened his back, setting both feet on the floor and resting his elbows on his knees as he stares at me.

"Yes." I nod firmly, glad I was able to grab his attention. "We saw how that worked at the mission to get rid of Oleg. And now that I'm running it, I really think we'd be great allies. We are responsible for neighboring territories, and as far as I know, we also deal with the same type of businesses. We could expand them, even internationally, since I have my men in Russia too."

"The Saints and the Romina Empire? Sounds impossible," Tony mutters to himself, but I can almost see the wheels turning inside his head.

Angelo is still quiet, his jaw set as he watches our exchange. He doesn't chime in or make any moves, knowing this is a decision only his boss can make. I can tell he's nervous though, the way his fists are clenched at his sides.

"Let's make history, Tony. We can be great allies. It wouldn't be the first time that two gangs put their differences aside to become greater, more powerful," I press, hoping my determination will be enough to convince him. "I also am humble enough to acknowledge I have a lot to learn, and I'd be happy if I could learn from someone like you. And Angelo. It'd mean a lot if I could have you by my side, showing me the way. I know this is not all it takes, but..." I take a deep breath, realizing I'm starting to ramble. "What I mean is that I don't want to be away from Angelo. And I'd never ask him to choose between me and you guys. And not only that, but I honestly think the Saints and the Rominas can build something great together, putting all the animosity behind us. We have so much more to gain from this than if we remain enemies."

"I see your point," Tony says slowly, his eyes set on me. "I can't say that doesn't sound like a great proposition, but there's so much to discuss before making that big of a decision. There's a lot of businesses and deals involved, conflicts of interest—"

"That will turn into a shared interest," I cut him off. "We split our profits fifty-fifty. Everyone wins. We double our task force, cover more ground, expand our networking...."

A deafening silence follows, and I decide to give Tony some time to consider my offer. It is indeed a big decision to make, and I don't want to force him into accepting or declining it because I'm too impatient.

One glance at Angelo is all it takes for me to calm myself. His eyes are soft as he stares at me. It's almost as if they can talk to me and reassure me all will be fine. That only makes me love him more. Even though he's also unsure of what will happen to us in case Tony rejects my proposal, he's still trying to make me feel secure and calm.

"You know what?" Tony finally speaks, and I shift my gaze to him. He has a small smile on his lips, his eyes looking playfully at me. "I think you're right. Becoming allies would be very profitable for both of us. Of course, we'll need to figure out how to deal with everything, and who's responsible for what, but I'm sure we can manage everything after a couple of meetings."

Excitement washes over me as I take his words.

"We have a deal then?" I ask, not wanting to make assumptions.

"We have a deal," Tony confirms, stretching his hand in my

direction.

I hold it as fast as humanly possible, afraid he'll change his mind if I don't. It's just a handshake, but I learned this means a lot in our world. So do our words.

"That's great! I'm looking forward to working with you," I add, glancing at Angelo for a quick second. We will have time to celebrate this later, but just seeing how relieved he also seems is enough to make me feel like I just got rid of a huge weight.

There's still so much to do, and the hard work is just beginning, but knowing I'll have Angelo and the rest of the Saints beside me is all the reassurance I need.

"Well, I look forward to working with you too," Tony repeats, getting to his feet and adjusting his blazer. "I have to run now, but Angelo–" He turns to his capo. "Make sure to set up a meeting with Tatiana and all the capos, from both gangs, as soon as possible."

As soon as Tony is out of the door, I run toward Angelo and jump on him, wrapping my legs around his waist and pulling him into a deep kiss.

"We did it," I murmur against his lips, pulling away just enough to get some air.

His hands are on my ass as he supports me, and the sexiest grin forms on his lips.

"We did it," he repeats, his voice slightly hoarse. His eyes darken as he stares at my mouth, and a wave of excitement mixed with arousal invades me as I realize what just happened.

This man is mine.

And we'll be able to be together.

Without a second thought, I crash our lips together once more, not caring about a single thing in the world other than the two of us. Everything else can just wait.

"Wanna enjoy the apartment a bit more before I have to hand it over?" I suggest when he starts lowering his kisses down to my throat.

"I absolutely do," he replies, nibbling at the sensitive skin under my ear and causing a shiver to run down to my core.

FORTY-FOUR
BLISSFUL

Tatiana

ANGELO TURNS us and presses my back against the cold brick wall of the living room. His kisses slide down my neck to my collarbone, and I tilt my head backward, the delightful feeling of his lips on my skin threatening to burst me into flames.

A soft moan escapes me as his fingers dig deeper into my ass. Heat pools at my core, and my fingers curl into his shirt as I hold onto him with all my might, anchoring myself to him. He presses his hips against mine, and I grind against him, wanting more, needing more.

A groan comes from deep in his throat as his grip on me tightens, and he holds me against the wall with the weight of his body as his hands start roaming up my shirt and reaching my breasts.

My back arches instantly as his fingers graze my nipples from under my bra.

I suddenly feel overdressed.

"Wait. I need to get rid of this blazer," I murmur breathlessly.

Struggling with myself, I try to focus on removing the blazer while Angelo's hands explore my body. Needless to say, this is a fucking hard task.

The blazer falls somewhere near his feet, but I don't bother to look. There are still too many layers between us, and it's annoying.

With precise skill, Angelo unbuttons my blouse in the blink of an eye, leaving me in my bra, tailored pants, and the pumps I decided to wear this morning to look presentable.

"I need to say this is a very sexy bra, but I will have to get rid of that too," he tells me at the same time he unclasps it. I help him slide it down my arms, but before I have the chance to do anything else, his mouth closes over my aroused nipple, nibbling and sucking at it as if he's starving and I have just offered him a full meal.

His hand grabs the other breast, his thumb flicking at it, making me delirious with need.

I can feel my soaked panties, and I need some friction to get rid of this pent-up energy threatening to explode inside me.

His member is hard against my core, and I rub myself on it, even through the fabric of our clothes.

"You're so fucking hot, baby," he murmurs against my breast, his hot breath fanning against my skin and giving me chills. My fingers thread through his hair as I keep his head in my chest, my ankles locking behind him so he doesn't get away from me.

I'm on the edge of losing my mind. I can't stand the idea of him getting away from me now, not even by an inch.

"I also have to say, you're sexy as hell as a boss, you know that?" he continues, his voice raspy as he massages my breast, rolling his hips forward against mine.

"Is that so?" I murmur, my breathing sharp and erratic. I slide a hand between us, down his abs, and grab his cock from over his pants, squeezing it lightly. "What if I start giving you orders then? Will you find it sexy too?"

"Hell yeah," he replies under his breath, staring up at me with his dark eyes.

"Good, because I need you to solve a little problem for me. Down here." I press his dick against my core. "But we're still overdressed."

"I'll fix that for you... Boss." He smirks, setting me down on the floor and quickly unbuttoning my pants. It drops to my ankles and I step out of it, kicking it away. His eyes scan me from head to toe, watching me only in my panties and heels. "Fuck... now that's a view."

I raise my brows at him, gesturing with my head to his clothes. He pulls up his shirt and shoves it over his shoulder, and I help him remove his pants and boxers.

"Up or down?" he asks me with that sexy grin.

I don't bother answering him, pushing him backward until he falls on the couch. I pull my panties down my legs before straddling his lap. His hands instantly grab my ass and pull me forward against him.

"Shit..." he murmurs, his eyes fluttering shut and his head falling back as I buckle my hips against him, my slickness sliding against his hard shaft.

His grip on me tightens, but I can't keep teasing him like this. The aching in my core is getting unbearable. If I keep this going much longer, I risk finishing before he enters me.

"What do you want me to do, baby?" I ask in a low voice, teasing him with my slow and deliberate moves against his tip.

His eyes find mine, wild and hungry, his control hanging by a thread.

"I want you to ride me until you can't feel your legs anymore. I want you to come undone around me. I want to hear you moan my name." His fingers find my folds and slide up and down, massaging me exactly where I'm aching the most for him.

His thumb circles over my clit and I squirm under his touch, grinding against his hand.

"You like that?" he whispers, adding more pressure to his maddening movements.

"Fuck yeah, I do," I reply. Heat consumes me, and I'm on the verge of getting out of control. Every fiber of my being is sensitive to his touch. I bite my lip, preventing a moan from escaping.

"Don't hold it in. Just moan for me, baby," he orders, speeding up. My vision starts to blur as I finally let out a groan.

"Shit, this is so good."

He inserts two fingers inside me, and all of my self-control goes to hell. I roll my hips, needing some release. When he pulls his fingers out of me, I don't give him time to think of his next move.

Placing my hands on his sculpted chest, I rise from his lap, only to sink down on him, taking him inch by inch. My walls stretch to accommodate him as he fills me up completely. I allow myself a second to adjust to his length and start moving, setting the rhythm I need to catch on fire.

A cry escapes me as I feel that strong energy coursing through my veins, every cell alight. He grips my thighs, watching me ride him as if my life depends on it.

"That's right, baby," he grunts, his voice rough, his self-control slipping too as he shudders beneath me.

Pure pleasure rips through me as he bucks his hips up into me, harder, his thrust growing clumsier and out of pace. His lips crash into mine once more, desperate, his tongue exploring every inch of my mouth.

His hands are everywhere—gripping my waist, my ass, my breasts—touching me as if he needs to feel me completely to keep himself from falling apart.

The coil inside my belly tightens, but I don't want this to end yet.

Breaking the kiss, I rise from his lap just enough to leave just the tip of him inside me, then I slide back down with a swift movement.

"Fuck, Tatiana. Don't do that or I'll..." He trails off, his words strangled in his throat as I repeat the movement a couple more times.

"Just fuck me, baby, and let's finish this together," I suggest, letting go of the last thread of control I was holding onto.

Angelo smirks at me, a wicked smile playing on his lips, and I allow him to finally take charge. He slides one arm behind my back and pulls me down against him, sinking deeper into me and hitting the most sensitive spot so far.

I gasp and sink my nails into his shoulders as his name blurts out of my mouth in a loud moan.

"Like that?" he taunts proudly against my ear.

I can't find the words to reply to him, finally taking that step into the abyss.

Angelo twitches inside me, and I close my eyes, just letting joy consume me entirely.

"You're perfect," he whispers as we both try to steady our breathing, then he places a soft, quick kiss on my nose.

I lean my forehead against his, feeling like the happiest woman on Earth.

"I love you," I say in response, unable to keep all the emotion flowing through my body to myself.

"I love you too, baby."

FORTY-FIVE
TIME OFF

Tatiana

"SO, what do you want to do now?" Angelo asks me as soon as we step out of the building. I've just returned the apartment key to the landlord, and even though I didn't even spend a whole day inside this place, it still feels somewhat bittersweet to say goodbye to it, knowing Lev was the one who rented it in the first place.

The suitcase he left with all the blueprints and documents regarding Oleg had been taken to the Saints' safe house when we were preparing for our mission, so there wasn't really anything left for me to take.

I still feel like I'm leaving a part of Lev behind, and it makes my heart shrink in my chest as I stare at Angelo.

"I'm not really sure," I tell him honestly. "I need to meet with my men. It can't wait any longer, especially if we're all going to meet with the Saints soon for the merger," I explain, following him to his car.

"Okay. What about now, though? Are you hungry?" he asks,

raising his eyebrows at me over the roof of the car, from the other side.

"Actually, I am," I answer, realizing I could definitely eat something before I call Guskov to see if he's set up the meeting.

Angelo drives us to a restaurant in Soho, and I order the most delicious pasta I've eaten in a long time.

Angelo and I share ideas on how I want to decorate the penthouse and when I plan to move in.

"If Guskov has it ready by tomorrow, maybe I could go the day after," he says. "I have so much to catch up on, I'm afraid I won't have much free time this week."

I pout slightly.

Angelo chuckles, reaching for my hand over the table. He squeezes it lightly and smiles at me.

"Baby, I'm pretty sure that's going to be your routine from now on," he points out. There's a hint of amusement in his voice, but I know him too well by now and notice the sadness behind it. It will definitely be different for us moving forward. "We won't have that much time together, at least not during the day anyway."

I nod slowly. "Yeah, I know. But you're going to sleep with me every night, won't you?"

"You mean when we're both not working?" he adds with a grin on his lips.

I grunt, rolling my eyes. "Is it too late for me to give up on everything and just travel around the world with you?" I joke.

Of course I don't mean it, but I just want to have a day where I don't have to worry about anything for a change. And thinking of traveling with Angelo without a care in the world sounds like a dream now.

He looks at me from across the table, his eyes darkening and his expression turning serious.

"Are you having second thoughts?" he pries, confused.

"No, I was just kidding. I.... You know why I did all of this. And I don't regret it. It's just... I'm realizing how hard it will be for us to be together moving forward. I am glad we managed to find a way to do it, though." I squeeze his hand tighter.

Angelo's shoulders relax, and he lets go of my hand, leaning back on the chair.

"Let's not talk about any of that for now. If you need some time off before hell breaks loose again, I'm giving you that. What do you want to do with the rest of your day?"

"I can't do anything, baby. I need to meet with the guys, remember?" I remind him.

"You can reschedule the meeting for the evening. Let's just enjoy a few more hours together, and I'll drop you at the penthouse before I have to go back to Staten Island."

I consider his suggestion. Maybe I can spare a few hours before having to formally start my obligations as the new head of the Romina Empire.

"All right," I finally agree. "Do you have any suggestions? I'm not sure what I want to do. Maybe you could take me around the city so I can properly meet New York? I haven't really had the chance to have a city tour ever since I got here. And I'll need to know my way around now that I'll be living here."

Excitement washes over me as I realize this is my new home.

I'm staying here for good.

I still need to figure out what I'll do with my house in Russia, but I can think about that later. One step at a time, so I don't get overwhelmed, I tell myself.

For now, a walk around New York City on this sunny day with Angelo by my side sounds like everything I need to feel refreshed and ready for a new start.

After he insists on paying for the bill, we step out of the restaurant and start walking around town. He shows me all the nice restaurants he loves, walks me through the cool parks around the city, especially Central Park, which I had been dying to see, and then we stop for an ice cream close to the Brooklyn Bridge.

Observing the view of the river ahead of me, I allow myself a moment to think of everything that happened that led me to this moment with Angelo. My life turned upside down from the moment I decided to follow Lev and Ilya to the United States. I lost them in the most traumatizing way, was kidnapped and almost forced to marry a man I hate, and, going against everything I believed would happen, I fell in love. I met Angelo and became part of his life in the most unusual way possible.

I can't imagine my life without him now.

"Life can be so unpredictable," I muse to myself, keeping my focus on the sun setting and casting the most beautiful golden rays on the water and the concrete buildings. But I know Angelo is listening when I see him turning to face me from my peripheral vision. "To imagine all I went through, all you went through, to get to this moment of our lives..."

He considers my words and nods slowly, returning his attention to the landscape before us.

"Would you change any of it?" he asks, his voice low and distant.

I exhale, considering everything this simple question implies.

Would I change the fact that I lost Lev and Ilya? Yes.

Would I change the fact that I killed Oleg? No.

But if anything had gone differently, would I have met Angelo? Would fate find a way to put us on the same path if anything had been different?

"Maybe," I reply honestly. "If I could, I would prevent my parents from dying, but then would we have met? Is it selfish to want it all?" I chuckle sadly, feeling slightly confused by my feelings and thoughts.

"I know what you mean. I don't think it's selfish. I think it's human of you to want everything that makes you happy," he reassures, smiling softly at me.

My eyes fill with tears, and I wrap my arms around his waist, feeling him pull me into a tight embrace. We stay like this for a few more minutes, and I lay my head on his chest, feeling his heartbeat and somehow letting it calm my racing heart.

"We should be grateful for one thing, though," I say suddenly after a long moment of silence between us. "We both found a partner in each other to share the adventures of this crazy world. It makes me feel less burdened to know you'll be here with me for this shitty ride," I point out.

Angelo hums against me, his chest vibrating against me. "I never thought I'd be able to have that, so I never dared to even dream of it. I am so lucky that you found me and decided I was worthy of you. It still seems insane to me when I think about it."

"You're more than worthy of it. And technically, you found me," I tease, getting on my tiptoes and placing a soft kiss on his lips. "Never thought I'd be grateful for being kidnapped." I pull away from his embrace and adjust my coat, raising my chin and putting on a serious face. "Now, I have a meeting to attend. Can you give me that ride you promised?"

"Sure can, ma'am." He leans down for another kiss and grabs my hand so we can walk side by side to the car.

As he drives to my new home, I prepare myself for what I'm about to face.

This will be my first meeting with the Rominas, and I need to make a good impression. They all decided to stay because they believe in me and somehow expect me to follow in my father's footsteps.

That's a lot of responsibility, but I force myself to be confident.

I can do it.

I am the daughter of Petr Romina, after all.

It's in my blood.

And I will make him proud of me.

FORTY-SIX
THE ROMINAS

Tatiana

MY HEART IS POUNDING SO hard and fast that I can hear the blood pumping in my veins as I ride the elevator to my penthouse. Angelo offered to come with me, but I didn't think it was a good idea.

This is my first meeting with the men who chose to follow me as their leader. Having a chaperone wouldn't give me the image of a leader they would be proud of—someone confident, strong, and reliable. And that's the exact image I want to give them tonight.

I know the reason why they voted for me has everything to do with who my father was rather than my skills, but I intend to make them proud of their decision. I want to be a leader they can rely on. I want to be someone they think it's worth risking their lives to protect every day.

When the elevator door opens to the living room, I am speechless and shocked by the number of people I see inside my new apartment. The place is packed, from left to right, not to mention the stairs, the balcony, and the second floor, with men dressed in black, all looking at me expectantly as I step inside.

Holy shit, there must be at least 500 people here.

All because they want me to be their new boss.

No pressure, I tell myself as I prepare to greet them.

Some of their faces are slightly familiar. I remember them from the time I spent at Oleg's mansion when he kidnapped me. They hadn't been mean to me back then, but even if they had, they'd have had no choice other than to follow the orders of their leader.

I wouldn't hold any of it against them.

Laura, the maid who was nice to me during that time, is here too, in the corner along with several other maids. Even they decided to come.

My heart fills with pride and gratitude for them, and I fight back the lump forming in my throat.

"Good evening, everyone," I finally greet them, speaking loudly so everyone can hear me.

They all bow their heads in my direction, and I need to hide my surprised face. I know they have their formalities, but it still feels odd to see them be directed at me.

I spot Guskov leaning against the wall across from me. He gives me a reassuring nod, and I notice a kind glint in his eyes and a small smile on the corner of his lips.

I'm so glad to have him as my right-hand. Knowing he was friends with my father only makes me more trusting of him.

"First of all, I want to thank you all for being here tonight. I can assume it wasn't an easy decision to make, but I want you to know how grateful I am for your vote of confidence," I carry on, my gaze roaming around the room so I can take in the faces of everyone I must treat as my family from now on.

It will take me some time to get to know all their names, but I'll do my best so they all feel special.

"For years, you've been working for a guy whose only goal was money and power. He never cared about anyone other than himself. He took everything from me—my parents, my freedom, my life... but this is going to change. You're my new family now. And yes, there will be major changes in the future, but I want to assure you that you'll be my priority too."

I can imagine some of them—if not most—won't take lightly the idea of merging with the Saints. It's been rooted in them to hate them as enemies for years, so this will be news I deliver in another moment. For now, I want them to see me as a better boss than Oleg ever was.

"Changes are not always welcome, but I want to make things better for the Romina Empire. And I'll be counting on you to help me along the way. I do have a lot to learn, and I will need some time to catch up with everything. But, if you need anything, please feel free to come and talk to me."

Applause erupts around me, so loud that it almost deafens me. I try to fight the smile forming on my lips, but end up failing. My eyes are filled with tears as I stare at every one of their faces, their eyes eager for a new perspective in life.

I don't know what led each of these people to be a part of this gang, but I want them to feel appreciated.

"Guskov will be my right hand, so you can talk to him whenever I'm not accessible. We will have a lot to deal with for the next few days, but most importantly, our main goal is to find Yakov and make sure he doesn't come after us, seeking revenge," I inform them, starting to pace around the room. The energy running through my system is starting to become too much for me to be able to stand still.

"Anyone who has any information on where he might be or what he might be planning, please tell us and we'll investigate." I offer a small smile to Laura as I pass by her, and focus back on the others. "I'll also have bigger news to share with you all, but for now, I need you to be prepared in case we need to go after Yakov."

"Yes, Boss!" they all shout in unison.

"Is there anything you want to share or address before I let you go for tonight?" I ask, staring at them, stopping close to the entrance once again.

Silence fills the room, and they all remain in the same position, their arms locked behind their backs and their chins raised.

Guskov steps forward, with his arms also behind his back, but in a more relaxed posture than the rest of the men. He comes toward me and stops by my side.

"I just want to speak for all of us when I say we are here to offer our lives for the mission of serving the Romina Empire and our leader," he begins, his voice firm and serious. I can still see the kindness behind his gaze, and it astonishes me that I can already read him so easily, even though we met only a few days ago.

The men shout in agreement and I feel my heart flood with a mix of emotions I can't interpret. I feel slightly overwhelmed with their loyalty, and it only makes me more eager to prove myself worthy of it.

"Thank you so much, Guskov. And all of you," I address the rest of the room. "I will schedule another meeting with you all soon. I just need to get informed about everything we have going on, so I ask for your understanding and patience while I do so. But as I said, my door will be open for any of you if and when you need me," I conclude.

I take a deep breath, trying to steady my racing heart as they all start applauding me again. They don't move out of their professional posture, but some of them risk whistling and cheering.

I let the widest smile spread across my face, showing them my soft side. I may not have the chance to do so moving forward, but I want them to see I'm a human being before a cold boss.

Slowly, they all start moving out of the apartment. Since there's only one elevator, it takes them a long time to empty the room. As they wait, they come to me to introduce themselves personally. They all reinforce their vows of loyalty toward me and the Romina Empire, and I take the opportunity to get to know them, asking some personal questions like how they ended up here and if they have any complaints.

Of course I don't have time to get too deep with any of them now, but at least now they know the path is clear for them to come to me at any time.

Guskov is the last one, and when there's no one else in the room but us, he comes to me.

"So, big news, huh?" he pries, and it occurs to me that he should be the first one to know before I tell the others. If Guskov is truly going to be my right hand, I need to be open with him about everything related to our empire.

"Everything happened so fast that I didn't have the chance to tell you my plans earlier," I say in an apologetic tone. I sit down on the couch and gesture for him to do the same, but he chooses an armchair across from me instead. "I had a meeting with Antony Bellini earlier today. I made a proposition to him, and he accepted. We're going to merge with the Saints."

Guskov blinks, staring at me in silence.

"I know this is shocking, but I honestly think it's a good opportunity for us to cover more ground in the city. Not to mention that the Saints are the biggest gang in the state of New York. You saw how well we fought together to take down Oleg," I press, trying to give him reasons to believe and support my idea.

"I see your point, and I think it can work. It might take some time to adjust, though," he finally says after a moment in silence. I was expecting him to disagree with me, but I'm glad he didn't. I wouldn't know what else to do to convince him.

"It will work," I assure him with a sharp nod. "I will need your help with everything, Guskov. And I need that to happen as fast as possible. I don't want to be caught by surprise by Yakov."

"Absolutely, Boss."

But, in the end, being caught by surprise is exactly what happens when I wake up the next morning.

There are several missed calls from Angelo and Tony on my phone, and when I open the last text message, I jump out of bed.

The sun is not even out yet, and I'm already being tested.

'Call me as soon as you see this message,' Angelo's message urges. 'Some of our guys were ambushed last night. It's Yakov.'

FORTY-SEVEN
RUSHED

Tatiana

YAKOV HAS FINALLY MADE A MOVE.

I was kind of expecting him to be a coward and just vanish from the world, start over somewhere where he isn't known, or any shit like that.

But he didn't. I have to at least give him credit for not going down without a fight.

As soon as I see Angelo's text, I call him back.

"Finally," he blurts as soon as he picks up. "I'm on my way to get you. Tony has requested the merger meeting to happen as soon as possible," he adds, not allowing me to say anything.

I planned for it to be a bit more organized than this, so I could prepare the Rominas first, but I can't refuse it. We need to come up with a plan to get to Yakov immediately. I'm quickly learning things don't always happen the way I want, even as the boss, which leaves me frustrated.

"Inform Guskov and tell them to bring everyone to the address

I'm sending you now," he instructs me, hanging up on me right after. I didn't even have a chance to speak.

I text Guskov the address and ask him to prepare everyone for a meeting with the Saints. I don't have time to explain anything else other than that.

I rush to put on some clothes and pull my hair up into a ponytail, and my phone buzzes with another message from Angelo.

'I'm here.'

I grab my purse and head for the door, double-checking whether I have everything I need with me. Now that I'm the head of the Romina Empire, I need to bring my gun with me everywhere. I put some knives in my purse as well just as reassurance. Even if I have my men with me, I still need to be able to defend myself if needed.

I'd be lying if I said I'm not at all nervous.

I'm in the dark when it comes to the reaction expected from both the Rominas and the Saints. I don't think they see any of this coming since Tony and I didn't have a chance to tell them beforehand.

I can only hope things will go smoothly. If anything, whoever disagrees with me can simply walk away. No one is forced to stay here, and this will be their last chance to leave before my leadership with Tony is officially established.

Walking out of the elevator, I stride across the lobby of the building, spotting Angelo's car by the entrance. I climb inside and give him a quick kiss on the lips.

"What really happened?" I ask as soon as he drives onto the streets.

"Max and a few other men were ambushed in one of our casinos in Harlem last night. There was another attack at the same time in one of our warehouses in Newark. Several guns were stolen," he informs me seriously, his jaw clenched and his eyes hard on the road ahead.

"Was anyone hurt?"

My stomach drops to my feet as I see him grimacing slightly.

"Max was shot. It wasn't pretty, but he will survive. He won't be able to fight for a while, though."

Shit, Max must be feeling terrible.

"I'm glad he's alive." My mind is in overdrive as I try to think of what we can do to get Yakov. "Do we have any idea of where Yakov went or how he caught them by surprise?"

Angelo shakes his head. "He has probably had some info on us for a long time. He took the opportunity to attack us, although we should have been prepared. We knew he was on the loose. I don't know what happened," he tells me honestly.

I nod but remain silent, deciding to keep my questions for myself. Maybe Tony will have more information to share.

Angelo takes us to a Saints safe house in Manhattan. I'm glad we didn't have to ride to Staten Island. Otherwise, I'd be biting my nails the entire way.

This house, different from the one I stayed in, is smaller on the inside, but has a bigger external area, which makes it easy to accommodate everyone in the same place.

Tony is already waiting for me in the garden, and in front of him, all his men are organized in lines. Guskov and the Rominas arrive at the same time as Angelo and I do, and they follow us inside. He sets my men beside Tony's, and it doesn't go unnoticed by me the way they all exchange confused glances between themselves.

"Morning," Tony greets them in a loud voice as soon as I join him. "I know most of you are not understanding what we're doing together, but Tatiana and I have some news to share. It might not be good news for everyone, but I can guarantee you that it is the best thing that's happened to us."

He's being enigmatic, and I appreciate that he's preparing them for the blow.

"We're merging both gangs. This might come across as something crazy, delusional even, but I ask you to give us both a vote of confidence, trusting that we're doing the best thing for the Saints and the Romina Empire," he carries on, his voice firm while his eyes roam over the army of men standing in front of us. We get murmurs and widened eyes in response, but Tony doesn't let that stop him from talking.

"As for the Saints, I ask you to treat Tatiana and the Rominas with the respect you've always afforded me, since she is now also your boss. I'm sure this will be a successful partnership," Tony concludes his motivational speech and gestures for me to take the lead.

I thank him and turn my attention to the others, focusing on my guys at first.

"I stand by everything Tony just said. I also ask the Rominas to keep the mutual respect between us, no matter our differences. We're no longer enemies, and no matter what happened in the past, I'm sure we can all put it behind us so we can focus on our future," I begin firmly.

"This alliance will grant us all new territories, but most importantly, it will send a message to the mafia world that this city belongs to us. We're a united front now, and whoever dares to cross us will have to face the Saints and the Romina Empire together. We'll be unstoppable," I encourage them. "I reinforce Tony's plea for your trust in us as we adjust to this new scenario. But most importantly, I want you to know that we're all going to be a big family now. We should count on each other and make sure we have each other's backs."

Shouts and cheers come from the crowd in front of us. Tony and I allow them a moment to express themselves, but when things seem to be getting out of hand, with a few of them getting overly excited and suggesting a celebration in one of the Saints' bars, Tony gestures for them to be silent again.

"I know you want to celebrate and get to know one another, but the celebration will have to be postponed. As some of you already know, the Saints were ambushed last night by Yakov Romina. One of ours was hurt, but thankfully, we didn't have any losses. However, Yakov managed to get his hands on several powerful weapons. We don't know what his plans are, so we need to prepare for a potential attack," he informs them, his voice cold and angry.

Angelo is standing on my right, in the back, blending in with the tall trees on the edge of the garden alongside Guskov. They are both watching the scene, but have decided to keep their distance to give us the space we need to address everyone.

However, when our eyes meet, I can see the spark of pride reflecting in them, and it gives me the strength and incentive that I need to keep going.

Someone in the middle of the crowd raises his hand.

"What is the plan?" he shouts.

I don't recognize him, so I assume he must be one of the Saints, but since I still don't know all my men, I can't be sure.

Before Tony or I have the chance to reply, another man rushes toward us and hands me a piece of paper. I thank him with a nod and open it, unsure of what to expect. If he had to deliver whatever message in the middle of our meeting, it must be urgent.

Tony leans over my shoulder to read it with me, and my blood freezes as my eyes scan the words written in a rushed calligraphy.

'Yakov was spotted near the docks. We think he might be hiding in one of the Rominas' old warehouses in the port.'

The teams trying to track Yakov have finally found a lead on where he might be.

I lift my gaze up to Tony, whose lips have turned into a thin line. His jaw is tense, and his eyes darken as he stares back at me.

"Looks like we finally got the motherfucker," he muses.

Adrenaline pumps through me, and a grin starts forming on my lips.

"Let's fucking get him then."

FORTY-EIGHT
THE WAREHOUSE

Angelo

WATCHING TATIANA BESIDE TONY, addressing the Saints and the Rominas, fills my heart with pride. I know deep down she is nervous, but she seems so comfortable that it's hard to believe she wasn't born for this.

It's definitely in her blood, and I must admit the role fits her perfectly.

I don't think I'll ever be at ease with her being in such a dangerous position, but since I can't do anything about it, I can only be thankful that she has this many people around her to help and protect her.

It soothes my heart a little.

Everyone seems to have accepted the merger, although I can see a few men still a bit hesitant about it, glancing at each other unsurely. But if I were to guess, it'll be just a matter of time until Tatiana and Tony can prove they made the best decision.

When Johnny comes rushing toward them and delivers a piece of paper to Tatiana, I know something is up. He's been in charge of the teams we have on the streets looking for Yakov and any of his minions.

I glance at Guskov and take a step forward while Tatiana and Tony read the message.

"Do you think they found something?" he asks me quietly.

I shrug, unsure of what to think.

"All right, everyone. We got news sooner than expected," Tony announces, straightening up and addressing all of us again. Tatiana is tense beside him, but I can see that glint of excitement in her eyes. She is ready to fight. "Yakov was found. Apparently, he's been hiding in the docks."

"Guskov," Tatiana calls, and the man beside me heads to the front of the garden where she's standing. "Do we have an old warehouse there? Is it possible to check and see if it's been used by someone over the past few days?"

Guskov nods sharply, already grabbing his phone from his pocket.

"I'll give them a call."

He walks to the side of the house, and we're all eager to hear his answer. My adrenaline has already kicked in, and I can't wait to get some action. The longer we wait, the easier it will be for Yakov to go missing again.

We can't let that happen.

Silence envelops our surroundings as we wait for Guskov to return with information. When he does, I notice I've been holding my breath this entire time.

"There seems to be movement in the docks, Boss. They didn't see Yakov specifically, so I asked them to check the surveillance cameras and give me a call. This might take a while," he informs her, looking at Tatiana.

"I suggest we end this tonight," she says. "Let's get prepared for an attack. If we get the green light, we won't have to waste time thinking of a plan." There's not a hint of hesitation in her eyes or voice.

"I agree. Let's plan a coordinated attack. We need to make sure we leave no loose ends," Tony adds from beside her.

When the sun sets, we're all headed to the docks. Guskov said it was confirmed that Yakov was hiding in the old warehouse, and as planned, we are all prepared, equipped from head to toe.

Tatiana and I drive in the same car, following the others in a convoy. We don't exchange any words other than going through our plan over and over. We park the car a few miles away from the warehouse and move in through the shadows of the containers piled throughout the docks.

It's hard to have a clear vision for an attack, but since we checked the cameras, we know some strategic places we can stay hidden and shoot from without being hit.

"Let's go," Tatiana orders through the earpiece device. "No mercy—and don't get hurt," she adds in conclusion.

I don't say anything, following her closely, holding my gun in front of me. Tatiana does the same, slowly moving forward.

TATIANA

WITH A BANG, Sal and Guskov kick the door of the warehouse open.

A wave of men storm inside, pointing their guns at whoever shows up in our way and taking them out with calculated shots.

I waste no time striding inside, my eyes searching for that one familiar face. I don't worry about protecting myself, knowing Angelo and the others have me covered. I told them I wanted to handle Yakov myself, and they easily granted me that wish.

I will have another death to my account, but I should start getting used to it. It will surely not be the last.

Knowing I'll be the one to put Yakov under the ground, just like I did with his father, sort of gives me a feeling of satisfaction I can't deny.

My eyes roam through the dark place, watching as people engage in fights, dodging punches, kicking, and shooting at each other.

That's when I see a pair of widened eyes staring back at me from behind a desk. It's dark and distant, but I'd have recognized them anywhere. My stomach churns and bile threatens to climb up my throat, and I know I'm right—the visceral reaction confirms my eyesight. Yakov.

I wasn't missing the feeling he gives me, that's for sure.

Pushing the repulsion away, I move forward, dodging to the left when he shoots at me from over the desk. He's clumsy, and the shot doesn't even pass close to me, but it angers me anyway.

"You fucking coward," I yell at him through gritted teeth, holding my gun so tight in front of me that my knuckles turn white. "Running away like a fucking rat. What? Don't you want to be the boss of the Romina Empire? Don't you think you should be fighting for it instead of hiding behind a desk? Instead of attacking us and running away? Where is that arrogance of yours, huh?" I taunt him, remembering the way he would stare me down as if he owned me when I was trapped in his mansion.

I get closer to him, and he shoots at me again. This time, I have to hide behind a pile of boxes, but I counterattack faster than he expected. The bullet hits his arm, making him drop his gun. Yakov gasps and crawls backward, hitting the wall behind him.

His eyes widen even more as I take a step forward, towering over him and pointing my pistol at his face.

"Come on, Tatiana," he pleads, his voice cracking as he stares at the barrel pointed at his forehead. "We're family...."

I scoff. "Family?" The word tastes like venom in my tongue. "You were going to force me to marry you."

I remember the feeling of his icy fingers gripping my chin and the way he gazed at me, eager to make me do whatever he wanted. My skin crawls, and I struggle to get my shit together.

Don't lose focus, I scold myself.

As if on cue, I feel someone moving behind me. I don't need to look to know it's Angelo. His scent invades me as soon as he steps close to me, and I instantly feel reassured. Protected. Safe.

One glance over my shoulder and I spot his gun raised and pointed at Yakov.

He doesn't do anything, letting me handle it as he promised he would, but knowing he has my back is enough to give me the necessary strength to finish this.

Yakov gets on his knees, bowing at me dramatically.

"Come on. Let me go, and I promise you'll never have to worry about me again. I won't come back to claim the Romina Empire. You'll never see my face in your life." His plea is ridiculous. It's obvious he's only saying this now because he's cornered. I don't doubt for a second that he'll come back to bite me in the ass as soon as he's out of danger. He's that much of a coward.

"And you thought you'd be a great leader. You're nothing but a bastard brat who thinks the world revolves around you," I spit, fury seeping through my every pore. "I won't leave loose ends. I hope you rot in hell with your beloved father."

I cock the gun, and with one decisive move, I pull the trigger.

Yakov falls forward, his limp body landing on the floor in a strange position, blood pooling beneath him. He's the third person I've killed, but I still don't feel comfortable enough to keep staring at him for long.

I look away, lowering my gun, my arms falling by my side. My heart is slamming against my chest, my breathing erratic, and the adrenaline is starting to wear off as I realize it is over.

For now, at least.

Warm and comfortable arms wrap around my waist from behind and pull me against a hard chest. I take a deep breath, closing my eyes and inhaling the best scent in the entire world, letting it calm me down.

Angelo places a kiss on my head. "You did great, baby," he tells me in a soft and low voice.

I nod, letting the peace he offers consume me completely.

FORTY-NINE
GETAWAY

Tatiana

I WALK inside the penthouse late at night, my body sore and my head aching. The rain is slamming the windows, the loud thundering and lightening making me jump as I remove my shoes and toss my purse on the couch.

The apartment is dark, except for a dim light coming from the second floor, more precisely my bedroom.

Angelo must be here already.

I climb the stairs, massaging my neck as I try to alleviate some of the tension in my muscles.

These past few weeks, my life has been nothing but pure chaos. I've barely slept more than four hours a night, catching up with every single business the Romina Empire has, getting familiarized with the finances and everyone who works for and with me.

I had imagined it would be hard, but I wasn't expecting it to be this much.

"Hey, you're here," Angelo greets me from the bed as I show up by the doorway. He's already showered and tucked under the sheets, leaning against the headboard with his phone in his hand. "Another tough night, huh?" he asks sympathetically, tilting his head as I stride inside the room, removing my blazer and tossing it over the chair.

"There isn't a single part of my body that doesn't hurt," I murmur, plopping on the foot of the bed and looking at him over my shoulder. "If I knew it was going to be this hard, I'd have thought twice before making a decision."

I don't mean it, and he knows it, but tonight, I honestly wish I could disappear from the face of the Earth for a few days.

"I'm sorry, baby." He puts his phone aside and gets up from the bed. "Do you want me to prepare a hot bath for you? I can maybe give you a massage," he suggests, stopping in front of me and pulling me into a hug.

I melt in his arms, inhaling his scent and letting myself relax.

"That actually sounds great. I might fall asleep in the tub, though," I joke, pulling away to look at him. His dark eyes stare back at me, and there's a little crease between his brows. He doesn't often say it, but I know he's worried. The way he's been taking care of me lately tells me he can sense how overwhelmed I am, and he's been trying to help me get through it.

"It's fine. I can take you out and put you in bed if you do. Just wait here until I fill up the tub."

He walks to the bathroom and I wait, fighting with myself so I don't just collapse on the bed and sleep until tomorrow.

Turns out I don't sleep in the tub, even though Angelo gives me the best massage on the shoulders and back. I doubt the best spa in the world would be able to make myself relax the way he did. He helps me put on my pajamas after I finish and sets me to bed. Then he lies beside me and pulls me into his embrace.

"I can't believe I'm only going to have a few hours of sleep before I have to be on my feet again," I complain, pouting slightly even though he can't see my face.

I don't normally complain about my new lifestyle, but tonight it feels like my body just can't handle it. I'm on the verge of collapsing.

"No, you won't," Angelo tells me simply, caressing my hair.

I frown, and lift my chin to look at him. "What do you mean I won't? I have so much to do tomorrow, I'm already dreading the morning."

"Guskov cleared our schedule for tomorrow and the day after," he informs me, as if this is the simplest thing in the world.

"What? Why?" I sit down in a swift movement, too shocked to stay still. Why would he do this? He never got in the way of how I led things in the Romina Empire. Why would he suddenly start interfering?

"You clearly need some rest. And I thought taking you on a weekend getaway would help you recharge." Angelo looks at me expectantly, and I must admit, it sounds like a dream.

"I can't be away from things, especially not now," I argue.

"It's not up for debate. Besides, Guskov said he can handle everything for a couple of days. He will let us know if something big happens, but honestly, nothing is going on that can't wait for you to return. You can go back to business on Monday. I'm sure everyone will understand."

I don't have the strength to fight him on this. Exhaustion is consuming every fiber of my being, and I honestly can't find any more reasons to refuse it. If he says Guskov is okay with it, maybe it won't be that bad if I step away for two days. It's been a hell of a month. I doubt my men will be mad at me for it.

I can give them some time off eventually, too, so they feel appreciated.

The next morning, I put together a small bag of clothes, and Angelo and I get into the car right after breakfast for our weekend off. He drives us to a Saints safe house outside New York, away from all the noise and madness of the city.

The place is a private retreat. It looks like a small cabin in the middle of the woods. It's cozy, silent, and most importantly, private.

There's no one around other than a couple of guards that Angelo called to watch the house.

I barely see them, though, and I bet Angelo ordered them to be invisible.

"It's really strange to be this... quiet," I murmur after we have settled down, having put our bags in the bedroom and lit up the fireplace in the living room. Angelo opens a bottle of wine and pours two glasses for us, and I offer to make us some pasta to have for lunch.

He turns on soft music while we eat, and for a moment, I forget about all of my problems outside the door.

It's just me and him.

Nothing else matters.

"This was an amazing idea," I tell him, sipping the wine as I finish my meal and set my plate aside. "Thank you for bringing me here and taking me out of the chaos for a change."

He shakes his head, getting up from the table and moving toward me. He takes my hand and pulls me toward the carpet in front of the fireplace. Then he sits on the floor, pulling me into his lap afterward.

"You'll eventually get used to it. Don't be too hard on yourself, though. You're doing great," he says softly, his fingers tangling in my hair. I close my eyes, enjoying the feeling it brings me.

"Am I?" I tilt my head, relishing his touch. "I feel like chaos will always catch up to us, no matter what we do."

"I know." He smiles kindly at me. "But I'll always be here to remind you of what really matters. As long as we find our way back to each other, there's nothing to fear, right?"

That was our promise. Be there for each other, no matter how hard things get along the way.

"Thank you for not letting me forget it," I reply.

For a few days, when everything caught up to me, I was afraid I was going to lose myself. I was afraid that I'd easily turn into a soulless person, someone who only cares about achievements and results.

But Angelo was always there to remind me that this is not who I really am.

It's part of the career I chose, sure, but deep down, it's what's in my soul that really defines who I am.

And I want to be the woman he fell in love with.

For that to happen, I need him by my side, to remind me of who I'm supposed to be every single day.

"I will never let you forget it," he whispers, his hand reaching for the back of my neck and pulling me into a kiss.

A kiss that quickly turns into desperation.

I cling to him as if I'm drowning and he is the only lifebuoy floating close to me.

Angelo lays me down, and I'm happy there's a carpet under us, because the floor must be fucking cold. Silently, we remove each other's clothes, and as soon as we're both naked, I pull him toward me, claiming his lips once more.

He spreads my legs with his knee and adjusts himself between them. The heat radiating from him is enough to set me on fire. I'm already dripping wet, every cell in my body desperate for him to possess me.

He teases me with the tip of his dick, and I arch my back off the floor, gasping when his tongue grazes my earlobe.

"A bit in a rush, are we?" he teases, nibbling the sensitive skin of my neck.

"That's not fair," I grumble, locking my ankles behind his waist and pulling him down on me. "And yes, I'm in a bit of a rush. I need you," I add, feeling as if I'm about to explode with all the pent-up energy inside me.

Angelo chuckles, and with a swift movement, he slides inside me, so easily and quickly that I'm left speechless for a second. My walls adjust to his length as I take him completely, and once we're both ready, he starts his thrusts, slamming our hips together as if he wants us to become one.

I bite down on my lip, not wanting to make much of a scene, knowing the guards are silent, but they are still somewhere outside.

My vision starts to blur as Angelo hits just the right spot, and I sink my nails into his shoulders, holding on for dear life as he threatens to push me off the edge.

"Baby, I'm close—"

The words get stuck in my throat as my toes curl and my walls clench around him. I feel him throbbing inside me, and I close my eyes, letting myself fall into the abyss of pleasure.

I don't think I'll ever get tired of how great this man makes me feel.

FIFTY
EPILOGUE

Tatiana

A YEAR LATER...

THE SOUND of my heels hitting the marble floor echo through the lobby of the new office building we have just acquired. This place will function as the new headquarters of the Romina Empire in Staten Island.

For months, I've been thinking of finding a new place, somewhere closer, to work with Tony and the Saints, and this was a great deal I couldn't turn down.

Lines of men from both my sides bow their heads at me as I head for the elevator, greeting me as soon as I arrive. It still astonishes me, even after all these months, how they address me with so much respect.

I earned my place, I know that, but it still surprises me.

At first, when I accepted this position, I was afraid they'd only follow me because of who my father was. But, with time, I proved myself worthy of it, and I can feel their loyalty through their every word and action.

I never take it for granted, though. And I never want them to feel unappreciated.

I know how that scars you.

We have been through so much together already. And they always had my back, walking through fire for me. I couldn't have asked for better people to go through all of this with.

As soon as I get to the top floor, I head for my office at the end of the hallway. It's late at night, so the place is empty, but as soon as I get to the door, I realize I'm not alone.

Angelo is waiting for me, seated on the leather couch, a glass of whiskey in his hand. He has removed the blazer from his suit and rolled his sleeve up to his elbow, revealing the anchor tattoo on his forearm that I love so much. He's decided to let his hair grow, so the curls are falling over his eyes and ears, and boy, does he look hot.

"Good evening, Boss," he greets with a sly smile, raising his glass at me.

I walk inside, closing the door behind me.

"Good evening," I reply, biting back a smile. "Last time I checked, this is supposed to be my office," I taunt, lifting my brows. "Yours is next door."

"Hm, didn't take you for a territorial woman." He sets his glass on the table and starts pouring another one. He then hands it to me, and I take it, sitting beside him on the couch.

I take a sip from the amber liquid, letting it burn down my throat and warm my chest.

This is exactly what I needed after a long day of work.

"It depends on what I'm being territorial with," I note, glancing at him sideways, scanning him up and down. I'm sure he can see the heat in my eyes.

He swallows hard, chugging the rest of the whiskey at once and looking away.

"Don't do that, or we'll have to break in your office." He grins at me, that sexy, cunning smile on the corner of his lips making me wonder why we can't do exactly that.

"Do what?" I tease, crossing my legs and leaning back on the couch.

Angelo sneers. "Aren't you a little tired for this?"

I am. But I could use some sex to relax, though I'd rather we wait until we get home. For now, I just want to enjoy this moment, giving myself some room to breathe and celebrate another victory.

"Fine. You're right. You're not escaping once we get home, though. I miss you. And we barely had any time together these past few days," I point out, looking at him with sorrowful eyes.

"Yeah... I miss you too. But now that you closed this deal, we have time to celebrate. Until you find something else to focus on, that is," he jokes.

He knows me so well by now. He knows that once I set my mind to something, I don't let it go until I get it. And I never wait too long until I find a new purpose.

That's the type of boss I became.

And I'm so glad he supports me, no matter what.

"You made it," he adds, finding my hand on the couch and squeezing it.

"We made it," I correct him, intertwining our fingers and scooting to the side to get closer to him. "I wouldn't have gotten where I am today if it weren't for you. And the rest of the guys, of course. So, thank you for staying with me." I didn't intend to cry, but tears swell in my eyes anyway as I stare at the man I love.

"Did you ever doubt I would?" he retorts, heat radiating from his gaze and body.

"Never."

Because it is true. No matter the hardships life throws at us, despite all my insecurities and inexperience, deep down, I always know I can count on him.

I turn my body to face him, tears rolling down my face at this point. Angelo widens his eyes at me, shocked to see me cry when we were just now taunting each other.

"I really mean it when I say I couldn't have done this without you. You're my family, Angelo, and if it weren't for you, I wouldn't have had the courage to do everything I did. To fight for myself. For us. For my father's legacy. For justice. You give me the strength I need to go through all of this, to face the hardest days, to want to keep moving...."

"Baby..." he murmurs, but I shake my head at him—wanting, needing to let it all out.

It's probably the most raw confession I've ever given, and tonight, I suddenly feel like I haven't shown enough how grateful I am to have him in my life.

"We have built an empire, with money and power... but this means nothing to me. All I care about is the family we have become. The family we're going to be one day," I continue.

Angelo raises his hand and gently wipes the tears from my cheeks, caressing my skin with his thumb. I tilt my head against his touch, relishing in it.

"I wouldn't have had it any other way." His tone is serious and firm, but I can feel the love and devotion it carries. "Meeting you was like being saved from the darkness. Like being saved from a life without love, hope, and dreams. When I lost Luca, life stopped making sense for me. I carried on with my days without worrying whether I was going to die or not. The only thing that kept me going was the rage and grief I buried in my heart. The thirst for revenge. It kept me moving forward, but those were not good feelings to hold on to," he confesses, lowering his gaze to his lap, ashamed. "It wasn't something I was proud of, but I didn't know how else to control those feelings inside me. So, I just let them move me. Until I met you. And then everything fell into place. Everything started to make sense again."

Angelo and I have exchanged countless 'I love yous' in the past year, but never once have we had this pure, intimate conversation.

Sometimes it feels like words aren't needed until they are said. Now that we're putting all our emotions and feelings for each other on the table, I'm finally realizing how powerful our love actually is.

It saved us both. From a life without hope. From a life of despair.

Both of us lost our families because of greed. But because of that, we also found one another.

We fought for justice. And we did it together.

It feels good to have someone to share all your burdens and dreams with. I never thought I needed that person until I found him.

"I love you," I state firmly, locking my eyes with his. "And I'm really glad you came into my life when you did."

Angelo smiles softly at me, cupping my face and pulling me slowly toward him. He places a kiss on my lips and pulls away, resting his forehead against mine.

"Thank you for sticking with me. I love and need you so much that it scares me sometimes. And I wanted to take this moment to reinforce my promise to you. I want to stay beside you for the rest of our lives. I can't imagine living a single day without you. That's why..."

Angelo releases me and stands, only to kneel in front of me. He takes my right hand, and with the other, he removes a diamond ring from his pocket.

My eyes widen in shock, and I gasp, covering my mouth with my free hand.

"What...?" I can't find the words to express what I'm feeling right now.

"That's why I want to ask you... Tatiana Romina, will you be my wife?"

I nod so fast that I almost get whiplash. The tears are falling freely down my face now, blurring my vision, but I don't mind. I simply let him place the ring on my finger before I toss myself on him, both of us collapsing on the floor, giggling.

"Yes! A thousand times, yes!"

ALSO BY BELLA MOONDRAGON

The Alpha King's Breeder series:

Bought by the Alpha: The Alpha King's Breeder Book 1

Loved by the Alpha: The Alpha King's Breeder Book 2

Lost by the Alpha: The Alpha King's Breeder Book 3

Luna of the Alpha: The Alpha King's Breeder Book 4

Legacy of the Alpha: The Alpha Kings's Breeder Book 5

Daughter of the Alpha: The Alpha King's Breeder Book 6

Descendants of the Alpha: The Alpha King's Breeder Book 7

Shadow of the Alpha: The Alpha King's Breeder Book 8

Son of the Alpha: The Alpha King's Breeder Book 9

Spare of the Alpha: The Alpha King's Breeder Book 10

Claimed by the Alpha: The Alpha King's Breeder Book 11

Atonement for the Alpha King: The Alpha King's Breeder Book 12

Rejected by the Alpha: The Alpha King's Breeder Book 13

Abducted by the Alpha: The Alpha King's Breeder Book 14

Wolf Shifter Fairy Tale Retellings series

Beauty and the Alpha Beast

Sleeping Beasty

Tangling With the Alpha

The Luna's Vampire Prince series:

The Culling

The Kingdom

The Conquered

Pregnant With Four Alphas' Babies

Chosen As the Breeder

Mated to Four Alphas

Threats Against the Breeder

At War for the Breeder

The Stolen Breeder

Four Alphas, Four Babies

Becoming the Luna Queen

Descendants of the Breeder

Desired by the Devil series

Whispers of the Devil

Banter of the Devil

Murmurs of the Devil

The Mafia Kings series

Indebted to the Mafia King

Loved by the Mafia King

Claimed by the Mafia King

Secrets of the Mafia King

Burned by the Mafia King

Kidnapped by the Mafia King

Dark Stalker Romance series

Tempted by Sin

Fated to Sin

Secret Billionaires series

Finding the Secret Billionaire by Olivia Bhelle Kildare

Falling for My Secret Billionaire by Bella Moondragon

Driven by the Secret Billionaire by ID Johnson

Wolf Shifter Alpha Kings series

Ravens and Ruins

Sundrops and Shadows

Snowflakes and Sabotage

The Vampire King's Feeder series

Claiming the Alpha's Daughter

Loving the Alpha's Daughter

Finding the Alpha's Daughter

Writing as B. Moon

The Boy Who Died

Sign up for Bella's newsletter here.

Or get a free novella from The Alpha King's Breeder series when you sign up here: The Beta and the Maid